THE
APARTMENT

THE
APARTMENT

K. L. SLATER

 THOMAS & MERCER

Published by Thomas & Mercer, Seattle. Previously published by Audible UK in 2019. This edition contains editorial revisions.

www.apub.com

Amazon, the Amazon logo, and Thomas & Mercer are trademarks of Amazon.com, Inc., or its affiliates.

ISBN-13: 9781542023917
ISBN-10: 1542023912

Cover design by @blacksheep-uk.com

Printed in the United States of America

THE
APARTMENT

PROLOGUE

His chance to speak to her comes in Starbucks on Kensington High Street, of all places.

He stands behind the queue of people who are silently debating whether to go for the vanilla latte or today's special: a Pumpkin Spice Frappuccino, according to the poster on the back wall.

When he arrived, the streets had seemed quiet, the warm air buffeting his ears, but here in the café it is busy and he finds it slightly claustrophobic.

He'd spotted her from the outside. She'd been scanning the cluttered bulletin board on the wall next to the window. Perusing the small white index cards, hastily scrawled by locals with details of items for sale, babysitting services, and a separate section at the side for homes available for rent.

He approaches quickly now, battling through the wall of noise rising from the packed tables. Her head, with its neat brown ponytail, is bent forward as she bites her lip and repeatedly runs a fingertip over the rental cards. The café atmosphere feels damp and cloying around him.

Michael picks his way past snivelling toddlers and families jostling for seats and positions himself in front of the board, right next to her.

He waits for her to look up and notice his frustrated expression. She doesn't.

Michael clears his throat. 'Sorry, I hate to ask but . . . would you mind awfully, if I just squeezed past?'

'What?' She looks up, startled.

Michael can see she is in no mood for chatting but that's OK, they almost never are. He grins conspiratorially. 'You know, coffee shops are quite a stressful experience when you think about it . . . all this chaos for little more than a cup of hot, frothy milk.'

Her face lights up with a brief but genuine smile. 'Yes, I suppose you're right.'

Michael reaches down into his overcoat pocket and plucks out the wedge of flyers. 'I wasn't sure whether to put these on the tables or' – he makes a big deal of looking at the dingy bulletin board as the coffee machines continue to whoosh out their steam – 'I could just pin one on the rentals board here. What do you think?'

'What's it about?' She glances at the flyer he's holding up. He sees her face is pale and drawn with worry. And no wonder.

'Nothing exciting I'm afraid. There's an apartment up for rent in my building. The tenant let me down, but if I can get a few flyers out today, it should be taken by the morning.'

'Must be a nice apartment if it's going to be snapped up overnight,' she says gloomily, sitting down.

'It's a *very* nice apartment,' he agrees, thinking of the distinctly average family home she has just been forced to sell. She'll be worrying now, of course, about where she and the girl will end up. 'A short walk to Hyde Park, built-in wardrobes and bills included. Ideal for the right person, I'd say.'

'Lucky them,' she mumbles to herself, and he almost misses the words amidst the background din.

'Ahh, now that's where you'd be wrong, you see. Because luck has very little to do with it.' Michael pauses, waiting for his words to register and reel her in inch by tantalising inch. 'The new person has to be *just right*. Has to fit in perfectly with the other five residents already living at Adder House.'

'Adder House,' she repeats thoughtfully. 'Sounds . . . interesting.'

'It is indeed very interesting,' he agrees.

'Can I take a look at one of those?'

Michael slides a flyer forward on the table and she reaches for it with fingers that are delicate but woefully neglected. Raw, rough patches pattern the top of her hand, and her nails are bitten to the quick. A narrow band of white shrunken skin is evident on the third finger of her left hand where her wedding ring sat for twelve years.

He watches as her burnished-brown eyes flick over the page, taking in the interior photographs of the apartment. She lingers on the impressive façade of Adder House itself. It always gets them in the end, even the really stubborn ones.

'It doesn't say how much the rent is on here.'

'That's because the amount payable is dependent upon the circumstances of the successful tenant. The landlord sets the level, and it's always a figure the person can afford.'

'Your landlord must have a screw loose,' she says, a thread of impatience unravelling in her tone. 'A place like that? Be at least a couple of grand a week, I reckon. Probably even more.'

'Maybe I *have* got a screw loose.' He chuckles. 'But money isn't my priority. Adder House is a very special place and that comes from the unique mix of residents. That's what makes it a special place, not their bank balances.'

'Oh!' She's flustered now. 'Sorry, I didn't realise it was *you* . . . that you're the landlord, I mean. I—'

'No offence taken.' He waves away her apology. 'Do you live locally yourself?'

'I *did*. The house has just been sold after – well, let's just say we have no choice but to move.'

But of course, he knows all about that. The whole sorry tale.

'I'll probably end up crashing with a friend for a short time.' She hesitates. 'Just until I can get something sorted. It's not easy when you have a little one.'

'You have a child?'

'A daughter. She's five.' A brief bloom lights up her face.

'How charming,' he says, thinking of the sweet girl he's watched Freya collect from school most days for the last couple of weeks. 'Sounds like you've got it tough at the moment. I don't suppose—' He laughs and shakes his head, as if embarrassed at himself. 'Ignore me, it doesn't matter.'

'What is it?' She sits up a little straighter. '*I don't suppose* . . . you were going to say what?'

'I was going to ask if you'd like to view the apartment at Adder House? If you were interested, that is.'

She stares at him and he bumps his forehead with the heel of his hand.

'Of course, I understand entirely. Take no notice of me blubbering on. You must think my offer bizarre, under the circumstances.'

'No!' She clears her throat. 'No, I don't think that at all.'

He produces his card and slides it across the table to her. His ticket of immediate trust.

'Dr Michael Marsden,' she reads out slowly. 'You're a doctor?'

'Not any more.' He smiles.

1

'A new house?' Skye screeches at the top of her voice, her face lighting up and then dimming just as fast. I don't have to ask why. She's thinking about Lewis.

I turn the radio down but Skye has already stopped dancing to the music.

She's thoughtful for a moment or two, her dark-blonde eyebrows knitting together as I clear away her tea plate and mug. 'And we're going to the new house *now*, Mummy?'

'Yes, we're going to view Adder House now to see if we like it. That's if you want to come?' I help her slide her arms into her little red jacket without waiting for her to answer. 'I waited until I picked you up from school because I thought it would be nice for us to go together.'

'Hmm . . .' I can almost hear the cogs turning in her smart little head. 'But if we do go to live somewhere new, how will Daddy know where to find us?'

And there it is in plain sight. The enormous shadow that constantly nibbles away at the edges of her happiness.

I pause in my attempt to help her get her coat on and kiss the top of her head.

'Your daddy always knows where you are, remember?' I say softly. 'Everywhere you go, he's with you, poppet.'

Lewis's death is still so raw. For both of us. It's only natural she's worrying.

It's hard to explain the terrible truth of what happened to Lewis to a five-year-old who simply can't be told all the details. The school counsellor said the first and most important thing at this young age is initially for her to understand and accept that her father isn't here any more.

I think we're getting there at last. I see the clues peppered between her normal everyday activities.

My heart squeezes in on itself every time I catch her staring into space when she's meant to be watching her favourite TV show. When she leaves a spare seat on the floor for her daddy at one of her soft-toy tea parties, or squeezes her hands into little fists when her friends' daddies pick them up at the end of the day. Just like Lewis would often do.

The counsellor said it shows she understands he's gone now and she's dealing with it.

In her own way.

It's more problematic for me. I'm still alternating between the extremes of emotion, caught in no-man's-land, usually somewhere between grief and fury.

I've read countless articles online advising how to discuss difficult matters with very young kids, but really, it all comes down to one thing. I'm the person who knows my daughter best, and I have to find the right way to break the truth to her as gently as I can.

For now, I've decided it's better to fluff the detail.

'You should see what might be your new bedroom at Adder House.' I muster as much enthusiasm as I can. 'It's got a real cherry tree blossoming just outside the window.'

'Pink confetti!' Skye claps her hands. 'When Petra comes over, we can stand underneath it and pretend we're guests at a wedding!'

Yet again, I push away the realisation that I'll need to speak to my daughter about changing schools very soon. I'll need to be explicit about the fact that her best friend, Petra, won't be at the new one.

All this is a very big deal when you're just five years old.

But even if Adder House falls through – which still seems a reasonably likely outcome judging by its grandeur on the flyer – we'll not be able to afford to keep living in this area anyway. I'll be forced to change Skye's school sooner or later.

I look around our small but functional kitchen with its clean lines and white fitted units. The duck-egg-blue kettle, tea and coffee canisters, and the toaster tone in perfectly; I took ages choosing that colour scheme. It seems ironic now that that sort of thing ever mattered to me.

It's true I've got Lewis's insurance money, but that won't last forever. I had no savings when Lewis died, and I've calculated I have about six months before the insurance money will run out, so I know I need to look out for a job well before it gets to that stage.

Despite my sadness in leaving our home, I thank my lucky stars every day I've managed to sell it; albeit for 10 per cent less than the asking price, which also removed any available equity.

I sigh and button up Skye's coat as she hums the theme tune from *Frozen*.

Two years ago, when he'd just had his promotion at work, Lewis and I were planning to take her to Walt Disney World in Florida. Since his death, I've been worrying about where we'll live and how I'll meet London rental costs and sky-high bills, especially while I'm not working.

Skye has coped so brilliantly, but I worry that more upheaval could push her over the edge. Sadly, moving house is one major change I simply can't avoid.

I bundle my daughter out of the house and pull the door closed, just as the black cab appears. I open the door and clamber in, totally unused to the luxury. Usually we have the grand choice of taking the bus or the Underground.

Travelling by cab is typically well out of my budget capacity, but before I left the café this morning, Dr Marsden insisted on sending one to collect and return us home, fully paid for.

'It's the least I can do, if you're genuinely interested in the apartment,' he'd said, and I'd felt more than grateful.

The driver says he's been given full instructions on where to go, so I settle back into the seat with Skye to try and relax and enjoy the ride.

She's a little live wire as usual, pointing out people, shops, and particularly dogs . . . which are currently her favourite animal.

'Can we get a puppy at our new house, Mummy?' She looks at me imploringly with her enormous blue eyes.

'First things first, Skye.' I smile, beginning to feel a little sleepy as I relax into the smooth ride. 'It's not actually our home yet, remember.'

'I'd love a puppy,' she says dreamily. 'I could take him for walks and I'd play with him *every* day and show him pictures of Daddy . . .'

I close my eyes, listening a little sadly as Skye disappears off into one of her wonderfully detailed imaginary worlds where everything is always perfect and Lewis is as he always used to be, as if all the crappy stuff never happened.

It's a kind of therapy for both of us, and my heart warms to hear her happy, even if it is make-believe.

The cab turns into Hyde Park Corner, then later on to Palace Gate. It begins to slow. 'Adder House coming up, love,' the driver announces.

'Wow!' I hear Skye breathe as she sits bolt upright, taking in the white stucco buildings that line Palace Gate like sentries.

The cab stops and I stare open-mouthed at what I can only describe as a mansion, nestled amongst similarly spectacular properties.

Surely, the apartment can't be located *here* and yet . . . I realise on closer inspection that this is the exact same building as featured in the photograph on Dr Marsden's flyers. Then I spot a pristine white sign with decorative black script above the door that reads:

Adder House

I thank the driver and open the door, holding it wide as Skye slips out of the cab and on to the pavement. She's still staring up at the buildings, too in awe to chatter. The diesel rumble of the cab fades behind us as we climb the short flight of stone steps that lead to the door.

A few houses down, a musclebound builder emerges on to the road, his arms full of old pipe work that he deposits unceremoniously into a skip outside.

He smiles in our direction and Skye gives him a little wave.

I chivvy her up the entrance steps, but before I can ring the bell, the door opens and Dr Marsden appears there, looking smart in his shirt and tie.

'Freya! Welcome to Adder House.'

Before I can answer, he bends forward and stretches out a hand. 'And you must be Miss Skye. I'm very pleased to meet you.'

'Hello,' Skye says in the small voice she uses when she feels a little nervous, but I almost burst with pride when she, nevertheless, boldly shakes his hand.

Dr Marsden nods approvingly at my daughter's confidence and holds open the door while we walk into the foyer of Adder House.

'I do hope you'll find our home is to your liking. I think you could both be very happy here.'

'Wow, this is *so* cool!' Skye gasps, staring up at the winding stair balustrade of intricate iron filigree that spirals up the centre of the building, all the way to the top floor.

Witnessing her disbelief at the grandeur is a bit of a wake-up call and it finally hits me what an utter fool I've been. I did try really hard to fully explain my circumstances in the coffee shop, but Dr Marsden has obviously still managed to completely underestimate my financial capabilities.

I mean, what on earth are we doing here, really? People like *us* simply don't live in places like *this*.

I know I have to say something to him right now, or I'm at real risk of becoming horribly embarrassed later on. I clear my throat.

'Dr Marsden, I'm so sorry but I think we're at cross purposes. You see, I'm on a very tight budget.' I drag in a breath as the corner of his mouth twitches with apparent amusement. 'You see, I'm not actually working at the moment, and there's no way I'm going to be able to afford the rent on a place this grand.'

'I can assure you there's been no misunderstanding from my side.' He chuckles, dismissing my concerns with a flutter of his thick manicured fingers. 'As I said before, I think you and Skye will be just perfect for Adder House and that is the only priority we have here. My advice is to put all such thoughts from your head and accept the fact that you have the chance – if you want it – to make a fresh start.'

I want to believe it, I really do. But I know only too well how it feels to not fit in, to feel like the outsider.

And I've had enough of that to last me a lifetime.

2

We follow Dr Marsden further into the spacious entrance hall.

Skye seems entranced, looking all around her, but it's a strange and new environment and I become aware that her small hand is feeling blindly for mine, and so I give it a reassuring squeeze.

The wood-panelled entrance is large and impressive but not so enormous that it feels impersonal. It is decorated in the manner of someone's home, not like an apartment building at all. It's perfect.

I step from the fitted door mat on to the gleaming wooden floorboards. The pleasant, faint odour of polish hangs in the air, and a Tiffany-style lamp on the antique console table adds a warm glow to an enclosed space that might otherwise be lacking in light.

Paintings line the walls; originals, I think, noting the brush strokes in the swirls of thick, coloured oils. Over towards the far wall there are polished mahogany stairs complete with the elegant balustrade Skye noticed earlier, snaking all the way up to the higher floors.

The three of us have fallen quiet for a few moments, and when I turn, I see that Dr Marsden is still standing near the entrance door, quietly watching us to gauge our reaction, I think.

'It's amazing,' I gasp. 'I mean, I haven't even stepped inside a property like this before.' *Never mind lived in one,* the cynical voice in my head adds.

He smiles. 'Let's go upstairs. Unfortunately, Adder House doesn't have a lift. There aren't many downsides to this property, but I suppose for some people, that might be one of them.'

It crosses my mind that without a gym membership these days, I'll need to learn to make friends with the stairs. With the park and gardens only yards away – I'd already spotted a row of Boris Bikes at the entrance when the cab turned – I think that, finally, I might actually be in a position to shift the extra weight that has crept on with all the stress of the past eighteen months.

Sadly, I'm not the kind of person who loses interest in eating when my mood plummets. I take solace in food and treat it like an old friend, particularly bread, cheese, and anything creamy and calorie laden. Eating is one of the rare times I actually feel secure again.

We follow Dr Marsden upstairs – Skye effortlessly negotiating the steep climb while I take it a little steadier – until we emerge on a wide, spacious landing with the same polished wooden floor as downstairs and a rather attractive red-and-gold-patterned Persian rug.

Two solid, wide panelled wooden doors with shiny brass numbers and knockers lead off the landing, one at each end.

'Mr and Mrs Woodings are in number three.' Dr Marsden points out the door. Without delay, he begins to climb the next flight of stairs up to the second floor.

Again, two impressive wooden doors stand off the main landing.

'Miss Brockley is at number four,' he murmurs. 'The residents who live at two and five are away at the moment. The third and final flight of stairs is coming up, you might be pleased to know.' Dr Marsden smiles.

He seems fit and isn't out of breath at all despite, I'm guessing, being in his mid-sixties. I hope he doesn't notice my own laboured breathing; not very impressive for a thirty-two-year-old.

The landing up here on the third floor looks a little different. It has a smaller floor area but is also a much lighter space, thanks to a larger window at the front that overlooks the road.

'Mummy, look!'

Skye is standing at the glass looking out with delight at a neat Juliet balcony filled with groomed topiary trees and other greenery. The smaller top windows are slightly ajar, and I can hear birds whistling from the nearby trees.

There are two doors up here, too. One big one without a number on the front and then towards the corner, a narrower door with a brass number six.

Dr Marsden walks towards the smaller door and waves a key card in front of the brass handle.

'You two will be the first tenants in this apartment.' He opens the door and signals for me to enter first. 'See what you think.'

Holding Skye's hand, I walk through a tiny entrance hall and into a large, spacious area that clearly serves as both a lounge and a kitchenette. Light floods in through a floor-to-ceiling window which overlooks the back of the property and the small, sheltered garden.

Skye pulls away from me and runs to the window. 'There's a swing down there!' she exclaims.

'It's a small backyard but, I like to think, perfectly formed,' Dr Marsden remarks, opening a door to the right. 'And here we have the master bedroom.'

A modestly sized room but with the same lovely view. I spot built-in wardrobes and a fitted dressing table and stool. I can visualise myself in here, taking pleasure in having an early night with a good book again like I used to before my life fell to pieces.

'It's perfect.' I breathe out.

We move on to the second bedroom. It's smaller but more than adequate and again there's a built-in wardrobe.

'This will be the young lady's room, I'd imagine.' Dr Marsden smiles.

Skye skips past us to the window and beams at one of the blossoming cherry trees she likes to call confetti trees.

'I love it here, Mummy!' she declares, her face open and flushed with joy. I feel my eyes prickling. Moments of unbridled joy for Skye used to be second nature, but for the last year and a half, they've been few and far between.

I reach for my daughter and squeeze her hand, smiling.

'And finally, we have the bathroom.' Dr Marsden opens the door to an ivory-tiled room with a sparkling white bathroom suite and a mirrored wall which makes it seem twice as big.

I'm mortified when I feel a tear escape from my eye, but I can't help it. After spending so long worrying what was to become of us, it feels like a miracle that we might actually get to live in a place like this.

I swiftly wipe my face with the back of my hand and take a breath before I turn around. I really don't want Dr Marsden to think I'm flaky.

'Can we live here, Mummy?' Skye tugs impatiently at my hand. 'Can we?'

'It's perfect, Dr Marsden.' I jiggle Skye's hand, signalling for her to let me speak.

When she does, I focus on trying to keep my emotions in check and my voice level. 'I can't thank you enough for this opportunity, I—'

He holds up a hand. 'There's really no need to keep thanking me, my dear. If you genuinely think that you and Skye can be happy here, then Adder House would love to have you. But there's

14

no rush, so feel free to take some time to think about it. After all, it's a big decision.'

'It's actually not a big decision at all.' I laugh, feeling lighter than I've done for ages. 'I'm certain we could be very happy here.' I glance at my daughter and her eyes are wide.

Unblinking.

'Perfect! Well, Skye and I are delighted, aren't we, dear?' Skye gives a single, decisive nod. 'Let's go back downstairs and I can give you a little more information.'

As we descend, I glance at the other doors again. 'Does anyone else have young children here?' I ask.

'No, no. Most of our residents are older, their days of raising a family behind them. But the ones who are home at the moment will love to see a youngster around the place, so you mustn't worry about that.'

Skye isn't a boisterous child, but the quality of the silence and the ambience here speaks of a different kind of life. A hidden pocket of a more traditional way of living in a modern world.

After a chaotic and energy-sapping time, I admit I feel more than ready to embrace a calmer lifestyle. Is it hopelessly naïve to believe that for once, fate has smiled on us and at last, we'll find a place we can begin to live again?

It's completely natural that Skye feels a little unsure at the prospect of leaving the only home she's really known.

But there's no doubt in my mind that Adder House would be safe and nurturing for Skye, and kids are so adaptable, aren't they? I feel sure she'd get used to the change in no time.

Sounds silly to say this so early on, but I do think we could be happy here. I've just got a nice warm feeling about the place, and when I turn and look back down the hallway of the apartment as we leave, I still can't quite believe my luck.

3

Down on the ground floor again, Dr Marsden beckons us towards a dim alcove I didn't notice when we first came in.

Partly concealed behind a cluster of tall potted ferns, I spot another of the outsize wooden doors. This one features ornately carved panels and an elaborate brass lion knocker about two-thirds of the way up.

He uses a large, old-fashioned brass key to open it.

'Welcome to my home. Sadly, Mrs Marsden – Audrey – couldn't be here to meet you today, but she's very much looking forward to doing so soon.' I hesitate in following him and look down at my footwear. 'Oh, don't worry about those. Leave them on.'

We walk into a large panelled hallway and then emerge into a very spacious lounge. French doors lead directly out into the garden at one end, and enormous picture windows sit at the front of the room, complete with textured beige drapes that trail stylishly on the floor.

Skye sticks to me like glue. 'Mummy, this apartment is massive,' she whispers.

'Sadly, this one's not up for rent, but you can drop in any time you wish, Miss Skye.'

I'm surprised Dr Marsden heard her; he must have very keen ears for his age.

Skye seems to forget her nervousness when she sets eyes on the multitude of treasures inside the apartment and walks a few steps ahead of me. I beckon her back, terrified she'll inadvertently knock flying some priceless vase or glass sculpture.

'Please, don't fret, Freya, just let her explore,' Dr Marsden urges me.

Two long pale-gold sofas frame an imposing and ornate Adam fireplace that showcases built-in oak bookcases at either side. My eyes gravitate to a large, fancy gilt mirror that hangs above the mantelpiece and a marble-topped coffee table sitting between the sofas, scattered with large hard-backed photographic books featuring art and travel.

'Wow, look at the elephant, Mummy!' Skye darts over to the antique sideboard where an enormous carved wooden elephant stands regally, its tusks looking suspiciously like real ivory.

'Don't touch, Skye,' I call out.

'Really, she's fine. I spent some years in Africa,' Dr Marsden remarks, stepping closer to Skye and watching her reaction with interest. 'This was one of the many treasures I brought back with me.'

Skye's small fingers trace across the intricate gem-studded wood. I move next to her and pull her hand gently away. I can hardly blame her for being amazed; to a curious five-year-old, this place must truly seem to be an Aladdin's cave.

I actually feel relieved that compared to this enormous living space, the vacant apartment upstairs seems like a very large, beautiful cupboard.

It sounds silly, but after living in mostly semi-detached converted properties in rather dubious areas, I know I'd struggle to feel comfortable amidst such large-scale grandeur. Dr Marsden's home seems visually perfect, and yet something is niggling at me about the place that I can't quite put my finger on . . . it's as if something is missing.

I'm suddenly aware I'm openly staring. 'Sorry, it's just that I don't think I've ever seen a place quite as beautiful.'

'Oh, that's very kind of you to say so,' Dr Marsden murmurs. 'I have dear Audrey to thank for the stylish interior design.' He hesitates. 'Please, Freya, won't you sit down and relax a little while Skye takes a look around?'

I perch at the edge of one of the couches like a coiled spring, trying to make myself smaller in the perfect beige and gold oasis. The carpet is a pale biscuit colour, and I'm terrified of making a mark on it with my shoe.

I keep my beady eyes trained on Skye's inquisitive hands as she stalks along the walls, oohing and ahhing at the contents of the shelves. Her shyness seems to have completely dissipated.

'Can I offer you a drink . . . tea perhaps? How does Earl Grey sound?'

'Thank you, but no,' I reply regretfully. 'We can't stay too long I'm afraid, our friends are popping by later.' That isn't really the reason, I'm not expecting visitors. But I can't trust myself not to spill tea or risk Skye breaking one of Dr and Mrs Marsden's many displayed treasures, and my heart rate is definitely increasing the bolder she becomes in reaching for the numerous objets d'art.

But that's not the only reason my shoulders feel knotted and sore. I'm continually worried my potential new landlord will soon discover his mistake in believing I'm the sort of person who can seamlessly fit in here.

I just can't shake the feeling that this is a world I simply don't belong in. I'm bound to show myself up somehow, and he'll have no choice but to reconsider my suitability for such a cultured and genteel environment. How long will it take for him to notice my awkwardness?

Yet my fears appear to be unfounded.

'If you think Adder House is somewhere you and Skye can settle, then you only need give me the word, Freya. I can then arrange for the paperwork to be drawn up without delay. You could move in as early as next weekend . . . if that suited you.'

My heart soars. Dr Marsden can't possibly know, but the couple who've bought my house are pressing to move in as quickly as possible. The estate agent only advised me yesterday to find somewhere else quick, or risk losing the sale.

I look at Skye, still totally absorbed in staring up at the elegant cornice with its carved cherubs and flowers. I think about the perfect apartment on offer upstairs, just down the road from one of the most beautiful royal parks in the country.

Don't we deserve a shot at happiness?

I fold my hands on my lap and look at Dr Marsden.

'Thank you, that would be wonderful. If you're sure, then we'd love to come and live at Adder House.'

Skye turns from her browsing and looks at me. I hold my breath in case she bursts into tears, but a tiny smile appears on her face. My shoulders loosen a little.

'Excellent! Then I'll speak to Audrey and we'll get things moving right away.' Dr Marsden beams. He looks genuinely pleased. 'Now, I don't want to keep you if you've company coming, so let me call for the cab.'

Having someone who wants to make life easy for us feels so refreshing. It seems to have been just me against the world for so long, I have to stop myself from insisting we can sort our own transport out.

While he busies himself looking for the number, I take a last look around the doctor's lounge, willing myself to believe that, incredibly, we'll soon be making a new start here.

Finally, as my eyes flutter over tables and sideboards and shelves, groaning under the weight of various beautiful pieces, I realise what it is that's missing from the room.

Photographs. There isn't a single framed photograph perched on the furniture or hanging on the walls.

No pictures of Dr Marsden and his wife, their grown-up kids, or grandchildren playing with family pets.

Nothing of that nature at all.

4

Palace Gate seems quiet as we walk up towards the congested traffic of Kensington Gore. In the end, I asked Dr Marsden to forget the cab. We'll get the Tube instead so I can show Skye the park.

'Mummy, all the houses are so big and tall here!' Skye gasps, tipping back her head to look up at the buildings.

Compared to living in Acton, in our tiny home with its minuscule backyard that's overlooked by at least five other houses, the pads here must seem like true palaces to Skye.

'And we're going to live in one of them.' I grin down at her, thinking how it still seems utterly surreal to me, too. 'Aren't *we* the lucky ones?'

She doesn't answer but she doesn't complain either, so I'll take that as a positive.

I grip her hand as we wait at the crossing to enable us to safely negotiate the crazily busy road at the top. Just a few minutes later, we are inside the railings of Kensington Gardens, walking up the wide path that leads towards the golden gates at the top of the incline.

Within a minute or two, the leafy calmness of the gardens works its magic, and it feels as if we've left the traffic behind us.

We stop at a small kiosk at the bottom of the hill, and I buy a pack of sandwiches and a bag of crisps before we carry on walking.

Skye seems quiet, her head turning this way and that, taking in everything that's happening around her. Runners, dogs, cyclists, people picnicking on the grass . . . the place is so alive.

I feel a pincer-like grip in my chest as I realise how few places I've taken Skye these last few months. I've been so absorbed in my own problems and worries – at times it truly felt as if I might drown in negative emotions – it was all I could do to keep functioning on a basic level each day.

I forgot all about taking her to the park to feed the ducks or to the cinema to see a film together. Instead I spent my time making lists so I wouldn't forget to complete mundane tasks like doing the laundry, paying the bills, and packing Skye's lunchbox each evening for the next school day.

I have a lot of making up to do.

Halfway up the hill, I stop walking. 'Close your eyes and tell me what you can hear,' I say. It's a game we used to play a lot when we went for walks as a family.

Skye squeezes her eyelids shut and waits for a few moments before blurting out, 'Birds!'

'Me, too. Birds and . . . and can you hear the leaves rustling a little in the breeze?' Eyes still closed, Skye tilts her head and a look of concentration crosses her face.

A sudden movement to my right takes my attention from my daughter's expression. I squint as a figure darts behind the enormous gnarled trunk of an oak tree. I felt sure that when I looked over, the person was holding up a phone as if they were about to take a picture of us.

'I can hear the leaves rustling, Mummy!' Skye exclaims, her eyes springing open again.

'Hang on, poppet, just wait here a moment.' I take a few steps towards the tree and then have to wait as a large group of tourists walk in front of me. When I get to the tree, there's nobody there.

I stand for a moment and pull in air as a wave of panic rolls over me. There's nobody there, it's just my imagination getting the better of me. I don't want that paranoia back again . . .

'What's wrong?' Skye runs over to me, concerned. 'Who are you looking for?'

'Nothing, I just thought I saw someone I knew,' I say, not wanting to worry her. My legs feel a bit shaky but I know a sure-fire way to distract her. 'Come on . . . race you to the top!'

'Yay, I'm the winner!' she announces when we get up to the palace gates. 'Stand there and I'll take your photograph, Skye,' I call.

A passer-by overhears and the lady kindly offers to take our photograph together. We stand beaming in front of the palace gates.

'If you look carefully, you might see Prince George waving from the window.' The lady winks at her as she hands me my phone back.

I have to drag Skye over to the grass after that or I think she'd stand there all day.

I take the sandwiches and crisps out of my bag. We wolf them down, the cheese-and-tomato filling tasting so much better in the fresh air, the way it always seems to do with an impromptu picnic.

My heart squeezes with pure joy. The dark shadow of what happened to Lewis has hovered above us for so long, I thought it had sapped the very life spirit out of us. There have been times anxiety has taken hold and I've honestly wondered if the light will ever fully come back into our lives.

Today, it feels as if it's shining upon us again.

The relentless ache inside that I've lived with since my childhood of endless foster homes, of being less than, of not belonging, may never be fully healed, but spending time with my daughter always acts as a soothing balm. I never wanted her to know what that ache feels like, but since Lewis has been gone, I think she has experienced it.

23

Here in the park, though, she seems happy.

'Come on!' I laugh as I stuff the picnic wrappings back inside my bag before standing up and reaching for her hand. 'Let's go grab an ice cream before we walk to the Tube station.'

Skye grabs my fingers and we start to walk towards the small gathering of people at the van.

I feel a prickle at the back of my neck, that kind of inexplicable feeling that someone is watching. As we shuffle up the queue another place, I turn around and scan the faces behind me and beyond.

No one is taking any notice of us, of course. It's just that destructive part of myself that likes to pop up to spook me when it can't accept things are going right for once.

5

A week later while we wait for removals, to my shame, I allow Skye to play back-to-back Candy Crush on my phone. Just this once, while I squeeze the last few bits into boxes.

Despite the excitement about moving to Adder House, she's been a bit clingy and tearful this morning.

'I'm so sad to leave my bedroom, Mummy,' she sniffed, and I know all the other lovely memories we've shared here with Lewis are probably on her mind. I know I've been thinking about them, too.

Our friends, Brenna and Viv, have come over to help out, and an hour later, we follow the loaded removals lorry to Adder House in Brenna's SUV.

The lorry rumbles up outside Adder House, and Brenna parks on the double yellow lines behind it. Dr Marsden appears at the front door before I can ring the bell.

'Freya, Skye, welcome to your new home.' He smiles when we climb the entrance steps.

I turn to my left to introduce the others.

'Dr Marsden, meet Brenna and Viv, our friends. They've very kindly given up their Saturday to help us move in.'

Dr Marsden smiles and performs a little bow. 'Very pleased to meet you, ladies. It's very kind of you to accompany Freya, but I'm happy to help out upstairs if you need to get yourselves off.'

'Oh no, we're staying to help!' Viv splutters. 'I've been dying to see this place for ages.'

I avert my eyes as we troop into the foyer. It's just the kind of comment that might be perceived as inappropriate in a place like this. Not for the first time, I question if I'll find myself out of my depth here at Adder House with all its perceived airs and graces.

'I see.' A thin smile settles over Dr Marsden's face. 'Freya, in that case, I'll leave you to it. The door to your apartment is already open. Please do pop down when you get a few minutes, as the residents who are home today are very keen to meet you.'

The apartment door opens behind him, and an older woman steps into the hallway.

She is heavily made-up and very elegantly dressed in well-cut black wool slacks and a simple charcoal-grey cashmere sweater. A discreet string of pearls adorns her neck.

I can't stop staring at her striking white hair; almost pure white and mainly short, it is swept back from her forehead in an astonishingly high quiff that seems to defy gravity.

'Ahh, I see the lovely Audrey has popped out to say hello.' Dr Marsden steps back as the woman glides over to us in her black patent pumps and extends a pale, liver-spotted hand.

'Audrey Marsden, delighted to meet you,' she says in a deep, cultured voice. I shake her hand, entranced by her powdered face and scarlet lips. When her misty grey eyes settle on mine, I get the strangest feeling; as if she's looking *into* me, rather than at me.

I clear my throat and smile. 'Hello, Audrey. I'm Freya and this is my daughter, Skye.'

'Welcome to Adder House, Freya.' She looks down on Skye. 'And to you too, little one.'

I feel Skye squeeze closer into my side.

'Michael has told me so much about you both. I do hope you'll pop down for tea, once you're settled in?'

26

'Thank you,' I say. 'We will.'

'We'll leave you to it, then.' Dr Marsden smiles and the two of them disappear back into their apartment as I attempt to peel Skye from my side.

'Why are you being silly? This isn't like you, munchkin.'

'I don't like that lady,' Skye whispers. 'She's got funny eyes.'

'Got to admit, there's definitely a touch of the Addams Family about her.' Viv sniggers.

'She could have *three* eyes for all I care, if she asked me to come live here,' Brenna quips, looking around the elaborate entrance hall open-mouthed.

I throw Viv a warning glance, uncomfortable in case we're still in the Marsdens' earshot.

I pop out to give the removals team instructions on where to bring the stuff and pretend not to notice the frowns when they look up to the top floor and register how backbreaking the job will be.

Back inside, I try and chivvy the others along. 'Come on then, let's go upstairs. Skye, get ready to move into your new bedroom.'

She gives me a little sad smile, and I know she's thinking about the old bedroom she's left behind. It was nothing special; quite small, painted pink with lots of stickers on the walls and a second-hand bunk bed that a school mum was selling. Skye begged us to buy it so Petra didn't have to sleep on a camp bed when she stayed over.

Despite that, I know Skye will miss her old room and the fun times she's had playing in there.

When we reach the third floor, everyone, apart from Skye, is out of breath. 'Holy moly, you'll either get fit living here or die try-ing.' Brenna pauses before attempting the last few steps.

'I'm definitely going to get fit. All part of my dynamic new-start master plan,' I say triumphantly. I push open the door to our apartment and gesture for everyone to enter before me.

I smile as I hear the impressed exclamations from Brenna and Viv, and when I hear Skye squeal in excitement, I know she's found her bedroom again. Her sudden happiness is like music to my ears.

I close the door and walk into our home, seeing the space anew again.

'Mummy! I found the confetti tree!'

I walk over to the window where Skye is standing. The tree is even more vividly pink than ten days ago when we were last here.

My daughter's face is glowing, her features alive with excitement, and I feel so thankful and relieved she likes it. Once she's settled in, I'm sure she'll be equally excited to start at the local school here. I'll broach the subject as soon as I feel she's ready.

'I think we're going to be very happy here, sweetie.' I pull her close and bury my face in her hair, which still smells of apple shampoo from last night's bath.

I can't hold on to her for long. She soon pulls away, full of plans for her new bedroom.

'I'd like my bed against this wall and my toy box under the window, please. Did you bring my rug? It's going to go just here.' She points to the middle of the small room. 'I can play with my figurines on there and still see the cherry blossom out of the window.'

I'm impressed with the level of planning she's managed.

'Look at the colour of those late rhododendrons!' I hear Viv shriek. She is a keen gardener, often out pottering in their tiny garden if the weather is fine.

I leave Skye debating where best to situate her props for her precious figurines, and join Viv at the window where she gazes down on the riot of colour. Again, it's even more vivid than when we visited last. 'The lupins are exquisite . . . and the peonies, too. Oh Freya, this place is just a dream.'

A man in grey overalls is kneeling by one of the flower beds, digging at the soil with a small handheld trowel.

'Oh look, there's the hired help,' Brenna quips, peering over my shoulder. 'You've fallen on your feet here my friend, no mistake.'

'So your initial doubts about whether I've been a bit hasty have faded away, right?' I say cheekily, remembering her comments about Dr Marsden when I called to tell her, and her questioning how everything had happened so incredibly quickly.

'No trace of any concerns whatsoever now that I've seen the place.' Brenna grins sheepishly. 'Creepy old doc's wife, or not.'

'I trust everything is in order here?' A voice fills the room.

My heart thumps when I look round and see Dr Marsden standing in the doorway. I didn't hear him come in, but the front door is wide open for the removals men, so there would be no need for him to knock.

I glance at Brenna and see even her face is flushing. Serves her right. I hope and pray he didn't hear her rude comment.

'Everything is fine, thank you, Dr Marsden. It's . . . just perfect.'

'I'll see you downstairs as soon as you're free then,' he says, throwing Brenna a blank glance before turning on his heel.

He pauses at Skye's bedroom door, and I'm just about to follow him down the short hallway, when two puffing removals men appear with the first sticks of furniture and some boxes.

In just over an hour, the removals company have completed their job. They didn't request a deposit when I booked, and when I query payment with the man in charge, he waves his hand dismissively.

'The bill has already been sorted, madam.'

I'm not going to stand there arguing about it, I'm sure they'll realise their mistake soon enough and send the invoice through, and having a bit longer to pay suits me fine.

There are heaps of packed boxes labelled by room stacked on the landing, and all the large pieces of furniture are in place. My stuff seemed perfectly fine in the old house but it looks a little jaded in here, kind of like when you repaint one room and then see how tired the rest of the house looks.

When the removals men leave, Brenna claps her hands. 'OK, first things first. Viv and I will go and find the most important box; the one with the kettle and the mugs. You stay here with Skye. Back in a jiffy.'

I nod, happy to defer to Brenna's bossy, organising nature. I can hardly believe we're here, in a beautiful new apartment, when only a few weeks ago I was trying to come to terms with the very real possibility of the two of us temporarily crashing in Brenna and Viv's spare room with its sole single bed.

When it comes to Adder House, I feel . . . I suppose the word is *unworthy*, in a way.

And yet this has happened, it *is* real, and we're here.

Skye runs in with what looks like a white credit card. She holds it out to me.

'Dr Marsden and Audrey gave me the special electronic key for you, Mummy. They said it was my job to make sure you got it safely.' Her chin tilts slightly with the importance of the task bestowed on her, and I smile at their cleverness in getting Skye onside.

'Thank you, sweetie.' I take it from her. 'And did they say anything else?'

'Nothing really.' Skye shrugs nonchalantly. 'Dr Marsden asked me what my favourite thing was about my bedroom, and I said it was the confetti tree.'

'That's nice.' I smile at her. 'It's such a pretty thing to have right outside your window.'

Skye nods. 'When they left I heard them say that the little girl who lived here before loved it, too.'

And off she skips down the hallway, smiling back at me as she goes.

6

I don't mention Skye's comment about the little girl to Brenna and Viv when they reappear with packing boxes marked 'kitchen' and 'essentials'.

I'm not sure why I decide to keep quiet, it just seems so bizarre and they're already a bit freaked out by Audrey Marsden as it is. The last thing I want is for any more embarrassing comments to be flying around.

Skye has such an active imagination, and besides, Dr Marsden has already said that we're the first tenants in the apartment.

Still, even as Viv and Brenna begin unpacking the boxes, it niggles.

'Listen, will you two be OK to stay here with Skye if I just pop downstairs to see the Marsdens? They've asked if I can meet a few people, and I don't want them to think me rude.'

'Sure,' Brenna murmurs, leafing through a Gordon Ramsay cookbook she just unearthed. 'Go knock yourself out with the *Dr Dee-ath* and his vampire bride. And don't worry, if you're not back in thirty minutes, we'll come looking . . . armed with a bunch of garlic and a silver cross.'

'Don't!' I quickly paste a smile on my face when they both look up at my snappy tone. 'You're freaking me out.'

'Hey, chill out, it's only a joke, Freya!' Brenna grins. 'Hurry up, we've got a bottle of fizz on ice to toast your new beginning here. That should loosen you up a bit.'

I pop my head around Skye's door and smile when I see she's deep in conversation with a circle of soft toys who are, by the looks of it, being treated to an impromptu tea party.

I decide to leave the apartment without disturbing her.

The house is blissfully quiet as I pad downstairs, and I'm already feeling brighter as I absorb my spacious surroundings and look out of the large windows at the front of the house, at the blue sky and fluffy white clouds.

Each landing is spotless. The wooden floors gleam and the ornate banister rails shine in the hazy sunshine that filters in through the glass.

I linger a little on the second and first floors, outside the grand mahogany doors, to see if I can detect the sound of voices beyond, perhaps a television or music playing. But there is nothing but the sound of my own breathing.

Back down on the ground floor, I stand on the bottom step for a few moments before tapping lightly on Dr Marsden's apartment door.

I hear footsteps approaching, and the door quietly clicks as it opens to reveal Audrey Marsden. Her skin stretches tightly, as if her face is struggling to accommodate the smile.

'Freya. How nice you've been able to pop down so quickly,' she says in that deep, hypnotic tone of hers. She tips her head to see behind me. 'But no little one with you?'

'My friends are looking after her for a few minutes,' I explain as she signals for me to step inside. I slip off my shoes at the door, and Dr Marsden himself appears, ushering me into the lounge.

'The removals went smoothly, I trust?'

'Yes, thank you.' I smile. Then something occurs to me. 'Thanks for recommending them, but they seem to think the bill has been already paid.'

'And so it has.' Dr Marsden beams.

'What? I mean . . . thank you, but there was no need. If you let me know how much it—'

'Think nothing of it, dear.' Audrey waves my concern away. 'We're good friends with the owner of the company.'

'Oh, I can't let you do that,' I say lightly.

'It's done,' Dr Marsden insists.

'Thank you so much.' My throat feels tight. That has saved me *a lot* of cash, but it still makes me feel uncomfortable that they've taken it upon themselves to pay without mentioning it to me first.

'Now. We thought it might be nice for you to meet one or two of our other residents on your first day here, but there's only one home apart from us,' Dr Marsden says, seeming to watch for my reaction. 'That's if you'd like to, of course.'

'That would be lovely,' I say, more confident than I really feel.

He looks pleased. 'We're quite a close-knit bunch here. Don't get me wrong, we don't live in each other's pockets by any means, but you can rest assured there's always someone around if you need any help. We pride ourselves on that.'

'This is not the kind of place where you will ever feel alone,' Audrey adds.

I draw in a breath. 'Actually, Skye mentioned something about the previous tenants . . .'

They both turn to look at me in unison. Silence descends on the room and the very air seems to still, hanging thick and heavy around my ears.

It's a ridiculous notion, I know, but it honestly feels as if the building itself is listening in, too.

7

'Skye is delighted with her new bedroom,' I say lightly, hoping it seems like a natural thing to bring into the conversation, but then I spoil it by stammering. 'She said . . . well . . . she thought she overheard you saying a little girl used to live in the apartment before us?'

Dr Marsden glances at his wife and shakes his head, obviously perplexed. 'I can't recall that I said . . . ahh, wait a moment. I *did* say that any little girl would be happy to have such a pretty tree outside her window. Perhaps Skye got mixed up.'

I smile. 'That'll be it. Skye can make a story out of very little.'

'The imagination of children,' Audrey declares, 'is a wonderful thing.'

'And to be admired,' Dr Marsden adds. 'I often think there's far too much emphasis put on grades and examinations these days, and that children aren't allowed to use their imagination at all.'

'Speaking of school, will Skye be attending St Benjamin Monks?' Audrey remarks. 'It's our closest state primary school.'

'Yes, in fact I've already spoken to the school office.' I feel inexplicably pleased with myself that I'm able to demonstrate I've at least got around to doing that. 'I have to arrange for us to visit. It's . . . on my list.'

'A very long list, no doubt.' Audrey chuckles. 'Just so you know, I'm a governor there. So if you need any help at all with the admission process, just let me know.'

'Thank you,' I say, genuinely touched by her kind offer. We're interrupted by a knock at the door.

'Come in,' Audrey calls out.

I sit up a bit straighter and force my hands out from under my thighs. I fix a pleasant expression on my face and watch as a thin, wiry man in his late thirties with slightly wild brown hair enters the room. His eyes dart around from side to side, as if he suspects someone might try and jump out at him at any moment.

His eyes flicker in my direction, but don't quite settle on me before he looks away again.

'Matthew! Good to see you.' Dr Marsden strides forward to shake the man's hand. 'Come and say hello to our new tenant, Freya Miller.'

I stand up, quickly wiping my clammy palms on my jeans. I feel weirdly vulnerable standing there in bare feet after shedding my shoes at the door. I hope none of them notice the chipped pink varnish on my toes.

The man advances towards me, still seemingly avoiding looking at me directly. He has allowed his hair to grow long enough for his dull curls to bounce around as he walks. When he gets closer, I see he has a full bottom lip which makes the top one seem thinner than it is.

'Freya, this is Professor Matthew Woodings. He and his wife, Susan, live at number three.'

'Hello.' I grasp his floppy hand and smile, but he still won't hold my glance. 'I'm very pleased to meet you.'

'Hello, Freya,' he says mechanically. 'Welcome to Adder House.'

'Freya has just moved in today. With her daughter, Skye.'

'You have a child?' He looks at me then, an expression of confusion on his face. 'I wasn't aware of that.'

Why would he be? And then I realise that Dr Marsden has no doubt informed the other residents to expect a new tenant and I would have thought he's told them a little bit about us.

'I believe Skye is five years old, is that right, Freya?'

'Yes, she turns six in August.' I feel a little uncomfortable as Professor Woodings now can't seem to look *away* from my face.

'Matthew?' Dr Marsden says gently.

'Sorry!' Professor Woodings shakes his head as if to dispel some kind of stupor. 'Sorry if I'm staring. It's lack of sleep. I was on the late shift last night.'

'Matthew is a scientist,' Dr Marsden explains. 'Works for the government on various classified and mysterious projects conducted in restricted areas, not open to the public.'

Professor Woodings gives a nervous laugh. 'You make it sound very intriguing, Michael, but I'm afraid it isn't that exciting at all. Not really.' He looks at me again. 'I *am* a scientist and I *do* work for the government, but it's not remotely as "Dr Evil" as Michael makes it sound, if you know what I mean. And my wife is a librarian, so no mystery there.'

Dr Marsden stage whispers from behind his hand. 'Don't let him fool you. She's head librarian at a private, members-only library . . . all a bit cloak and dagger if you ask me.'

'Really, Michael.' Audrey rolls her eyes and I catch a glimpse of her bright-blue eyeshadow.

Professor Woodings grins and I smile back, warming to him a little. I wonder why he was so stand-offish at the start. Perhaps it was just initial shyness.

'Well, it's very nice to meet you, Freya, but I really have to get some rest now. Susan and I will both be around this weekend, so do give us a shout if there's anything you need. I know my wife would really love to meet your daughter.'

Dr Marsden nods approvingly.

'That's very kind, Matthew. Thank you,' I say, touched by his friendlier manner.

When he's left, I turn to Dr Marsden. 'He seemed a bit surprised to hear there's going to be a child living here,' I say. 'I hope the other residents aren't going to mind having Skye around.'

'On the contrary, my dear,' Dr Marsden says emphatically. 'I think everyone will appreciate having a young person around the place. You have to understand that—'

'It's a little delicate, but I know you'll be discreet,' Audrey interrupts her husband. 'Matthew's wife, Susan, had a miscarriage just a few months ago. It was her third loss in the past eighteen months.'

'Oh no.' My hand flies up to my mouth.

'Yes, it was all very upsetting. Everyone tried their best to find ways to help them in any way they could, but it's such a private matter. They really had to just work through it themselves.'

'Of course,' I say in a small voice.

Dr Marsden coughs. 'Well, it's better you know about it. With you lucky enough to be a mother, and all.'

'Thank you for confiding in me.' I'm already feeling guilty for being lucky enough to have a beautiful daughter. But I'm humbled that the professor thinks having Skye around could please Susan, his wife. I do hope he's right, it sounds like she's suffered so much and seeing a child here could prove painful.

'Just take the time you need to ease in slowly to life at Adder House,' Audrey says kindly. 'You're part of our family now, so relax.'

She looks over at her husband and something . . . some kind of silent understanding, seems to pass between them both.

I make my excuses and head back upstairs.

8

By the time Brenna and Viv leave, we have all the basic things in place in the apartment, including a gorgeous Nelson and Forbes bronze hare they gave us as a housewarming gift that now sits in pride of place in the lounge window.

Our beds are up – thanks to the removals men assembling them as part of their job – and we've now made them up with clean linen. The seating, television, and coffee table are in the living area, and the kettle, crockery, and the most important utensils are in the small, integral kitchen.

I could spend the next twelve hours unpacking the boxes, measuring up for curtains, and making a list of things I need that for whatever reason I was unable to bring from the old house. I could stick Skye in front of Netflix or give her my iPad to play games on so I can get on, but I don't do any of this stuff.

Instead, I say to my daughter, 'Trainers on . . . we're going to explore the garden.'

Skye's face lights up. 'What . . . *this* garden, with the swing?'

'The very same one. The unpacking can wait for now.'

Skye immediately dumps the iPad down on the seat cushion beside her and bounces across the room.

'I'll get my shoes on now, Mummy!'

I have to smile to myself. There aren't many situations where I ask Skye to get ready to go out and she reacts with such enthusiasm. Particularly during this past week, which has been difficult at the best of times as she's alternated between staying put in Acton and wanting to move.

Five minutes later, we're heading downstairs. 'Careful, the stairs are quite steep.'

'Who lives behind these doors?' Skye hesitates on the second floor and stares at the large polished wooden doors.

'Different people, different families but some people are away at the moment. Dr Marsden introduced me to one of the residents called Matthew this morning, and he seemed very nice.'

'I want to meet new people, too,' Skye says.

'And you will. But we've only just got here and there are lots of jobs to do and people to meet . . . including the teachers and children at the lovely school near here.'

Skye starts to hum but that's OK. I'm just sneaking the idea of a new school in when I get the chance for now. There's no rush and it's important it's done properly, so Skye doesn't feel threatened by it.

We don't see anyone on the way out of the house, but I find myself almost tapping at Dr Marsden's door to tell him we're just popping out to look at the garden.

Obviously I've no intention of doing so, but I just have this weird sense that he expects to know where we are at any given time. Completely imaginary on my part, I know, but there's a bit of a strange feel about the people here that I can't quite put my finger on yet.

'I love it here already, Mummy,' she says as we walk down the front steps and around the side of the house. 'But when I think about our old home, it still makes me feel sad, here.' She prods her own tummy.

'I know, poppet. I feel sad, too. It's always difficult, leaving a home we've loved . . .' I hesitate, not wanting to mention Lewis. 'But we had no choice, so here we are, and we must count our blessings that our new home is lovely, too.'

Seconds later we're in the leafy, walled oasis of the Adder House residents' garden.

It's still warm out and the lawn and flower beds are bathed in sunlight while the verdant canopies of mature oak trees provide a seductive shade.

Skye races down to the bottom end of the garden where a rope swing hangs from a mighty oak bough.

'Hang on, Skye, wait for me!' I pick up my pace. 'I need to make sure it's strong enough first.'

For all I know, it could have been hanging there unused for years, the rope rotten and perilous.

'It's quite safe.' A strange voice floats into my ears. 'The swing, I mean.'

I freeze and look around me but there's nobody here but us.

Then, a slight movement catches my eye at the edge of a large rhododendron bush. I step a bit closer and peer around it.

A slightly built woman is sitting there on a small wooden bench. She looks a little older than me, maybe in her late thirties. She has a neat dark-blonde bob and wears no jewellery at all apart from a thin gold wedding band. She's dressed in a long white cotton dress and has bare feet with unpolished toenails.

'Hello, I didn't see you behind there,' I say, a little awkwardly.

She looks so pale and her eyes are like dark, sorrowful smudges under her long fringe, with not so much as a flicker of light discernible.

There's a sort of frailty about her despite her young age, and I wonder if she's supposed to be in this garden or if she has just wandered in with the side gate being unlocked.

'This is my little piece of heaven.' She smiles weakly. 'It's where I come to recalibrate.'

I glance down the garden to check on Skye and see with relief that she's moved slightly away from the swing now and is happily skipping and singing around the trunk of another large tree next to it.

'I'm Susan Woodings.' She doesn't stand up or offer her hand. 'I think you met Matthew, my husband, earlier.'

I realise then it's Professor Woodings' librarian wife, who has just lost another baby.

Now I understand that the shadows in her eyes bear witness to her repeated heartbreak, and a sudden ache fills my chest.

'I'm so pleased to meet you.' I give her a warm smile. 'I'm Freya and the noisy one over there is Skye, my daughter.'

As soon as I refer to my child, I feel guilt instantly nip at my throat, even though I know it's illogical. I just hope seeing Skye around the place doesn't deepen the rawness of her grief.

I walk closer to Susan and see that a little enclave has been fashioned there behind the bush.

There's the pretty carved bench she's sitting on and a tiny paved area cluttered with brightly coloured pots planted with lavender and rosemary. Small glittering charms and three wind chimes hanging from various flora and fauna that act as a natural screen from the openness of the main garden.

A slight breeze carries the wonderful calming scents of the potted herbs up to my face.

'What a lovely space you've made here,' I sweep my hand over the area. 'It's like a little peaceful retreat.'

'I call it my memorial garden.'

I feel a squeeze in my heart.

'It's beautiful,' I say softly. 'And I love your chimes.'

'One for each child,' she says faintly and flicks the silver wind chime next to her, causing a harp-like flurry of notes to ripple through the air. It's captivating and a little eerie.

'What's that?' The noise has attracted Skye, who runs up, bumping into my side. 'Oh!' She sees Susan tucked behind the large bush.

'Hello, Skye, I'm Susan.' The briefest sparkle flickers in her eyes before it's gone again.

'Hello,' Skye says shyly, screwing the toe of her training shoe into the grass.

'I live at Adder House, too.' Susan smiles at Skye's obvious preoccupation with her garden. 'Would you like to tinkle my wind chimes?'

Skye nods and tiptoes around the plant pots on the little patio, reaching towards the silver chime. The flurry of notes dances around us and a wide smile spreads across Skye's face.

'She's called Clare, and this one' – Susan points to a bamboo chime with a long middle pendulum – 'is Clara.'

Skye wiggles the pendulum and a deeper sound resonates.

'What's this one called?' Skye reaches towards an intricate chime consisting entirely of beads and coloured shells. A delicate tinkle scatters the stillness of the air.

'Ahh, she's called Clarice.' Susan smiles.

'Why do the names all sound nearly the exact same?' Skye frowns. Susan stares into the middle distance but doesn't answer.

Goosebumps prickle my arms and I give them a rub as I address Skye.

'Right, come on then, scamp. Let's head for the swing, we've lots of unpacking waiting for us to do upstairs.' As Skye picks her way around the pots, I turn back and smile. 'It's really lovely to meet you, Susan, we'll no doubt see you around the place.'

'I could look after her,' Susan suddenly blurts out, clasping her small, pale hands together. 'While you get your unpacking done, I mean. Or if you need a babysitter one night, perhaps.'

She looks longingly at Skye, who's already skipping back towards the swing.

'Oh! That's very kind of you, but—'

'She could bring her dolls. I have lots of tiny baby clothes that would fit.'

Her face is so full of hope and yearning, I could cry. I rack my brains for a sensitive reply.

'That's really kind of you, Susan, but I've given her a bit of responsibility in unpacking and placing her own stuff in her bedroom. So she better understands how things are organised, if you see what I mean.'

'Of course!' Susan says a little too brightly. 'It's a good idea, Freya. You seem like a really good mother.'

'Mummyyy!' Skye shrieks and I breathe a silent sigh of relief at the distraction.

'Oh dear, better go.' I set off walking before hesitating and turning back again. Susan is staring at her hands. 'When we're properly settled in, it would be lovely if you could pop up for a cup of tea with us. Skye is into soft toys more than dolls, but I know she'd be delighted to show you each and every one of them . . . if you have the time.'

A smile brightens her face. 'Thank you, Freya,' she says. 'I'd really love that.' Then she walks back inside, her shoulders sagging.

9

I push Skye for ten minutes or so on the swing.

Susan Woodings is right; the swing is in good repair and I wonder if Dr Marsden keeps it maintained because other residents here have grandchildren who visit Adder House on occasion. Skye would love to make a few new friends, if so.

Again, my mind wanders back to Skye saying she thought another little girl used to live here. Maybe part of her wishes there were other children to play with.

When we get back inside, Dr Marsden surprises me by meeting us at the door.

'I hope you've had a nice time out there in the garden.' He smiles at Skye as we move into the foyer. 'I saw you high up on the swing.'

I remember the Marsdens' French doors overlook the garden.

'Do other children play on the swing?' Skye asks in a forthright manner.

'No . . . at least not any more,' Dr Marsden murmurs.

What does he mean by that? When I asked him about a child living here, he didn't say one used to, he just dismissed it. I feel twisty inside as if I might not be getting the full truth for some reason.

'If you have a moment, Miss Skye, I have something for you in my apartment,' he says to her.

Skye shuffles closer to me again. 'Can Mummy come, too?'

'Of course she can.'

We follow Dr Marsden into his apartment. He walks over to a long mahogany cupboard built in under the vast stretch of bookshelves. It has deep drawers and doors with polished brass handles.

'Now. How about a little welcome present for our youngest tenant?' He has Skye's attention now, and she takes a step away from me in an effort to see what's inside the cupboard. 'This one . . .'

Skye's eyes widen as he holds up a beautifully plush white unicorn with a shimmering multicoloured single horn on its head.

Just as I'm trying to think of a nice way to say we can't possibly accept such a generous gift, Dr Marsden presents a second choice. 'Or perhaps you'd prefer this one?'

In the other hand he holds an expensive-looking teddy bear. *Surely*, I think, eyeing the distinctive round white label with black writing, *it can't be a Steiff bear?* I knew someone years back who collected them and I know they're devilishly expensive.

This is too much after them paying for the removals.

I'm about to protest when a door opens at the other end of the room and Audrey appears. She pads elegantly over to her husband and Skye and watches them without comment.

'Now, which one will it be?' Dr Marsden says in his deep, velvety voice. This room feels too warm with all the glass, and just listening to him after our busy day is starting to make me feel a bit sleepy.

Skye points shyly at the unicorn. 'I'd like this one, please.'

'So, that's your choice, is it?' They both seem entranced by my daughter.

'Yes.' Skye nods firmly. I feel relieved she didn't choose the *Steiff* or I'd have had to intervene.

'It's only fair I should point something out, Skye. This one' – Audrey holds the bear aloft – 'costs four times as much as this one to buy.' She shakes the unicorn with her other hand.

I'm not sure where they're going with this, but I watch, intrigued.

'So, I'll ask you one final time.' Dr Marsden leans forward. 'Bearing in mind what Audrey just told you about the value of the two items, which one would you like to take as your present today?'

'I'd like the unicorn, please,' Skye says without hesitation.

'Then that is the one you shall have,' Dr Marsden says and hands the toy to her. 'Welcome to Adder House, Miss Skye.'

'Thank you!' Skye cuddles the unicorn close as she beams up at me, delighted. Audrey stares at Skye, as if she's baffled by her choice.

'This is so very kind of you both.' I feel I have to thank them even though I'm a tad irritated. 'It's certainly not necessary but it's very much appreciated. Thank you.'

'I haven't forgotten you, my dear. I shall be offended if you don't accept a tot of my finest sherry. We must toast this very special day.'

'Thank you,' I say, hiding a grimace. I've always disliked sherry.

Audrey pours three small glasses from a heavy crystal decanter and places them on a round silver tray. We follow her over to the big cream couches.

Clutching the unicorn, Skye finally leaves my side. She's still fascinated by all the beautiful trinkets Dr Marsden has around the place; exquisite bronze sculptures on strategically placed plinths, carved wooden boxes that have probably come from somewhere exotic.

I take the proffered glass and sniff it. It's only teatime and the smell is so strong I can't help but jerk my face back.

'Wonderful aroma, isn't it?' Dr Marsden says, drawing in a long inhalation above his own glass. 'Barbadillo Versos 1891, a rare limited-edition sherry dating back to the nineteenth century.'

'It's . . . very distinctive,' I say, desperately trying to keep the look of distaste from my face.

I force myself to take another sip. To my uneducated palate, it tastes just like cough medicine.

'Don't rush now. You have to sip it slowly to fully savour its bouquet,' Dr Marsden insists.

I fight another flash of irritation in my chest and put down my glass on the table. 'Sorry, it's really not my thing,' I say as politely as I can. 'I'm not a big drinker.'

The Marsdens actually look shocked that someone openly dares to have a different opinion to them.

This place is like living in an over-inflated bubble of luxury. Don't they know there are people just a few streets from here living rough, struggling to find their next meal?

Then I catch myself, feeling like I don't belong again and my last foster mother's words replay in my head. *You'll never make anything of your life. You'll see.*

But she was wrong. I *am* making something of our lives here. It's just going to take a bit of getting used to.

◆ ◆ ◆

It's 2.40 a.m. when my eyes spring open.

The glowing red digits of the clock don't get the chance to move on a minute before I start feeling a little queasy.

I prop myself up with pillows and lie back in the soft glow of my single bedside lamp. It must have been drinking sherry at the Marsdens' on an empty stomach like that . . .

What on earth was I thinking?

I'd only had a few sips before putting down my glass, but it was strong stuff. I'd felt the warming effect of the alcohol when we came back upstairs, but I hadn't had enough to feel remotely drunk.

I'd made Skye a simple tea of fish fingers and peas, but I hadn't bothered having anything myself simply because I felt so tired. That had clearly been a mistake.

I take a sip of water from the glass I brought to bed with me last night and allow my head to sink back into the pillows. I don't know why I feel restless, I should be counting my blessings.

Yet I can't help asking myself why they are so accommodating, pushing gifts on my daughter, paying bills that have nothing to do with them. Some folks might think I'm crazy for even questioning their motives, but it makes me uncomfortable. Simple as that.

They could fill this place a hundred times over for the peppercorn rent I'm paying, there's no doubt about that. So what's so special about us?

Dr Marsden told me he chooses tenants on the basis of how they fit in here. But a single mother with various hang-ups and a precarious financial status? A little girl who's struggling after the death of her father?

We seem a world apart from the existing Adder House residents. I sigh and close my eyes, tired of turning it all over in my head.

It's so blissfully quiet here. There's no traffic noise and, as our apartment looks out over the back of the house, no sounds from people returning home from a night out in the surrounding houses and apartments.

48

Most people around here seem older, more conservative than the diverse mix of neighbours we had in Acton. I'm far from missing the place but feel a little squeeze of concern that once we're properly settled in, I'll need to ensure I'm mixing with younger people, too.

There is more to life than antique vases and vintage sherry, although the Marsdens don't seem to think so.

I look around my apartment at the newly painted smooth walls, the modern and functional Roman blind at the window, and the spotless beige carpet. This place seems to have literally everything we need.

But I've no intention of living in the landlord's pocket, and I need to make that crystal clear as soon as I get the chance.

10

We set off for school early Monday morning. We have to walk up the road to the bus stop and then get the first of two buses to Skye's current school, Grove Primary in Acton.

I could have easily kept her off school for the remainder of the summer term. It would certainly be easier than trawling across London on various buses twice a day. But I thought it was really important to keep the routine going, particularly as I hadn't had a chance yet to inform Grove about Skye's transfer to a new school.

But before our moving day, I rang St Benjamin Monks Primary, the school just down the road here where Audrey is a governor.

It's a state school, rare in this area with its sea of independent private primary schools costing up to twenty thousand pounds a year for each child. It's located on Kensington Church Street, and Ofsted have graded it as 'Outstanding' for the last three inspections. Plus, the school's examination results rank in the top five best state primary schools in the whole of London.

It's a no-brainer which school Skye is better off attending.

When I called, the school office put me through to the head-teacher, Mrs Grant.

'It's probably neater if Skye finishes the term at her current school, if you're able to travel there in the meantime,' Mrs Grant suggested. 'We hold a holiday club all through the summer break, so Skye can come in a few times and get used to the school and meet some of the children who'll be her new classmates in September.'

This had sounded like a great plan, and I was heartened by the thought of Skye making new friends before the autumn term started.

Once her old school closes down for the summer, there are no other facilities offered. There are no holiday clubs, no residential camps. Already I can see the benefit of my daughter attending a better-funded school with such useful additional holiday activities, particularly when the time comes for me to find another job.

It's mid-July, so there is only a week and a half of the school term remaining.

Although it takes three times longer to get to Grove Primary from our new address, we won't have to do it for long, and it will give Skye a chance to say goodbye to her teachers and friends.

I get an uncomfortable pulsing in my throat every time I think about telling her. I've done everything the wrong way around. I should have dealt with this stuff while we were still living in the old house, but our moving date came around so quickly, I barely had time to think.

I haven't even spoken to Kat, her best friend Petra's mum.

Skye skips along the pavement, excitement buzzing like a layer of electricity under her skin.

Before all the awful things that happened with Lewis, she used to remind me of an effervescent bath bomb, fizzing with energy and a joy for life. He left us for another woman first and then he died.

Unsurprisingly, tragedy sucked that joy out of her, and I've become accustomed over the past year to her new, more reserved nature. *Too* reserved, some of the time. For a healthy five-year-old anyway.

So it's lovely to see a little of her old *joie de vivre*.

'I'm going to tell Petra all about us moving to Adder House today, Mummy.' She dances around me like a mini boxer as I steer her to the bus stop. 'Can she come over to ours soon? I know she'll want to help me unpack all my Sylvanian Families and see my new bedroom. Oh, and she'll need our address so her mummy can bring her over. But I'll still see her every day at school, won't I?'

'And you might be able to finish your painting today in art class!' I say quickly. 'We can stick it up on your bedroom wall.'

Thankfully, we spend the rest of the journey talking about the art supplies she'd like for her birthday which falls at the end of August.

I breathe a sigh of relief when I drop her off and finally beat a hasty retreat from the playground, grateful not to have bumped into Kat. We're not big friends ourselves but we're both under no illusions that our girls are close buddies and that the friendship means a lot to each of them.

Once I tell Kat exactly where Adder House is, she'll know immediately that Skye cannot practically continue attending this school. But the last thing I want is for Petra to know that Skye will be leaving Grove Primary before my daughter herself does.

I head for the bus stop and blow out a long exhalation of air. I resolve to speak to her this evening. It's the right thing to do.

Impulsively, on my way home, I decide to pop in and see Brenna. A quick chat with her over a coffee will be sure to cheer me up.

As a respected professor in the field of psychology, Brenna occasionally guest lectures at universities throughout the UK, but mostly prefers to work from home writing her academic research papers.

Her partner, Viv, works away a lot, and as such, we've always spent quite a bit of time together; and she's been a godsend in looking after Skye at short notice.

The last time I visited her at home was just after I'd met Dr Marsden in Starbucks. 'I'm so glad you called in, I have great news,' she'd said cryptically when I rang the doorbell. She signalled for me to sit at the breakfast bar while she made coffee. 'Viv has a friend in phlebotomy who's looking to rent out her apartment while she takes a sabbatical year abroad. It's a little small and further out of town, but Viv has visited her there and she says it will be just perfect for you and Skye, at least until you get turned around.'

Brenna and Viv knew just how worried I'd been about finding a suitable place to live that fitted my budget. They had already kindly offered us their own spare room if we needed it temporarily.

Brenna had smiled expectantly, waiting for my reaction, which would have been an ecstatic one, if I hadn't got some news of my own.

'That sounds really great, but actually I came to tell you something,' I'd said tentatively, wondering how I was going to word it. 'I've found somewhere amazing for me and Skye to live. In fact, we're moving in there next weekend.'

Her mouth had fallen open as I explained about the opportunity at Adder House. I'd watched as the smile slid from her face, the way her hand froze in mid-air before pulling out a couple of mugs from the cupboard.

It sounded crazy; I knew it did. But I also reminded myself it was real. Amazingly, it was real.

She'd stared at me. 'You're seriously telling me that some random guy you met in a coffee shop just signed you up to an apartment in South Kensington?' Her voice shot up an octave. *'For five hundred a month?'*

'I know, I know, it sounds dodgy, but it's true. It's all above board. I've been to view the place, fully checked it out.' I could barely keep the smile off my face despite Brenna's concerned expression.

'But you have checked *him* out, right?'

'He's a retired doctor,' I'd explained. 'He lives there, at Adder House, with his wife.

He's such a nice man, Brenna, you'd understand if you met him.'

'But he could easily be a conman of some sort. Believe me, some of the doctors I've met over the years, they're unstable and prone to—'

'He's not like that.' I'd rolled my eyes. 'I can just tell.'

'But you read about this stuff all the time; people running off with rental deposits and that sort of thing. Aren't you worried?'

I'd nodded. 'Oh yes, really worried . . . I keep worrying he'll change his mind.'

But he didn't change his mind, and now, as I ring Brenna's doorbell again, I shrug off the niggling worries I have about the slightly odd Marsdens and Susan Woodings.

I've been so desperate to make a new life for us both and to feel fully accepted. As far as I'm concerned, Adder House fulfils both of those caveats.

11

Brenna beams when she opens the door, and I follow her into the kitchen. 'Well, this is a nice surprise. How's it going at the palace?'

I can tell there's going to be a lot of mileage in this nickname.

'Great. Still loads of unpacking to do, but I thought I'd take an hour out to visit my old mucker.'

'Hey, less of the old!' She frowns, having recently celebrated her forty-fifth birthday, which prompted Viv's annual tease that she was eight years younger than Brenna. 'Anyway, I'm glad you dropped by, because you've forced me to take a break. I've been working like a Trojan since six o'clock this morning trying to get my paper finished.'

'What's this one about?' Brenna's work is always interesting, and I like to get her talking about it when I can.

'Oh, just exploring some historical stuff,' Brenna says vaguely, spooning coffee into two mugs. 'How we can still learn stuff today from experiments of the past.'

I wait for her to elaborate but she's already moved on. 'That guy, Marden—'

'Dr Marsden,' I correct her with a grin.

'I really don't want to rain on your parade, but I know Viv will say it if I don't . . .'

'Go on.'

'Well, despite all I said before, he seems a decent-enough sort, even if his wife is a bit creepy, but I just want to reiterate that you need to keep your wits about you. That's all I'm saying. The place is fabulous, but you can't be too careful, especially—'

'I know, I know.' I sigh. 'Especially with what we've already been through this last year or so. But that stuff is also exactly why I couldn't afford to pass up the chance we were offered, Bren.'

'I know Skye is always your priority, it's just that she's been through so much . . .'

I'm aware that Brenna's suspicious thinking is only in defence of us, and I silently acknowledge that I'd feel exactly the same if a stranger offered Brenna and Viv something similarly fantastic. I could just do without hearing it all right now.

He offered, I accepted, and I want to keep positive and optimistic about our new life in Kensington despite one or two early reservations, like our weird neighbours, and little details that niggle me, like the lack of photographs in the Marsdens' apartment.

'I actually think living there will be wonderful for Skye. I've just got to work out how to tell her she'll have to leave Grove Primary and her best friend, Petra, behind. It might not sound like much, but it's a very big deal to her.'

She nods. 'Of course, it's a big deal for any kid, but she'll get over it.'

I don't think Brenna has ever seen the full force of Skye's wrath. If she had, she mightn't be as flippant. To my irritation, she returns yet again to the subject of Dr Marsden.

'Do you think you're just a tiny bit too impressed with your new place, though? Too willing to trust the old fella from the outset because he's a doctor?' She takes her mug over to the sink.

Brenna has won numerous accolades and awards for her groundbreaking research, but sometimes, she allows her imagination to get the better of her.

I smile and shake my head.

'He's never pressured or coerced me once, Bren. In fact, he asked me to go away and think carefully about whether living at Adder House was what I really wanted before giving him the go-ahead to prepare the tenancy agreement.'

'And did you take him up on it and say you'd think about it?'

'Not likely; I'd have been mad to dither! There'd be a thousand people snapping at my heels to move there in a matter of hours.'

Brenna smiles wryly in a thoughtful sort of way, as if she thinks I'm being naïve. I can't deny it narks me, but I push it away.

I did google Dr Michael Marsden but surprisingly little came up to match the name. None of the results referred to him. But I get the impression he hasn't worked for a while, probably retired ages ago not needing the money. More to the point, nothing came up saying a Dr Marsden got struck off or was involved in a terrible scandal. Maybe I'll ask him at some point if I get the chance, but for now, I'm really not worried.

'Well anyway, I really must be going. Lots to do.' I drain the last of my coffee and take the mug over to the sink. 'I'll go and have a think about how I'm going to broach the subject of starting a new school with Skye later. Wish me luck.'

'I'm sure you'll handle it brilliantly.' She gives me a hug. 'And if you get any vibes that all's not well at the palace, give me a shout and I'll come over. I can figure out where the Marsdens might be on the Levenson psychopathy scale. Although I could probably hazard a guess right now . . .'

She nudges me playfully.

There are very few people I can count on these days, but Brenna is one of them. We met on my first day as an administrator at the clinic – we'd both reached for the last cheese-and-ham sandwich in the café – and we've been friends ever since.

Brenna is also Skye's godmother and she is the singular person I'd trust to look after my daughter if I wasn't able to. Brenna is just one of those rare people you can count on to watch your back in life.

Skye and I often go over to Brenna's house for one of Viv's legendary Hungarian stews with sour cream and homemade bread. Divine.

When my marriage broke up eighteen months ago, before the terrible events that followed, I realised too late that most of my friends were Lewis's, too, and they were *his* before mine.

So, when he left, most of them went with him, and the few friends I had made disappeared like wisps of smoke within weeks.

Moving around with foster families from a young age, I never really got a chance to make any lifelong school friends like lots of people do. I guess a natural distrust of people, thanks to my fostering experiences, precluded me from making acquaintances as I got older.

So I'm sort of left with nobody. Except for Brenna. She stuck around.

12

You get to Grove School in good time for the children's mid-afternoon break. You have already found the exact spot which affords you cover without appearing to skulk.

One has to be very careful these days, around schools and parks and other public places. It's another sign of a world obsessed with correctness at the price of almost everything else.

You sit on the bench which some bright spark in the local planning department decided to situate under the canopy of a very old oak tree. The gnarled and sap-marked trunk, of some considerable girth, sits right in front of the bench, blocking the view but affording unrivalled privacy, right next to the wire-fenced playground of the school.

The package was delivered about half an hour ago. You watched as the courier took it inside and you received the emailed confirmation that it had been signed for at the front desk.

Only when you're satisfied there is nobody else around and nobody observing you, do you take out the camera. And then you wait for a long four and a half minutes until the classes begin to emerge, one by one, from the main school building.

The children come out in twos and threes and group together in bigger numbers when they get out into the space of the school yard.

Soon there seem to be hundreds of them, although you can't see the girl at all. Your nails are digging into your palm. Have they kept her inside for some reason, you wonder? Is she distressed?

You push away the disappointment of not being able to observe her reaction as you had hoped.

Instead, you slip on your soft gloves, reach into your bag and take out the hand-stitched journal that's filled with Beatrice's own thoughts. It is written in her neat and surprisingly eloquent hand, and you never tire of looking at it.

You calculate you must have read her words a thousand times, but this time feels special.

This time, everything means so much more because the woman and her child are finally here, at Adder House.

You turn back to the very beginning of Beatrice's journal, dated June 1920, and begin to read . . .

◆ ◆ ◆

'Beatrice?'

As I walk down the corridor, I feel myself freeze at the sound of Dr Rosalie Rayner's voice. The cold walls and stark floor seem to reverberate around me as every fibre of my being urges me to carry on walking as if I hadn't heard the doctor speak.

But of course my manners stop me from doing so.

I twist my hands together before wiping my brow. I feel old-fashioned next to Rosalie with her modern look, her neat bun and small white cap.

Rosalie places her hand on my arm.

'I wondered if you have given consideration to Professor Watson's request, my dear?'

I feel such a heat in my cheeks. A damp spot collects in the slight dip at the bottom of my spine but I try to appear unflustered.

Professor Watson's request has been looming large in my head. It has robbed me of sleep on a few nights, in fact.

'I'm sure you'd agree that it is such an honour to have an eminent professional, such as Professor Watson, interested in your child. It is, without doubt, an astonishing opportunity.'

'I – I'm very grateful for Professor Watson's interest in my son, Rosalie, but . . . he's a rather sensitive boy and I don't think—' I stammer. I can't help it, she is so bold and insistent.

'Why, the child has such a pleasant temperament! I've seen him around the hospital with others, so sociable and content.'

'He might seem that way, but as his mother, I—'

'Of course, Professor Watson is a very influential man. You know he sits on the hospital board and has the ear of all the decision makers? I assume you've heard the rumours concerning the reorganisation of the hospital's maternity wing?'

I have indeed heard the rumour, which had begun quietly and grown with troubling speed until all the employees of the maternity wing were bracing themselves for an announcement any day.

I, together with many other people, have endured sleepless nights and fretful days, imagining what life might be like without my job. How we would survive.

My wages as a wet nurse in the maternity wing are minimal but adequate for our meagre lifestyle.

When a baby's mother sadly dies or, for whatever reason, is unable or unwilling to feed her child, myself, or one of my colleagues, is allocated responsibility for the child.

My job is to feed and nurture my tiny charges until such a time as they are able to thrive independently. In my humble opinion, it is certainly a healthier choice than the dubious use of infant formula milk that the hospital's doctors generally disapprove of.

It is true that I gain a great deal of job satisfaction in my work. It might not seem important to some, but my milk saves babies' lives.

If I become a casualty of the hospital's reorganisation, the loss will be catastrophic for me in a number of ways. I will lose both my job and my home on the hospital campus.

The consequences are unthinkable.

Still, that does not alter the churning in my stomach when I think about the nature of Professor Watson's request.

There is something about the whole scenario I find uncomfortable that I can't quite articulate. He is such a powerful, senior man and I am . . . well, I am nothing.

'So can I tell him you're pleased to accept his esteemed offer?' Rosalie's smile stretches across her dry, flaky lips.

Yet she knows I don't really have a choice.

'Very well,' I say quietly, my heart sinking down in my chest.

Back at the house, you place the journal in its rightful place on the antique oak writing desk that belonged to your grandfather.

Next, listen to the first recording of the professor again, read by Professor Watson himself in a dated, scratchy-sounding voiceover.

1920 Johns Hopkins University Hospital, Baltimore

Extract from the confidential case study diary of Professor J. Watson

OVERVIEW

The subject is an eleven-month-old male child. For the purposes of anonymity, I will refer to the subject hereon as Little Albert.

He appears plump and of a mild, content temperament.

He exhibits no signs of fear or anxiety and is familiar with the hospital environment.

It has been agreed that Beatrice, the mother of the child, will remain present during the sessions.

Session one takes place in a controlled environment, the private office of myself, Professor John B. Watson. Also present is Dr Rosalie Rayner and Beatrice Barger, the subject's mother.

STAGE ONE

The child is inquisitive and responsive to noises and visual cues around him. The initial introduction of stimuli commences and the following are presented in a relaxed manner to the subject: a white rat, a dog, a monkey, masks featuring both hair and cotton wool.

The initial reactions are as expected; Little Albert shows no fear.

On the contrary, he seems fond of the animals and appears particularly fascinated by the white rat.

STAGE TWO

Following a short break where the mother is encouraged to interact with the child, Little Albert is presented with a single stimulus: the white rat.

As he reaches for the animal, a steel bar behind him is hit with a metal rod. The noise is loud and jarring and the child visibly jumps.

This procedure is repeated twice before the session is brought to a close.

BASELINE REACTIONS:

Albert jumps and falls forward the first time the steel bar is struck. The second time, the child begins to whimper and reach nervously towards his mother.

Session one is then concluded.

Subject is returned to his mother with instructions to return in one week.

13

After coffee at Bren's, I spend a backbreaking day unpacking boxes at Adder House.

I have a lot of stuff to throw out, too. As we moved so quickly, I had to bring absolutely everything with us.

The hours fly by, and in the afternoon, I head back to Skye's school to collect her at the end of the day with a spring in my step.

The sky looks moody with pale-grey clouds blocking the efforts of the sun to break through. It's on the cool side for mid-July. Still, it hasn't been too bad this year, as far as English summers go.

I catch the first bus to the terminal where I then board the second bus, which drops me a few streets away from Skye's school. As I walk the short distance to the gates, I reflect on how she's been happy here at Grove Primary.

She first attended nursery at the age of three, before her first reception year in school, and has now nearly completed her time as a Year One pupil.

My daughter is bright and very capable and has done so well at Grove. Her class teacher, Miss Smith, and the headteacher, Mrs Vince, have been so supportive during our troubled times, and I'll miss them both myself, too.

They even arranged for Skye to see a school counsellor for a few sessions, which I think really helped her begin to come to terms with what happened. Between them, they offered Skye a safe place to release her feelings without guilt or pressure.

They went out of their way to speak to me regularly, too, asking how I was doing and if there was anything else the school could help with.

A sickly feeling rises in my chest. I hope she's in a good mood when I pick her up and open to the news I have to give her.

I'm a few minutes early getting to school and one of the first parents to reach the gates. I cross the playground and enter reception to pick up the transfer forms I'll need to complete.

Mrs Desai, the office manager, looks up as I enter the reception area. She picks up the phone, says a few words, and replaces the receiver before sliding open the glass hatch. I smile and ask her for the necessary forms.

'It's very short notice, so please bring them back tomorrow fully completed,' she says curtly and hands them over to me without smiling back.

She's always seemed very friendly up to now, so I figure she must be just snowed under with end-of-term work, judging by the unwieldy pile of papers on her desk.

As I turn to leave, the secure inner door that leads into the school opens and Miss Smith peers apologetically around it.

'Is there any chance I can have a quick word, Mrs Miller?' She pushes her wispy, light-brown hair out of her eyes and exchanges a glance with Mrs Desai.

How did the teacher know I was here, in reception? The classroom window overlooks the inner courtyard so she can't have seen me coming into school. Then I remember the office manager's discreet little phone call as I arrived . . . she must have tipped her off that I had arrived. But why?

'Yes, of course.' My heart thumps a little faster as I walk towards her. 'Is everything alright?'

'You can come through now, if that's OK.'

Miss Smith holds the door open and I slip through, following her down the corridor that's just starting to fill with children searching for their lunchboxes and coats. Her small heels sound officious as they clip the scuffed wooden floor as we walk, adding to the unsettled feeling that's growing rapidly in my stomach.

'My teaching assistant has kindly agreed to dismiss the class, so we can speak privately in here. She's going to hold on to Skye for a few minutes when the end-of-school bell sounds, so no need to worry where she is.' She opens the door of a room barely bigger than a large cupboard, which contains only a single desk and a couple of pupil-sized chairs.

'Is there something wrong?' I ask when she indicates for me to sit down. I remain standing, waiting with bated breath for an explanation.

Miss Smith presses her lips together regretfully. 'Mrs Miller, I thought it was important to let you know that Skye has been rather upset in class this afternoon.' She pre-empts my next comment. 'The office did try unsuccessfully to call and text you several times to come in, but in the end, I'm afraid they had to leave a voicemail.'

One hand fruitlessly scrabbles around in my bag and I inwardly curse when I realise I must have left my phone at home in my rush to leave the apartment.

'Is Skye OK? Is she ill or—'

'Skye is fine physically,' she interrupts. 'But it was the sweets, Mrs Miller . . . and your note. I think if you had let me know what to expect today, I could have handled it better and avoided—'

'Sorry,' I interrupt, placing the tips of my fingers lightly on the desk. 'I don't know what you're talking about. Sweets . . . and a note, you say?'

'Yes, they arrived in reception at two o'clock with instructions for them to be brought directly to class. The gift basket was

67

wrapped so beautifully in cellophane and ribbons and addressed to Rowan Class. As you can imagine, the children were excited when Mrs Desai brought them through.' She hesitates. 'But I'm afraid it all turned rather sour when I read out your note.'

I feel like I'm inhaling fog.

'Sorry, I need to stop you right there. I haven't sent a package to school today,' I say a little breathlessly.

'Oh, I see.' Her hand drifts up to her mouth as she considers the implications of this. 'Let's sit down a moment.'

The child-size chair feels insubstantial beneath me. 'What . . . did the note say?' I manage.

She opens the exercise book she's carrying and hands me a small lined piece of paper. I read it aloud, in disbelief.

> *To all my friends in Rowan Class,*
>
> *Me and Mummy have just moved into our new house, and I will be leaving Grove Primary to start a brand new school a long way from here.*
>
> *It's too far to visit so I will miss you all, especially my best friend, Petra. Enjoy the sweeties!*
>
> *Love, Skye Miller*

'This is crazy,' I tell Miss Smith as firmly as I'm able to, crossing my ankles under the small chair to steady my legs. 'I didn't send this to class. I haven't even told Skye she's leaving this school yet.'

'That explains her reaction,' Miss Smith says, watching me carefully.

'I just can't imagine how this has happened.' I listen to myself, realising how terribly thin and unconvincing my voice and words must sound to her.

But it's true. Literally nobody knows this information. With the exception of Brenna that is, and – I start at the sound of a sharp knock.

The door opens and Tana, Rowan Class's teaching assistant, steps inside, holding Skye's hand.

My daughter's cheeks look swollen and damp, and her usually vivid blue eyes are cast with a dull light.

I jump out of my seat and envelop her in my arms as the two women look on.

'I'm so sorry this has happened, darling,' I whisper in my daughter's ear. 'I want you to know that Mummy didn't send the gift basket or the note.'

When she pulls away from me, her eyes wide and tinged with fear, I realise I've made a mistake in saying so.

'But if you didn't send it, Mummy,' she says, sniffing back tears, 'then who did?'

14

Thankfully, by the time I finish talking to Skye's teacher and we leave the school building, the other parents and children outside the gates have mostly dispersed.

I really don't fancy bumping into Kat, and having to explain everything to her in front of an already traumatised Skye. No doubt little Petra is really upset too; the pair of them have been inseparable since their first day at nursery school here.

I make a mental note to give Kat a call later.

For once, Skye allows me to carry her *Frozen*-themed backpack. She usually has to be surgically separated from it, but today she willingly lets go and holds my hand limply.

My mind is full, whirring with disturbing thoughts about the candy delivery and vicious note someone sent to Skye's class. Whoever did it must have known it would upset Skye, or why bother in the first place?

I've racked my brains, and I'm certain the only people who knew I'm planning to move Skye to St Benjamin Monks are the Marsdens and, obviously, Brenna after my impromptu visit for coffee this morning. None of them have reason to upset us like this. The Marsdens have a vested interest in keeping us happy in our move to Adder House, and Brenna is our dear, loyal friend who would detest the thought of Skye being hurt.

The only other possibility is that someone unknown to me has found out about Adder House and wants to cause trouble in some way. Even if it means causing distress to an innocent five-year-old.

Janine Harworth's mean, pinched features instantly fill my mind. She's the woman Lewis left us for before he died. Understandably, there is no love lost between us, and I'm sure she'd revel in the upset caused today.

But for Janine to find out such personal information would mean she'd have to have been regularly covertly watching, perhaps even following, me. And I can't cope with a thought like that, not because it scares me but because it makes me feel so angry and also protective of Skye.

My thoughts gravitate to the figure I thought I saw watching us behind a tree in Kensington Gardens. Could it be . . .

I shake my head free of the awful puzzle. My daughter has to come first right now. 'Want to play the "count the car colours" game?' I say brightly as we walk up the road towards the bus stop, hand in hand. 'I'll take red ones and you can have your favourite, silver—'

'No thank you, Mummy,' she says quietly. 'I don't want to play that game today.'

'Hey, guess what I've got us for tea? Pepperoni pizza, your favourite!'

'I'm . . . not hungry.' My girl, who is always ravenous after school.

She stares down at her feet as she walks. No skipping ahead or singing her favourite songs today.

Thankfully, we're only waiting a couple of minutes before the bus arrives. We board and take our seats and still Skye is so subdued, I feel desperate to explain what must have happened to help her make sense of it.

'It seems someone has played a nasty trick on us, sending that mean note to school.

But you know, we really mustn't let it spoil our exciting news about moving to Adder House.' I squeeze her hand and look down at her.

'But why do they want to be mean to us?' she asks, her voice flat. She doesn't meet my eyes.

I'm trying to work out the very same thing for myself, but now isn't the time to dwell on it and I don't want to frighten her.

'I don't know,' I say lightly. 'Some people can get jealous when others have something exciting happening. They can tell fibs to cause trouble. And having a pretty confetti tree outside your bed-room window is certainly exciting . . . have you thought of a name for it yet?'

'Petra wouldn't talk to me after Miss Smith read out the note. She said Martha Fox is going to be her new best friend now.' She looks up at me, her eyes shining with renewed hope. 'But it's not true I have to move schools, is it, Mummy? The jealous person was just telling fibs.'

I smile tightly and pat Skye's hand, pointing out things from the window I hope might distract her.

The bus trundles on and passes the bottom of our old street. I can't help myself; I glance across at the detached house on the corner.

It's painful, even now after everything. Even though it's all over.

I still remember the raw feeling inside when Lewis first left us to live in that house. It belongs to Janine. I spent so many hours imagining them both entwined in that upstairs bedroom. It used to torture me to the point that I couldn't sleep.

Someone moving in the front bay window draws my gaze. At least I think that's what I saw. I crane my neck, but it's so hard to see anything from this angle because the light is reflecting off the glass, rendering it opaque.

I used to count Janine as a good friend. Not any more. Now, she's forever identified in my mind as the woman who took my husband, the catalyst for every terrible thing that would ensue.

Whatever doubts I might have briefly entertained over whether moving to Adder House was the right thing for us, if I ever needed a sweetener or an extra push to leave the area, then escaping Janine Harworth and the view of her house is it.

My husband's lover celebrated her fortieth birthday at the beginning of the year, making her seven years older than me. I've heard plenty of stories about men leaving their wife for someone younger, but not once have I heard of the other woman being *older*. Sounds silly, but at the time, it felt like an extra slap in the face. If it was possible for things to be any worse.

During the short time they were together, Janine seemed to take pleasure in constantly stirring things up between me and my husband, often over the smallest issues. Like when he insisted on bringing Skye back home on a Sunday at 8 p.m. instead of 7.30 p.m. as I'd asked. When he sent her home one day with a large bag of Haribo sour sweets, though he knew full well I went to great lengths to keep her away from confectionary like that.

I'd have been foolish to expect Janine to melt into oblivion when tragedy struck. Still, she managed to surprise me; came out fighting like a banshee rather than shrinking back even an inch in grief.

The focus of her belligerence was Lewis's 'estate', as her lawyer grandly referred to the meagre assets my husband left behind.

It soon became apparent to Janine that the only real asset worth fighting for was Lewis's small life-insurance policy, which she claimed he was in the process of legally changing to name her as beneficiary. He was also, apparently, *in the process* of starting divorce proceedings, which he'd never so much as mentioned to me.

After paying off some joint debt that passed to me when he died, I'd calculated that I had enough to last me about six months at our current level of outgoings. But the smaller Adder House rent meant I could now survive financially for longer before getting a job, giving me more time to spend with Skye while she settles in.

Janine had first confronted me in the street two weeks after Lewis's death, and when I refused to talk to her, she shouted through the letterbox and only stopped when I threatened her with a court injunction. I didn't want my already traumatised daughter having to witness all Janine's crap on top of everything else.

In reality, I hadn't got the funds to start any kind of legal action, but I must've given a convincing performance because she appeared to back off a bit after that.

When Lewis died, I was still the legally named beneficiary on the insurance policy. Whatever she said he was in the process of doing, *I* was still Lewis's wife in the eyes of the law.

Once, he had loved me with all his heart. I hung on to that fact like a lifeline. But Janine was having none of it.

'We were planning to get married at the end of the year. He intended telling you any day.' She'd spat out the words after rushing across the road while I fiddled with the awkward front-door lock. 'He was with *me*, he'd already left you. You and your brat have no right to that money.'

At that moment, I truly understood what it must feel like to want to impulsively harm another human being in a moment of madness. I just wanted to silence her.

I met her heated glare full on and spoke calmly. 'In the eyes of the law, I'm still his wife, Janine. And Skye is his daughter . . . his own flesh and blood. On paper, you're simply his bit on the side and, as such, are entitled to precisely nothing.'

74

Thankfully, my front door had sprung open as I finished speaking, and I stepped smartly inside, shutting the door in Janine's twisted-up face.

Once inside, I had to lean against the wall and take a few deep breaths, to avoid retching in the hallway.

During the weeks that followed, I came home to broken eggs dripping down the front door, deliveries of manure and topsoil with drivers demanding cash on receipt, and numerous communications from companies regarding the setting up of expensive funeral plans featuring biodegradable coffins of all things.

Of course I knew perfectly well who was behind it all. Who else could it be?

None of it was particularly sinister. It would take more than infantile tricks like that to scare me. I'm not easily unnerved after what I'd been through as a fostered kid. The one advantage of being passed like an unwanted package amongst foster families is that it takes a lot to rattle me.

Still, it was annoying and inconvenient when I was trying so hard to keep it together for my daughter's sake.

One day, I came home to find two full wheelie bins – my own and the couple's upstairs – upended on the front garden when there was barely any breeze outside at all. Doesn't sound like much, but when there's rotten food and soggy teabags and other people's rubbish to scrape up, it's unpleasant to say the least.

I'd had enough and got as far as calling the local police station out of pure frustration.

I explained the short history of what I saw as revenge incidents, and I told them who I thought was responsible, but they wouldn't send an officer out because there had been 'no wilful damage or threats', and there was zero proof Janine was involved.

The last few months before leaving the house had been quiet. Uneventful. But I'd never been able to shake the impression that she was always watching. And waiting. For what, I didn't know. It was just a feeling.

Somehow, during the second bus journey home, I finally manage to get Skye off the subject of attending a new school by talking about taking a tour around Kensington Palace at the weekend.

'Can we take Petra, too?' she says, a weak smile finally returning. 'I'm going to watch *really* carefully and try and spot Prince George at the window of the palace, Mummy.'

'I'll give Petra's mum a call a little later on.' I smile. Maybe I can rescue this situation, just be honest with Kat and explain everything to her. I'm sure she'll understand about the mix-up under the circumstances.

As for Janine Harworth, if she's responsible for the gift-and-note dirty trick, and she thinks it will somehow scupper our move, then she's got another think coming.

It'll take more than *her* to ruin our happy new beginnings.

15

When we get back home, Skye says from the doorway, 'Can we call Petra and her mummy, tell them that someone was telling fibs in the note? And can we tell them that I'm not leaving Grove Primary? Then she might still be my friend.'

'One second, poppet,' I say to buy time, even though I want to weep for her. 'Just let me sort out this paperwork.'

I make Skye's tea on a tray and she sits watching television, finally seeming to be a little more settled now.

I gently close the lounge door and the sound of the TV recedes.

In the narrow hallway, I tidy our shoes and bags and hang the coats on the hooks near the door. I stand there for a minute or two, leaning against the pristine magnolia-painted walls.

The apartment is so clean and cool, and as I take a few long calming breaths in and out, I massage the back of my neck and feel the taut wiry tendons give a little.

Now that I'm alone, I can admit to myself that what happened at school today shook me up a bit. The promises I'd made to myself when I was around Skye's age always make a reappearance as a mantra in my mind at any sign of trouble.

Don't show them you're scared. Don't cry. Never cry.

There had been an abusive foster carer who took me to A & E three times with broken limbs before my sixth birthday, until someone finally twigged he periodically came home drunk and threw me down the stairs.

I'd also nearly died from pneumonia when I was twelve after another foster family locked me outside in the rain for tramping mud through the house. When they eventually let me in three hours later, I was made to sleep in the wet clothes all night and keep them on the next day.

Still, I survived.

As I got a little older, I was a loner. Never had a gang of friends or even a close best friend. My nickname at school was Robot on account of my never showing any emotion or, as I saw it then, any weakness.

I liked to think I was made of sterner stuff. It took a lot to unnerve me, and I was almost never surprised by what life could throw at me.

When I met Lewis, I honestly thought those days were long behind me.

But I admit, that day he told me our marriage was over, I wasn't expecting it. Wasn't equipped to deal with it on top of all that existing hurt.

I squeeze my eyes against the sting of tears and the pain of a life now lost, take a deep breath, and walk into the kitchen.

Shake it off.

It can only still hurt me if I allow myself to feel it.

I make my own tea and take it through to the lounge to sit with Skye. She's absorbed in her television programme and doesn't look up at me.

Kids are so resilient; I honestly think she'll be OK about the new school. I'm pretty sure that—

My phone rings just as I finish eating my beans on toast, interrupting my thoughts. I'd forgotten to check it when I first got back in, after Miss Smith said the office had left me an answerphone message.

Skye glances up at the noise and then back to the television screen.

The ring is muffled and I realise it must have slipped down between the seat cushions, which is probably why I forgot to take it with me.

My fingers locate it and I pull it out and look at the screen. My throat feels full when I see who's calling. It's Kat, Petra's mum.

I push my tray and empty plate to one side and spring up from my seat.

'Hello?' I walk out of the lounge and close the door behind me, go into my bedroom and sit on the edge of the bed.

'Freya? It's me, Kat.' Her voice sounds sharp and to the point.

'Hi, Kat! I was going to call you after tea, I—'

'Is it true that you've moved house and Skye is leaving Grove Primary?'

I hesitate. My instinct is to be vague, stall for time, but I can't. I have to tell her the truth.

'Yes, it is true. I'm sorry, Kat, I should've told you, but things have moved so fast and—'

'Petra's heartbroken. She's in pieces, but then you'll know that because Skye would be exactly the same if we'd pulled a dirty trick like that.' Kat's voice sounds shaky, like she's genuinely shocked at the news, but I need to put this into perspective.

'It's hardly a dirty trick!' I exclaim. 'It's *life*, Kat. You know I had to sell the house after Lewis died and that we'd be moving.'

'I thought you'd be staying local, and if not, that you'd at least have the decency to tell me you were moving to the other side of London, so I could have warned Petra.' She pauses to take a breath and starts again before I can respond. 'It's unforgiveable, what you did today. To let her find out like that in front of the entire class.'

'It wasn't me who sent the note or the gift,' I say, keeping my voice level.

'What? Who did then? Frankly, it fits in with all the other self-ish things you've done recently, like neglect to keep us up to speed with your major life changes.'

She's starting to really annoy me now. Kat is secure in her nice middle-class home surrounded by an extended family that means there's always someone to look after Petra if she and Bryn, Petra's dad, want to plan one of their regular date nights she's so fond of posting on Facebook . . . in the days before I closed my account.

I sigh. 'Look. I've apologised for not telling you earlier, but I was only offered the apartment just over a week ago. Skye's going to finish the summer term off at Grove, and she'd like Petra to visit our new apartment this weekend. We can make up for what's happened with a tour around Kensington Palace. How's that sound?'

There's a tense silence on the end of the line for a few moments.

'You must have lost your marbles if you think I'm going to let that happen.' I can hear her words squeezing out between clenched teeth. 'Petra's still crying over the news. You might as well know I've already left a message on the school answerphone to see Mrs Vince in the morning to request that Petra sits next to Martha, and not Skye, in class from now on.'

'I can't believe you'd be that petty.'

She gasps but I can't help myself. However angry she is, she shouldn't take it out on Skye like that.

I hold the phone away from me, but I can still hear her shouting. I end the call and toss the handset across the bed, lying back and staring up at the ceiling. I know Skye leaving the school hasn't been dealt with in the best way, but I've had so much to do in a short space of time.

I feel myself harden inside, a metaphorical digging in of the heels.

Stuff Grove Primary and stuff Kat and her precious daughter, too. Audrey Marsden has already mentioned that as governor at the new school, she's more than willing to help me get Skye admitted there.

Maybe, just maybe, she can help me with Skye's transfer, too, so she doesn't have to go back to her crummy old school at all.

16

The next morning, I sit in the lounge and stare out of the large picture window at the blue sky and fluffy white clouds beyond.

It's a tonic to my sore insides and heavy eyelids, even though what I'd really love to do is crawl back under the covers and shut out the light completely.

When I came out of the bedroom yesterday after my call with Petra's mum, I bumped into Skye in the hallway. Turns out she'd overheard most of the call.

'Is Petra still coming over at the weekend?' she'd asked fearfully, tugging at a lock of hair.

I had to tell her. Had to be honest with her about the new school.

'So the nasty note was true?' Her bottom lip quivered. 'It said I was leaving Grove Primary.'

'No! It wasn't true, not then, anyway.' I crouched down and pulled her close, but I could feel her resistance.

'So I can stay at school with Petra?'

The hope in her voice broke my heart. At five years old she was tying me up in knots.

I knew I'd never have a better moment to explain, so we went back into the lounge and I turned off the television.

We sat together and I held her hand.

'You know, sweetie, life is full of surprises. We don't always know what's around the corner, but sometimes it can be a good thing. Like when you won the junior art competition and you were in the local paper. Remember that?'

The frown lines broke up when she smiled.

'And like when Daddy bought my trampoline and set it up in the garden for when I came home from school? That was a good surprise, too.'

'That's right.' I nodded, eager to move on from the mention of her father. 'But sometimes life throws us a surprise we're not quite ready for.'

'Like having to change schools?'

I pulled her close and kissed the top of her head. She was as bright as a button. 'There are times we really don't want to do something and then find out it's the best thing that happened to us.' She looked up at me doubtfully as I continued. 'Sometimes, we have to be brave enough to give life's surprises a chance. Like moving to Adder House, like starting a new school. Do you think you can be brave, Skye?'

She nodded and blinked her watery eyes. I'd fallen short in my explanation, but it was the best I could do.

Sometimes, life was just so damn hard.

Even after our chat, Skye had a bad night. We both did.

After her waking for a third time at 4 a.m., I didn't go back to sleep. I drifted a little before finally getting up at six and making coffee.

Now I still feel a bit shaky.

I haven't seen Skye upset like this since those first awful weeks after Lewis died.

Last night took me by surprise when her night terrors returned. To witness her sitting bolt upright and calling out with those wide, sightless eyes . . . I thought we'd seen the last of it after her therapy.

I open the window a touch. I can hear a blackbird singing even though I can't see him. He must be sitting in the foliage of the magnificent oak tree that stands adjacent to the main window, blessing us with his song.

If he visits us regularly, I get the feeling his singing will quickly become a joyous part of our breakfast, and goodness knows, we both deserve a little joy.

Skye looks up from the rug where she lies now, half-heartedly colouring. She tilts her head to listen to the birdsong and we smile weakly at each other.

I sip my coffee. I've calmed down a bit now. Yes, the Marsdens are a bit odd, but I can put up with that. Soon I'll work out their routine and how best to avoid them.

I don't know who sent the anonymous gift and note to Grove Primary; perhaps I'll never know. Whoever did that was undoubtedly spiteful and mean. They'd be delighted to think they were responsible for our upset and worry.

The most powerful thing I can do for myself is not to fret endlessly who it was, but to put it out of my mind.

As I sit here, I feel much more relaxed and I know it won't be long until it feels like home. Skye will slowly settle down.

We'll build a routine like we had at our old house: eating breakfast together and chatting about the day ahead. Soon Skye will be telling me about her latest dream. They're always so vivid, and sometimes the details stay with her throughout the day, particularly if she's had a nice one.

Like the time she relayed the pure joy she'd experienced riding on a unicorn.

'She just grew and grew, Mummy, until she was the size of a *real* horse and then I climbed on her back and she flew so high! Over mountains and trees and lakes . . . I saw it all!'

It was wonderful to listen and to watch her excitement; it was as if the experience really had happened.

The last few years, until taking this career break, I'd worked in a clinic within a hospital. It's situated in a smart standalone building and it specialises in phobias. Sadly, some of the clients there experienced the power of Skye's dreams but at the opposite end of the scale.

As the senior administrator, I had sight of client records, people whose sleep was continually and severely disrupted because of recurrent nightmares that seemed as real to them as events that happened during their daytime waking hours.

Night terrors. The thing they feared the most would crawl into their slumbers, torturing them all night long and impacting their careers, relationships, and in the worst cases, their mental health.

One woman in her early forties suffered from arachnophobia. She was constantly plagued during the day by the fear that a spider might descend from the ceiling and become entangled in her hair. But at night, her dreams were filled with spiders that poured out of the ceiling-light fitting, landing on her face and getting trapped in her hair and ears.

Through the night, it happened again and again, making sleep almost impossible. As she was employed as a private driver for a prominent politician, the cumulative sleep deficit made carrying out her job safely and efficiently pretty much impossible.

Another patient suffered from koumpounophobia; he was terrified of buttons. Funny, right? But think about it.

Buttons are everywhere, and when just setting eyes on one can put you into a state of abject panic, such a phobia can become very dangerous.

The client was a high-school teacher before his phobia became unmanageable. Surrounded by students, all wearing the standard uniform featuring buttons, it became impossible for him to function.

This is the power of our minds, our dreams. Defying logic and common sense. Our imagination has the power to control us and ultimately destroy us.

If we're willing to let that happen.

17

Skye clambers up from the rug and ambles over to the window to look for Mr Blackbird, as she's now named him.

'Mummy, there's a lady in the garden. She's feeding the birds!'

Encouraged by the sudden interest in her voice, I cradle my coffee cup and walk over to the window. When I look down into the garden, I see there's a diminutive older lady there who appears to be deep in thought, methodically stocking the bird tables that are dotted around the lawn from a bag full of what looks like seed.

'Can we help her, Mummy? Please? I want to help feed the birds.'

We're in no rush today to be anywhere. Thanks to last night's telephone call from Kat, I've decided not to send Skye back to Grove Primary.

Yes, there are probably a hundred boxes still to unpack in the apartment, but I figure that feeding the birds and meeting a friendly neighbour is exactly the sort of thing that might help Skye feel a little better.

'Come on then,' I say, slipping on flat sandals and grabbing a cardy to drape over my thin floral dress. 'I don't know who the lady is, but I'm sure she won't mind a keen little helper.'

Skye rushes to the door, pulling up her wrinkled pink leggings as she moves and shoves her feet into her My Little Pony pumps without unlacing them first. 'Quick, Mummy, or the lady might go back inside!'

It's refreshing to see the change in my daughter's mood. My eyelids feel a little less heavy.

I think about brushing Skye's hair before we go downstairs, but her urgency to get out there is infectious and, anyway, what does messy hair matter?

Five minutes later, we're walking around the side of Adder House and into the garden. Although it's still quite early, the sun kisses my face and warms my shoulders. I feel brighter already, and judging by Skye's purposeful stride, she does, too.

Once we get into the open garden, the air feels a little cooler in the shade of the leafy green canopies and the shadow of Adder House itself.

'Hello! Can I help you feed the birds?'

I feel so pleased at Skye's forthright manner in addressing the lady. It's not like her to turn shyly into my side as she does whenever Dr or Mrs Marsden speaks to her.

The woman turns and I see she is a good deal older than I first thought, possibly in her early eighties. She wears a gentle, soft expression that instantly puts me at ease. Her hair is silver and her eyes a very pale blue. I immediately feel myself warming to her.

'How kind! It's not very often I have a little helper around here; what's your name, sweetheart?' Her voice is strong and clear and sounds like it belongs to a much younger person.

'My name is Skye Miller. And this is my mummy, she's Freya. We're new here.'

I think my heart might burst with pride. Skye's eyes are wide with amazement as she stares at the plethora of different varieties of birds clustered on the various feeding tables dotted around the edges of the garden.

'Well, now this *is* a surprise. I heard you were coming to live at Adder House, and I've been very much looking forward to meeting you both. I'm Lilian Brockley and I believe I'm your downstairs neighbour at number four.'

I smile and step forward, holding out a hand.

'We're in number six, above you. It's very nice to meet you, Miss Brockley.'

'My friends call me Lily.' She shakes my hand and smiles at Skye, who is still distracted by the wildlife. 'I get the feeling we're going to be good friends because I can see you love birds as much as I do.'

Skye nods, her eyes darting from one bird table to the next.

'A goldfinch, a chaffinch, and . . . ooh look over there, Mummy, it's a collared dove!'

'Now, that *is* impressive!' Lily immediately furnishes Skye with a handful of seeds from her carrier bag. 'If you stand on that log, you can reach to sprinkle them here, see? It's where most of the birds land . . . that's right, perfect! I can see you're already a professional at this, Skye.'

Lily winks at me.

'I've nearly finished now, all today's seed is gone, but do you think you could help me tomorrow morning at the same time . . . and perhaps at the weekend, too?'

'Oh yes,' Skye says. 'I can help every single day, Lily.'

'And what partners we will be!' The old lady turns to me. 'Now that we're properly introduced, I'd like to invite you both this afternoon for tea and cake at three, if you're free?'

'We are free, aren't we, Mummy?' Skye jumps in.

I smile. 'Thank you, Miss Brockley. That would be lovely.'

As I turn to walk back towards the house, a sudden movement at one of the upper-floor windows catches my eye.

I look up, expecting to see one of the other residents waving, perhaps, but to my surprise, there's no one there at all; so perhaps someone just walked past the glass without pausing to look out.

I do a quick calculation in my head, working out what number apartment the window must belong to, and I conclude it's apartment number three, which is the home of Matthew and Susan Woodings.

18

We say our goodbyes to Lily and go back upstairs. We both have a renewed spring in our step after such a positive intervention in our morning.

Back in the apartment, Skye grabs her favourite red fleecy blanket and lies down on the sofa, holding the corner of it up to her mouth for comfort. I stroke her hair and her eyes begin to close. She'll feel so much better if she can claw a few hours of sleep back.

I'm tempted to join her, but there's something more pressing that needs sorting out.

I've saved the number for St Benjamin Monks Primary into my phone. I creep into the kitchen so I don't disturb Skye and close the lounge door quietly behind me.

Two minutes later, I end the call in frustration. Apparently, the snooty office manager informed me, there's 'no possibility' of Skye starting school so late in the term.

'I'm afraid it's quite impossible,' she said haughtily.

'My daughter's very upset about having to leave her old school,' I implored her. 'It would really put my and her mind at rest if she could just come in and—'

'As I say, it simply can't be done Mrs . . .'

'Miller.'

'It simply can't be done, Mrs Miller. Mrs Grant hasn't a single space for an appointment in her diary before the end of term.' She sighed. 'The best I can do is relay your message to the class teacher.'

Reluctantly, I thanked her and ended the call.

There is no sense in making an enemy of the school office, but why is this proving so difficult? We're talking about a five-year-old for goodness' sake, it's not as if she has advanced geometry to catch up on.

Meeting new classmates and possibly making some little friends she could see again over the summer would have really helped her make the leap from the upset with Petra and what happened in class and put Grove Primary firmly behind her.

Now it's abundantly clear that's not going to happen anytime soon. Then I have a bit of a brainwave. Maybe all's not lost.

I creep into the hallway and peek through the gap in the lounge door.

I can tell by her breathing that Skye is now sleeping deeply, and judging by her fractious night, she'll probably stay that way for a good couple of hours at least.

Should I risk it? It's still strange and unfamiliar here in the apartment to her, but it's not as if we're in a hotel somewhere. We're home. And Skye knows she's safe here.

If my little plan works, then it could make a big difference to her settling in here. I slip my feet into scuffed ballerina pumps and head for the door, praying she doesn't stir.

I'll be back in a few minutes and Skye will be none the wiser.

I stand on the ground floor and ring the doorbell by the grand entrance door of apartment one. I feel a bit cheeky just turning up like this. I ought to ask for Dr or Mrs Marsden's telephone number and then I can call first if I need them.

I hear footsteps on the other side of the door, and Audrey herself appears. She's dressed in tailored jeans, a white pussybow

92

blouse, and a knitted navy jacket with white edging. I feel like a slob in comparison.

'Oh, I'm – I'm so sorry,' I stammer. 'Did I catch you as you're going out?'

'Not at all, dear.' She smiles. 'I'm at home all morning, but I'm afraid you're too late for Michael, he's already at his gentlemen's club.'

Gentlemen's club? Sounds a bit dodgy . . . aren't those places full of young, scantily clad dancers and expensive drinks? She must be the only woman in London who doesn't give a jot that her husband so openly frequents one.

She cranes her head around me, this way and that. 'No little one with you today?'

'She's upstairs asleep,' I say, and then worry she'll think me a negligent mother. 'She had a bad night and didn't get much rest. I didn't want to wake her.'

She nods and shifts her weight from one foot to the other. Cartier Love Bracelets clash prettily on her wrist, and I can smell her distinctive perfume.

The Marsdens are always dressed so formally. Don't they ever crash out in their comfies like the rest of us?

I stifle a grin at the thought of Audrey in a onesie and force my thoughts back on track.

'I hope you don't mind, Audrey, I wanted to ask you something.' I hesitate. 'It's a rather big favour, actually.'

'Of course!' She beams. 'Name it, my dear.'

It becomes fairly obvious I'm not going to get an invite inside and it makes me feel slightly flustered again, as if I'm disturbing her.

'I've got a problem with St Benjamin's, they—'

My flow of words is interrupted as I catch movement behind her at the end of the hallway. The lounge door is open, flooding the wood-panelled space with light, and a tall, broad figure has just walked across the room. A man.

Audrey raises one eyebrow slightly. She knows I've spotted someone in there but clearly doesn't feel the need to explain herself.

'You were saying there's a problem with the school. In relation to Skye's admission there, I gather?'

I explain how Skye is becoming increasingly anxious about starting at a new school and that I think it would be really beneficial for her to at least visit there before the end of term.

'I'm afraid the office manager wasn't very helpful. She said it was impossible to arrange anything this late in the term.'

'Leave it with me. I'll speak to Iris Grant, the head . . .'

Her voice fades out a little as I wonder if the man in the lounge is Dr Marsden. But why would she say he's out at his club if, in fact, he's home? *This man is taller though, I'm sure of it.*

Audrey's brow furrows very slightly but not as much as it should do. Probably a touch of Botox, I conclude.

'Freya? I asked if anytime is good for you if I can get you an appointment.'

'Sorry, yes! Yes, thank you, anytime is good.' I take a step back, remembering I've left Skye sleeping. 'I'm really grateful, thank you.'

I head for the stairs and she calls me back again.

'There was something I wanted to ask. Have you got a moment now?'

'Yes, of course.' I walk back to the door.

'We'll need to get a security camera fitted in your apartment,' she says briskly. 'Unfortunately, we didn't have time to complete the work before you moved in. It'll be sometime this week, but there's no need for you to be in while the work is being done.'

She nods as though in telling me, it's already been agreed. But I'm puzzled. 'Do you mean you want to put a security camera *inside* the apartment?'

'Yes, dear. Just inside the hallway.' She smiles tightly. 'It's standard procedure here at Adder House where all the apartments benefit from our internal CCTV system.'

'I see. Well, I wouldn't want you to go to the trouble of installing one in our apartment,' I say lightly. 'It's only tiny, anyway, with nothing valuable in it, and I feel quite safe here.'

Audrey stares at me, her nostrils flaring slightly.

'Better to be safe than sorry, that's always been my motto. It's a lovely area, but you can never tell when there might be . . . an unpleasant incident.' For just a second, the corners of Audrey's mouth curl down, but then, when I don't reply, she smiles brightly. 'Right. That's settled then. I'll tell Michael you're happy for him to go ahead.'

I chew the inside of my cheek and I don't walk away. It all seems a bit odd. I'm familiar with external security measures like this, but it seems an invasion of privacy to have someone monitoring what's happening *inside* our home.

'I'd rather think about it,' I say lightly. 'If that's alright with you.' Actually, I'm going to think about it, whether it's alright with her or *not*.

'Sorry?' Her eyes widen slightly. I don't think Mrs Marsden is used to people challenging her in any way.

'I'll need to think about the camera, I don't feel comfortable with the idea of it.' My heart is galloping but she won't know that.

'Very well,' she says coldly. 'But as I say, it's for your own good entirely.'

And with that, she closes the door and I'm left in the entrance foyer with nothing left of her but a fragrant cloud of her trademark *eau de parfum*.

That, and a growing sense of unease.

19

When I get back up to the apartment and let myself in as quietly as I can, I'm relieved to find Skye hasn't moved an inch. She's still fast asleep and remains that way for another hour.

I can't find the energy to unpack a box, so I sit in the chair and doze myself. A blissful hour of peace and quiet. It's one of the things I love about this place already.

When Skye wakes up, she's refreshed and a little brighter. I make us a sandwich and relent when she asks for a few crisps on the side.

'We don't want to fill up too much, do we? Don't forget we're off to Miss Brockley's for tea and cake this afternoon.'

She beams and nods happily without speaking, her mouth full of bread, cheese, and tomato.

At precisely three o'clock, we stand outside Miss Brockley's door and I tap discreetly on the polished wood just beneath the gleaming brass number.

I look down at my daughter and smile. She is quite taken with the idea of afternoon tea and cake and, before we came downstairs, insisted on changing out of her leggings and T-shirt into a pretty yellow summer dress with a matching pink-and-yellow hair slide to hold her fine blonde hair out of her eyes.

The door to apartment four opens and Lily's soft, lined face breaks into a wide smile.

'Goodness me, what lovely guests I have visiting today. And what a delightful dress, Skye, to go with that beautiful name of yours. Please do come through ladies.'

Skye beams and glances up at me, shy flushed cheeks making her look happy and glowing with no trace of tiredness now. Sadly, I don't think I look quite as bright eyed and bushy tailed.

'It's so kind of you to ask us over,' I say, slipping off my shoes and stepping into the dim but spacious hallway. As we walk towards the light at the end of the hall, I see that it's a big apartment, just like Dr Marsden's, and there is a lot of traditional wood panelling in here.

I look up at the ceiling near the entrance and see there is no security camera located there.

We file through the door at the end and step into a bright, light lounge at least twice the width of the one we have upstairs. I realise our own lounge must be directly above here, but only for about a third of the width. The other space must be taken up by the apartment next to us.

'This one is much bigger than ours, too,' Skye remarks crossly.

'What's that, dear?' Lily asks, plumping cushions and indicating for us to take a seat.

'Skye isn't impressed that we appear to have the smallest apartment in Adder House.' I grin. 'But trust me, we're delighted to be here and very, very grateful.'

I wonder if the other residents know about my 'special' agreement with Dr Marsden. Paying a fraction of the going rent because we are deemed a 'good fit'. I find myself hoping that they don't know. It makes me feel guilty if we're getting the place cheaper than everyone else, and I don't want them to resent us being here, Lily Brockley included.

'Well you see, Skye, I have lived here at Adder House for many years now. Perhaps when you and your mummy have been here for a long time, you might move into one of the bigger apartments, too.'

Skye considers this and nods, seemingly satisfied with her response.

'You've furnished this room so beautifully,' I compliment Lily as I take in the muted Laura Ashley wallpaper and soft furnishings. The large picture windows that span an entire wall have the dramatic effect of bringing the garden inside. Here on the second floor, there's a sense of being even closer to the leafy trees.

As we watch, a squirrel scampers up the same oak tree our breakfast blackbird favours.

Although it's pretty, I wouldn't necessarily want to live with so much floral busyness myself, but I do think it seems perfect for Lily.

'Thank you, dear. I do like to surround myself with beautiful things. There's so much ugliness in the world, don't you think? So much distrust and focus on negative events, rather than on making peaceful progress so that the world is a better, more informed place for our future generations.'

'I agree,' I say, surprised at the strength of her feelings on the matter.

'Now, bear with me a few minutes and I'll get our tea. Skye, could I trouble you to help me to carry in the cake?'

Skye nods with no hint of shyness. Compared to her cautiousness around Audrey, she seems more than pleased to be involved in helping Lily.

The two of them disappear into the kitchen, and I close my eyes for a few moments, savouring the peace and tranquillity. Although I can hear the hum of their voices and the odd clink of china in the kitchen, it feels so relaxing here. I can almost imagine

Lily being my grandmother and Skye's great-grandmother. How it must feel to have a—

'Ta-dah!' Skye appears in front of me carrying a most impressive homemade lemon drizzle cake on a floral china platter.

'Goodness,' I exclaim. 'You baked that really quickly!'

'I haven't made it, silly.' Skye giggles. 'Lily has.'

She places it carefully on the coffee table and stands back as Lily comes in with a tray loaded with a china teapot, cups, and saucers. She sets everything down and begins to pour the tea.

'So. Have you met the other residents yet?'

'We've met Dr and Mrs Marsden. And I've met Mr and Mrs Woodings.'

'Ahh, you've had the pleasure then.' Her eyes twinkle. 'Milk?'

'Yes, please.' I smile as Skye hands me a slice of lemon cake on a china plate, a look of pure concentration on her face as she focuses on keeping the crockery level.

Miss Brockley serves my tea in a delicate bone-china cup and saucer.

'I don't know what your initial impression of them is, but try not to tar us all with the same brush,' she says candidly. 'I'm sure the residents here can seem a bit strange to a newcomer, but most of them are quite harmless.'

Most of them? Sounds a bit ominous.

Lily keeps her voice perfectly pleasant but I get the feeling she's thinking something quite different. I'm not sure how to ask for the meaning behind her comment without sounding rude, and I don't want to spoil the ambience of our afternoon.

'I'm sure you're right.' I sip my tea. 'Everyone seems very nice.'

Miss Brockley's pale-blue eyes settle on me. 'You're very polite, Freya, but you don't need to be. Not with me, anyhow. They're harmless enough, but don't let them get to you with their strange ways. That's all I'm saying.'

Here's my chance to ask a few questions. I take a breath.

'The Marsdens do seem a bit obsessed with security,' I begin. 'They want to install a camera inside my apartment, but I've said I want to think about it. I've already decided I don't want it though.'

She looks surprised. 'Really . . . a *camera*?'

'Yes. They said it was for my own security, so they could monitor the entrance to my flat.' I put my cup and saucer down on the coffee table. 'Seems an odd thing to do.'

'Indeed.' Lily looks thoughtful. 'You did right standing your ground like that. Make sure you put them in their place.'

She doesn't offer an opinion on whether she thinks they are obsessed with security, but seems to approve of my reaction.

'They said all the apartments have them installed,' I remark lightly.

'Well, mine certainly doesn't,' Lily says bluntly. 'Like you, I wouldn't entertain it.'

'Dr Marsden said a couple of the apartments are empty because the residents have gone travelling.'

She pauses before answering. 'That's true. I don't know when they'll be back. You might think me rude but I say good riddance. The place is better without them.'

I'm just trying to get a handle on this house, the people in it, how they work together.

I'm hoping Lily might give me a bit of extra information that helps me make sense of the setup here.

Right now, Adder House seems like one of those expensive but intriguing chrome-and-wood puzzles that look attractive enough to put on display. Only when you get closer, you see something about it is just a little off-kilter, making it almost impossible to solve.

Later, when we get back upstairs after visiting Lily, I make sure the latch has engaged behind us. I glance down and see a piece of paper on the floor that's clearly been pushed under the door.

I pick it up and turn it over and read the spidery black handwriting.

> *Skye may visit St Benjamin Monks at 10:30 tomorrow morning. Meet me in the foyer at 10:10 a.m.*
>
> *Regards, Audrey*

I marvel at the speed of this result after pleading with the school office myself and getting precisely nowhere.

It seems Mrs Audrey Marsden has quite a powerful reach around these parts.

20

Later, when I've put Skye to bed, I pour myself a gin and tonic and sit listening to a chill-out playlist on low volume.

It feels decadent with everything I've still got to do, but slowly, I feel the tension begin to seep from my bones.

This afternoon, for the first time in a long time, I saw my daughter forget her troubles for an hour or so, and become an ordinary little girl again with no worries.

Lily seems to have this way with her that just puts Skye at ease. There was no clinging to me nor snuggling shyly into my side. Lily brought out some beautifully illustrated bird books and the two of them sat together, leafing through the colourful images.

Lily pointed to a bird, and nine times out of ten, Skye identified it correctly within a second or two. Lily seemed genuinely impressed at Skye's knowledge, and I prickled with pride as I watched them.

I'd never known my own parents and obviously had zero interest in making contact again with any of the families I'd had to endure growing up, so Skye had no grandparents from my side. Lewis's dad died when he was a teenager, which only left June, his mother.

When Skye was around three years old, we noticed worrying behaviour from June. She'd constantly repeat herself when chatting and forget where she'd put important things like her purse and diabetes medication.

There had been a big move in the media to raise dementia awareness, and one day, when June had collected her pension in cash from the post office and called us in distress because she'd put it 'somewhere safe' and couldn't recall where, Lewis and I just looked at each other and we knew.

The sad thing was, dementia had sunk its horrifying claws in but hadn't got a real foothold yet. June still had periods of lucidity and would often realise she'd repeated herself or forgotten what she'd popped into Tesco for.

It was so cruel to witness.

Between us, we visited June twice a day and she came to stay with us for part of the week. Then, within a couple of months after leaving home, Lewis had inexplicably taken the decision to put June into a care home specialising in dementia.

I was heartbroken for her and tried to discuss it with Lewis, but he wouldn't entertain the idea of bringing her back home.

'Nothing to do with you, Freya,' he said shortly when I tried to raise it. 'Like Janine says, it's for her own good.'

June died a few months later.

Still, it was so nice to see Skye enjoying that kind of grand-mother-type connection today, with Lily.

I close my eyes and take a sip of gin, enjoying the delicate clink of the ice cubes as the liquid sloshes them together.

I suppose seeing the cold, unfeeling way my husband treated his own mother, I should have been prepared for what came next. But that wasn't the case. Instead, he shocked me to my core.

When Lewis first moved in with Janine, about eighteen months ago now, we agreed to preserve certain boundaries when he came to pick up Skye for the weekend. He agreed he would ring the buzzer and wait outside until I gathered her things and brought her to the door.

We also agreed that when he brought her back home on Sundays, he'd text me to say they were outside, and I'd go out to bring her safely inside.

It might sound a bit of a rigmarole, but I was really struggling. I knew if he constantly came in to wait and sat in his regular armchair like nothing had happened, it would totally screw me up. So I asked him for his key and made it crystal clear that under no circumstances did I want Janine anywhere near the house again, and grudgingly, he agreed.

So when the door buzzer sounded early one Sunday evening just a few weeks after he'd moved in down the road with Janine, I was somewhat surprised to see Lewis's broad shoulders and his face pressed up to the glass.

He'd taken Skye for the weekend and it was only four o'clock; they weren't due home for another couple of hours. As I approached, he knocked impatiently and loudly announced he needed to come inside.

Still achingly raw every time I saw him, I opened the front door with a strained smile and wide arms to greet Skye. My smile soon faded when I saw Janine hovering just behind him on the doorstep.

Skye dashed past me into the house, giving me a super-quick hug on the way. 'I've got to go and get something, Mummy,' she said breathlessly, before disappearing up to her bedroom.

'Sorry to spring a visit on you like this,' Lewis began. At least he had the decency to look a little bashful while Janine glowered behind him, clearly unrepentant. 'I wondered if . . . if we could just have a quick word?'

I took a breath, ready to square up to Lewis, to say that Janine wouldn't be setting foot inside the house; but I felt mindful of my daughter despite the guidelines we'd agreed to.

I didn't make a scene about Janine coming in. Instead, I took a few steps back into the hallway to give them both room to come inside. It was important to set an example, to be civil and tolerant.

Lewis looked around, as if he'd completely forgotten the fact that he'd recently lived there.

Janine, on the other hand, gave a cursory sweeping glance at the slightly shabby hallway together with a disparaging sniff.

Lewis's eyes met mine and I instantly recognised the 'silent pleading' look he'd always favoured using when trying to urge me not to kick off in company. This unnerved me a little, made me wonder exactly what was coming.

But I didn't ask. I simply folded my arms and waited.

Those nights in the weeks before he left, Lewis would be continually late home, and I'd spend hours watching the clock worrying. Then I'd start repeatedly calling him when he still hadn't arrived home from work at nine o'clock at night, and his phone repeatedly went through to voicemail.

Like a fool, I'd feel sick with worry that he'd had an accident. He told me he spent a ludicrous number of hours driving around the country.

Little did I know he was just down the road, screwing my posh new best friend.

Janine closed the front door behind her and Lewis shifted his weight, one foot to the other. It all felt painfully drawn out, but I wasn't in the mood for playing the perfect hostess.

'Could we . . . just go through for a moment?' Lewis nodded to the lounge door. 'It won't take long, but I want to explain everything to you properly, make sure you understand.'

Understand what, exactly?

A slow grinding started in my lower abdomen, but I didn't let on I felt worried. 'You'd better come through,' I said in my best snooty voice, and I led them into the lounge.

21

You are delighted the child will be moving schools earlier than expected. It will be so much easier to monitor the reactions of the mother and child.

They're trying very hard to be happy, anyone can see that. The woman has a toughness about her, a shell she's clearly built around her in reaction to her environment.

She has also got an air of entitlement to her, as if she has claimed a better life and nothing can stop her self-proclaimed 'fresh start'.

She likes to listen to music, to enjoy a drink on her own at night. She is more alone in the world than anyone you've ever met.

She could not be more perfect for what you have in mind, but everything will be ruined if you rush. Slowly does it.

You put on the gloves, open Beatrice's old journal, and begin to read.

◆ ◆ ◆

Leaving via the front entrance of the hospital, I pull my coat closer, glad of my hat because the fine day had gradually become cooler until now, at the end of the late shift, I am positively chilly.

I long to get home, where my sister, Dorothy, minds little Douglas until I finish my shift.

'I'll make us some cocoa,' Dorothy says when I get home. 'Douglas is sleeping.'

I slip off my coat and look in on my beloved Douglas, fast asleep on the bed we share. His thumb is in his mouth and his face belongs to an angel. I lean forward and kiss his blond head, relishing his sleepy warmth.

I love my boy, I only want the best for him. The professor is an intelligent man, a respected academic. As Rosalie says, I must not worry, he is entirely proper and professional in his intentions.

When I come out of the room, I see that Dorothy is watching me. 'You look troubled, Bea. What's wrong?'

I quickly alter my expression, I was not aware I have been wearing my concern so blatantly.

Dorothy has a muscle-wasting disease that is getting rapidly worse. Soon she will be forced to give up her job as a housemaid and my wages will need to support us all.

The last thing I want to do is worry her, but still, it feels good to talk to someone. 'Professor John B. Watson is an eminent psychologist at the hospital,' I begin. 'He has written some very important medical research papers and sits on the board. He is very well thought of by the directors of the hospital.'

Dorothy nods. 'He sounds like an important and respected man. Have your paths crossed?'

I give a troubled sigh. 'I have agreed he can do some kind of a study on Douglas. It's the second session tomorrow and . . . well, the study seems quite harmless, but Dougie has been unsettled since my first visit. Fractious and gloomy.'

'What sort of things happen in the sessions?'

'Well, he shows Dougie a rat and some other things and makes a loud noise. It doesn't sound much I know but it startles him and—'

'I don't really see the problem.' Dorothy shrugs. 'I'm sure the professor knows what he's doing.'

But Douglas isn't just one of the poor hapless rats I've seen caged in the labs. Douglas is my son.

◆ ◆ ◆

You replace the journal in its rightful place on the antique oak writing desk before removing the cotton gloves and listening to the professor speak.

◆ ◆ ◆

1920 Johns Hopkins University Hospital, Baltimore

Extract from the confidential case study diary of Professor J. Watson

OVERVIEW

The mother of Little Albert reports that the child has been rather more fractious than normal since his visit.

He appears slightly thinner but still of a mild, fairly content temperament. Beatrice, the mother of the child, is to remain present during the sessions. Session two takes place in a controlled environment, the private office of myself, Professor John B. Watson. Also present is Dr Rosalie Rayner and Beatrice, the subject's mother.

STAGE THREE

Little Albert is again presented with a single stimulus: the rat.

As he reaches for it, a steel bar behind him is hit. The noise is loud and jarring. This identical procedure is repeated three times.

Albert is then presented with the rat alone with no accompanying noise.

Two more presentations with the rat *and* the noise are made, followed by a final repeat of presenting the rat alone.

Total rat with noise procedures completed: 7.

BASELINE REACTIONS:

Following all presentations (with and without accompanying noise), Albert finally reacted to the rat alone by immediately crying. He pre-empted the noise.

He turned to the left and crawled quickly away from the rat towards his mother. Session two is concluded.

Subject's mother is instructed to return to the office in five days' time.

22

As Lewis and Janine took their seats opposite me in the lounge, I couldn't think of anything else but why Lewis seemed so suddenly desperate to speak to me. More to the point, why he'd brought *her* into the sanctity of what used to be our family home.

Instead, I silently berated myself that after getting back from lunch at Brenna and Viv's, I'd changed out of my best jeans and pale pink cashmere-mix sweater and pulled on some baggy old sweatpants and a grubby-looking T-shirt.

My eyes narrowed as I studied Janine, elegant as ever in her trademark Armani jeans and pristine white silk blouse. She'd had her glossy brown hair newly highlighted, too. Half a dozen new buttery shades that seamlessly blended together to give a flattering frame to her immoveable face.

It seemed even Lewis didn't do casual any more, judging by the Paul Smith sweater he'd paired with taupe chinos. No evidence at all of the scruffy combat shorts and battered lime-green Crocs he used to favour when he wasn't working.

The two of them perched on the edge of their seats. I felt gratified to see they looked as if they were suddenly on the back foot a bit.

Janine had kept on her towering heels, obviously feeling no pressure to comply with her own 'shoes off at the door' rule that I recall she was keen on enforcing in her own house. In the days we were still on speaking terms.

I glanced down at my own sock feet, one chipped toenail poking through a hole I hadn't even realised was there. Until now. I tucked the offending foot behind my other leg.

There were brief sounds of Skye moving about upstairs above our heads before Lewis cleared his throat.

'We wanted to talk about . . . I mean, we have something to tell you. About Skye. I'm hoping you won't—'

'For goodness' sake, Lewis, just tell her!' Janine snapped.

'I'm getting around to it,' Lewis said carefully.

His eyes darkened, but the flash of resentment had already gone by the time Janine turned to him. Her eyes searched his as she waited for him to speak.

I could tell by the expression on her face that she had no clue as to how to read him.

The set of his jaw, the faint squint of his eyes. It all meant nothing to her yet. Things were too new, too nice. Things were still too *fake* between them.

I knew him, though, and I could see he was nervous. He was feeling resolved about something.

Lewis cleared his throat.

'I've given it a lot of thought and I want to formalise the custody arrangements for Skye. In fact . . . I'll be applying for sole custody.'

In that moment, I can honestly say I hated him. All at once, his voice sounded distant from where I was sitting.

'I'm quite happy for you to be part of her life, of course, but Skye's wellbeing is paramount, and I know she'll get the necessary stability she needs living with us.'

Blood rushed to my head, and my legs felt tingly and numb in equal measure. I made a gargantuan effort not to let it show, but I don't think I succeeded.

'I'll fight tooth and nail if that's how you want to play it. You . . . and *her*' – I didn't look at Janine – 'are the ones messing up Skye's life. I'm sure any court would see quite clearly where her stability lies.'

The look Lewis gave me sent a chill down my spine.

'The last thing I want to do is fight dirty, Freya,' he said softly. 'But rest assured, if needs be, I will do so. If I need to, I'll use anything and everything.'

Panic flashed into my throat like a scorch of heat.

Lewis had lied constantly, thought up elaborate excuses on the spot to conceal his affair with Janine. What might he be prepared to use to take Skye away from me?

Janine coughed before adding a snide contribution. 'Skye needs a stable home, and if we decide to do so, we have the money to engage the best lawyers in the business to fight for her, if necessary. You can't compete with that, Freya.'

A look of triumph passed between them. I felt heat rising from my throat into my face and a sickening wave of fluttering started up in the pit of my stomach.

Skye barrelled into the room like a whirlwind of frothy net.

'Mummy, WE'RE GOING TO DISNEYLAND PARIS!' Skye screeched, bouncing into the room in her yellow Belle dress complete with paste-jewelled tiara. 'Have you told her yet, Daddy?'

I couldn't respond, couldn't speak. It was clear they were buying my daughter's cooperation. I couldn't compete with *that*, either.

'Skye, darling, pop back upstairs and play with your toys for five minutes while the grown-ups talk,' Janine said.

She placed her hand lightly on Lewis's thigh and his face flushed pink.

'I'll thank you not to tell my daughter what to do in this house,' I said, feeling my heartbeat begin to race. A confrontation was far from ideal in front of Skye, but I knew I couldn't afford to give Janine an inch. 'Lewis and I will deal with this issue. It's actually got bugger all to do with you.'

Skye gave a little gasp behind me.

'Oh, for goodness' sake.' Janine rolled her eyes. 'Mistakenly, I thought Skye was the only child amongst us.'

'Let's all just calm down a bit, shall we?' Lewis raised his hands.

'You can't buy her affection with a holiday. She can't go in term-time, anyway, the school won't allow it.'

'I don't care about school. I want to go to Disneyland and THAT'S IT!'

Skye stomped out of the room and headed for the stairs, a furious blur of blonde curls, frothy net, and yellow satin.

'All this has been a lot for her to cope with,' Lewis remarked quietly. 'A break will do her good, Freya.'

'I assume by "all this" you mean your having an affair and moving out?' I hissed in an effort to dampen the volume of my voice.

'Can't you just try to think of what's best for Skye? Rather than . . .' His voice trailed off and I ignored his stony stare.

'Rather than what?'

'Rather than just thinking about yourself,' Janine provided. 'For once, think about your daughter and what's best for *her*. We can give her so much more.'

I stood up, turned my whole body towards Lewis, blocking Janine completely. 'I think it's best if you leave.'

Lewis and Janine both stood up without saying anything. A few moments later, I closed the door behind them.

I exhaled slowly and closed my eyes, resting my forehead on the cool stained-glass inserts in the door.

I heard Skye singing softly from where she sat at the top of the stairs. I hoped she hadn't heard too much of that last piece of conversation.

I didn't know what I'd do if they took her away from me. I needed her in my life like I needed to breathe.

A feeling like falling washed over me and I held on to the door frame to steady myself. The floor felt so soft and unstable under my feet . . . everything I thought was certain just ten minutes earlier was fracturing into brittle pieces and falling away.

The truth was, I knew if it came to money and legal advice, Lewis definitely had the upper hand when fighting in the courts for our daughter.

In any event, fate intervened, and thank goodness they never got around to putting their callous plans into action.

I swallow down the tender ache that's creeping from my chest into my throat.

No one can hurt us now.

I'm here in a safe new home with my daughter. Lewis has gone and Janine no longer features on my radar.

Silence fills the room as the playlist ends and I open my eyes.

I feel a sudden prickle at the back of my neck at the sound of voices . . . not raised exactly, but seemingly in discussion.

I spring up and move over to the window. I only have one lamp in the room at the moment and that's over in the other corner, so when I look out of the glass, the reflection isn't too bad. I see there's an outside light illuminated in the garden, but there is nobody out there talking.

I wait and listen. There it is again. Definitely voices.

I tiptoe down the hallway and peek out of the spyhole. The big chandelier that hangs down from the tall ceiling is still on – they turn it off about 9 p.m. – but the landing outside my door is empty.

The talking seems to have stopped now. Strange.

I check on Skye on my way back to the lounge. She's fine and breathing deeply in the same position I tucked her up in an hour ago.

I turn to leave and see that one of the wardrobe doors next to her bed is wide open. I know it was closed when she went to sleep. Must be a strained hinge, I think.

I make a mental note to tell Dr Marsden about it tomorrow.

23

We both sleep well and Skye is a little ball of contradictions. Half of her is rebelling against the new school visit, half of her seems to be quite looking forward to it judging by her various questions about where it is exactly and what they might show her.

While she's eating a bowl of cereal and watching a bit of television, I take a critical look around the flat.

There are still lots of jobs to do, and I'm itching to get the place organised as we're tripping over boxes and bulging bin bags lined up along the hallway and piled in the corners of all the rooms. Progress is slow when there's only one person to do everything.

As an only child, Skye is more than happy playing in her bedroom organising her belongings and throwing tea parties for her soft toys, but despite all the tasks still left to do in here, I reckon they can all wait until another day. I've promised myself I'll try and do things differently, and now is a good time to start.

'Grab your cardy, we're going for a little early-morning walk.' I peer into the dusty mirror I'd hung on a hook I found in the hall. I haven't found the time to clean it yet. I give up finger-combing my shoulder-length brown hair and instead scrape it roughly back into a bobble.

'Are we going to see the palace again?' Skye asks.

'Not this time.' I grab my key card and pop it into my purse. 'We're going the other way for a change.'

I make sure the apartment door latch catches behind us, and we step out on to the landing. I remember the voices I'd been so sure I heard last night. There had been nobody out here when I looked through the spyhole. I suppose it's not beyond the realm of possibility that I could have been mistaken, it takes time to get used to how sounds carry in an old house like this.

I look down and see that the red Persian rug is rucked up along the edge opposite our apartment door.

'Come on, Mummy!' Skye tugs impatiently at my hand and we walk downstairs. Weak sunlight streams in through the small stained-glass windowpanes at the top, freckling the cream walls with shimmering blobs of colour.

As we walk past the wide wooden doors of the apartments on the floor below us, I slow down to see if I can hear any signs of life behind them, but it seems so silent, as if there are just the two of us in this house.

For all that I feel insanely grateful for the opportunity to live here, something about this place makes me want to creep around on my tiptoes and whisper.

But that's no example to set for Skye. We both need to feel comfortable here, so it's important we're not treading on eggshells around the place. We need to feel we belong.

'Which door is Miss Brockley's, Mummy?' Skye asks in hushed tones. Even she feels the expectancy of restraint that hovers in the air here.

'This one, remember?' I say as we approach it, the brass number gleaming in the sunlight.

I hesitate as the door creaks slightly, and I think I hear gentle knock sounds from the inside as if someone is pressing up against the door. I look at the convex spyhole just above the brass knocker.

But of course it's impossible to tell if someone is watching through it from the outside.

When we get to the foyer, I sit Skye down on the chair by the lamp table. 'I just need a quick word with Dr Marsden, sweetie. Wait here.'

She sits happily playing with a little fairy figurine she pulls out of her pocket. I walk over to the leafy corner, and I'm about to knock on the Marsdens' apartment door when I see it's already slightly ajar.

I push it open a little way further and I'm about to call hello when I involuntarily suck the breath right back in without speaking.

There, in front of the bright light of the lounge window, Audrey is in the embrace of the tall man I spotted before. He's casually dressed in jeans and a simple white T-shirt and looks quite a bit younger than her. I can see he is most definitely *not* Dr Marsden.

I back away quickly and gather Skye up, chivvying her outside. What the hell is it with this place? Nothing is as it seems.

Of her own admission, Audrey told me Dr Marsden frequented a dodgy gentlemen's club and now *she's* snogging some guy in their own home!

Must be what they call an 'open marriage', I think sourly. Well, I intend to keep away. No more Earl Grey or ancient sherry in there, if I can help it.

At the bottom of the entrance steps of the house, we turn left and walk along the road in the opposite direction of the park.

Two doors away from Adder House, another grand mansion stands, its redbrick grandeur marred by a web of scaffolding across the entire frontage.

'There's the smiling man again, Mummy.' Skye squeezes my hand.

I look up to see that the builder who was there when we moved in is watching us again. He smiles and nods at me from the second floor of the structure.

He's wearing a sleeveless T-shirt and his tanned arms are toned. Maybe he was in that famous Diet Coke advert, I joke to myself.

He raises his hand and Skye waves back.

I look quickly away, feeling my cheeks heating up. I'm not used to male attention and I wilt under it. I'd rather be invisible than have someone stare hard and take in all my faults.

There's a wolf whistle and an older man leers down from the other end of the scaffolding.

I curse myself for looking up again, but I catch the younger builder's head whipping around. He scowls and barks something at the whistler. He must be senior to him as the other man lowers his eyes and resumes working on the fascia of the building.

'Ooh, he gave you a whistle, Mummy!' Skye gives me a cheeky grin. 'Hey!' I jiggle her hand and she giggles.

We walk down to the bottom end of Palace Gate where it joins Gloucester Road. The buildings suddenly become far less grand and the shops less exclusive. I breathe out. I definitely feel more at home around here.

'Can we look in here, Mummy?' Skye pulls me towards the door of a small gift shop featuring a display of hobby-horse sticks with unicorns' heads in the window. 'They match the unicorn Dr Marsden gave me perfectly!'

Fifteen minutes later, we're sitting outside a small pavement café and Skye is petting her new toy. It might be the less posh end of the street, but I still only got a penny change out of the twenty quid I handed over for it. I feel sure I could have picked one up for half the price or even less at a nearby market.

Still, it's nice to see Skye happy and lighter than she's been since the troubling sweeties-and-note-delivery incident at school.

She seems to read my mind. 'Mummy, when can Petra come over for tea?'

'Soon, poppet. When we get a bit tidier in the apartment, we'll send her an invite,' I say quickly.

I *will* send a little card over to Kat as a peace offering, but then the ball is in her court. Somehow, I don't think she'll allow Petra to come, but I'll be keeping my opinion to myself on that.

Skye strokes the unicorn's shiny rainbow mane.

'I want Petra to see my bedroom and the cherry tree,' she says carefully. 'And I want to talk about who might be our teacher in September at Grove.'

She's testing me. She's letting me know that just because we're visiting the new school, she hasn't given up hope on returning to Grove.

'Ooh look, a Great Dane.' I silently thank the owner of the enormous caramel-coloured dog about to walk by us for grabbing Skye's attention. 'Isn't he big?'

Skye's face lights up, her plans for Petra's visit forgotten. She stretches out her hand and I touch it by way of a gentle warning.

'Remember what you need to ask the dog owner?' I prompt her. 'Is he friendly?'

Skye shyly asks the lady holding his lead.

'He certainly is.' The woman beams. 'His name is Archibald, but we call him Archie for short.'

Skye coos at him and, with Archie's full approval, rubs his soft, floppy ears. 'He's *so cute*, Mummy, I'd love us to have a doggy as big as this one.'

I laugh and shake my head at Archie's owner, a tall lady in her forties with crinkly, smiling eyes. 'We've just moved into a *very* small apartment here. I don't think our limited space could stretch to taking in an Archie, however handsome he is.'

'Close by, are you? I'm just around the corner, been here for two years now.' She looks down the street. 'It's a nice area. Buzzy and interesting. Everyone is friendly enough.'

'We live at Adder House,' Skye volunteers. 'Near the palace.'

'Really?' Her smile fades a little.

'It's not as grand as it sounds.' I laugh. 'Our apartment is very small compared to the rest of the house.'

'I see.' The woman jerks Archie's lead and he steps away from Skye. 'Well, must be going.' Her tone has grown cooler, and she looks at Skye in this sort of strange, regretful way. 'Keep your eye on her, won't you? She seems such a lovely little thing.'

My hearts starts to hammer. I don't like the way she's changed like that as soon as we mentioned Adder House, but I don't want to scare Skye by asking pointed questions.

She turns and walks briskly away.

'Bye, Archie! Bye, lady!' Skye calls out in a sing-song voice.

'Sorry, just wait one moment!' She stops. I jump up and run a few steps to catch her up. 'Is anything wrong . . . I mean, it was just a strange thing to say.'

The woman takes a breath as if she's going to speak and then blows air out and shakes her head.

'I didn't mean anything by it. I'm sure you've got everything under control, you look sensible enough.'

With that, she turns and strides off again and although I watch her until she turns the corner, she doesn't look back at us once.

24

We finish up our drinks and make our way back home. I walk at a relaxed pace while Skye happily canters ahead on her new unicorn stick.

Weak sunlight permeates the thick cloud covering, and when I look up, I see chinks of cornflower-blue sky pushing through the fluffy white.

I still feel uncomfortable about what the woman outside the café said, but when Skye breaks into song, I join her, even skipping along at the side of her unicorn trot to her delight. I ignore the inquisitive glances from passers-by.

Nearing Adder House now, we're still singing and skipping along when I hear someone shout. I'm mortified when I look up to see the builder whose smile is now replaced by a full-blown belly laugh.

'No need to stop, I was enjoying that.' He clambers down the scaffolding, impressively nimble in his heavy steel-toe-capped boots. I watch Skye skip on, up towards Adder House.

'Wait for me,' I call to her.

'Nice to see someone around here letting their hair down a bit.'

I take a step back from him, instantly on my guard.

His teeth are white and healthy when he smiles, and I notice a tiny chip on the corner of one of his front teeth, a small imperfection that somehow enhances his looks. He wipes a dusty hand on his overalls and holds it out. 'Mark Sutton. Pleased to meet you.'

'Freya,' I say cautiously without giving my surname.

'You've just moved in here, yeah?' He scans the row of enormous houses up ahead.

'Yes.'

'That's why I spotted you were a newbie in the first place. You get to see the same faces around here. People are creatures of habit, coming and going. I've been working on this place for six weeks now, doing a full refurb.' We both look at the glowing redbrick mansion behind the scaffolding. 'Got about the same number of weeks ahead, too, until it's finished.'

'Well, I'd better let you get on.'

'That your little girl?'

I nod and follow his eyes to Skye darting in and out of the mansion gateways on her unicorn.

'Which one are you in, then?'

'I'm sorry?'

'House. Which is yours?'

'Oh, we're just renting a really small apartment in the big white one.' I laugh. 'The whole house isn't mine, sadly.'

His smile fades. 'Is it the one they call Adder House?'

'Yes, that's right.' What is it with people around here? The woman outside the café, now the builder. 'You look worried.'

'No, not worried. Well . . .' He collects himself. 'It's just after what happened there, you know.'

My chest tightens. 'What is it . . . that happened?'

I try to keep my voice level so I don't scare him off from talking about whatever it is he seems reluctant to talk about.

'That woman and her kid who lived there. You know, all of it.' He shivers. 'Gives me the creeps just to think about it.'

Icy fingers trace the back of my neck. 'What happened to them?'

Mark seems to register that what he said might be inappropriate given I've just moved in there.

'Sorry,' he says sheepishly. 'I'm sure you don't want to talk about all that.'

'I . . . I didn't know,' I manage. 'But I'd like you to tell me what happened.' The sounds of the street fade out and I can hear myself breathing.

He holds up his hands. 'All I know is what I've heard second-hand and that is, about eight months ago, a woman who lived there killed herself.' He watches me nervously for a reaction. 'That's what I heard, anyway.'

My forearms prickle and I give them a rub. 'What was her name, the woman?'

'No idea. Barry, my foreman, he knew the woman's sister apparently. That's how he heard about it 'cos they keep suicide stuff out of the papers, don't they?'

'Do they?'

'Oh yeah. Thousands of 'em every year in London, aren't there? They keep it hush-hush. Don't want to freak people out, you see.'

I feel a bit light-headed. The thought of something like that happening in our apartment is too horrible to even consider.

'You OK, Freya? It's a terrible thing that happened, but I didn't mean to scare you.'

'I'm fine.' I pull at the neck of my T-shirt to get some air circulating. 'I hadn't heard about it, that's all.'

'Barry's on holiday but he's back Friday. You should ask him about it.'

I nod and look up the street for Skye and feel instantly sick. Palace Gate is clear.

There is no sign of her.

'Skye!' I yell and run towards Adder House. The road at the top is so busy . . . oh God, she could have fallen off the kerb on her unicorn. I shouldn't have taken my eyes off—

'Mummy!' I see the unicorn's head first, then her sweet face follows, beaming at me as she darts forward from behind the hedge. She clocks my expression and her cheeky grin falters. 'I was waiting to make you jump!'

I grab her hand tightly and jerk it. 'Don't ever do that again, do you hear me?' Her eyes instantly fill with tears and I look around guiltily. 'You scared me, poppet, that's all.' I soften my voice and release her hand, shocked at my own reaction.

I look down the street at Mark again. He signals to ask if everything is OK, and I nod, wave back at him.

'You were talking to that man for *ages*,' she objects, her lip trembling. 'I was bored.'

'I'm sorry. But you mustn't play tricks when we're out, Skye. You really made Mummy panic.'

'Sorry,' she says in a small voice, and I pull her to me, her words muffling into my side. Then she gathers herself and looks up. 'What was he talking to you about?'

'Just about how nice the street is,' I say brightly, pushing his shocking revelation from my mind. 'He said we're lucky to live here. His name is Mark, he seems quite nice.'

I look up at the towering façade of Adder House in front of us. At this dramatic angle, it looks foreboding.

I hesitate, a thousand things swirling around in my head. Everything I first loved about this place is being swamped by a rapidly growing sense of apprehension. I'm pinning so much hope on our new life here, and Skye has had enough upheaval to last her a lifetime.

The critical voice from the past echoes in my head again.

You muck everything up; you never stick at anything.

My last foster mother would say it every time I got a low mark in a test or started attending a kids' club and gave it up. She was so critical, as hard as nails, and I know that. Yet . . . it's who I believe I am. Someone who makes a mess of everything she does in life.

Skye pulls on my hand and we climb the steps together.

But before I can reach for the keypad, the door opens seemingly of its own accord.

25

I jump away from the entrance of the house as the door flies back. It gapes open, revealing the dark mouth of the wood-panelled hall behind it.

Skye squeaks and looks up at me fearfully.

Dr Marsden steps into the light from behind the door and holds up his hands. 'Sorry if I startled you, Freya. I heard footsteps approaching and thought I'd save you the bother of . . .' He peers at my face. 'Is everything alright? You look a little upset.'

Skye ducks under his arm and into the house on her stick unicorn. Dr Marsden's head tracks her.

'Excuse me, young lady, you need permission to keep a pet here!' he jokingly scolds, and Skye bursts into a flurry of giggles as she canters inside and disappears from view.

Dr Marsden is dressed in a pair of black trousers, an open-necked shirt, and a burgundy knitted pullover that he's knotted around his shoulders.

He looks back towards the stairs and the sound of Skye singing there.

'Let's get you inside,' he says kindly, waiting to close the door behind me. 'Is there a problem?'

My heart sinks as I step inside the house. I can hardly just blurt out, *Did someone die in our apartment?*

My fingernails are pushing deep into my palm as my chest tightens.

We can't stay here if it happened, we just can't! I have to keep my daughter safe at all costs. As this occurs to me, I feel like the great weight of my own self-disappointment has gained its foothold again.

Can't I make anything work any more? Why does every chance of happiness seem to dissolve around me? What is it doing to Skye's own feelings of safety and groundedness, experiencing all these big life changes in so short a period?

My heart sinks to my boots when I think about going back to Brenna with my tail between my legs and asking if we can stay in the spare room after all, until I find a job with a good-enough salary that will pay double my Adder House rent and come up with a better plan of where we'll live.

'Someone out there . . . a builder working next door. He just told me something shocking and—'

Dr Marsden stares at me. My face feels hot and I gulp in more air, but it still feels like I can't breathe deeply enough.

It's not so much what might have happened here, it's more the worry about why they never told me in the first place. Putting that together with the other odd things around here, it makes my skin prickle.

'Come through, come on.' He sweeps his arm towards his apartment before turning around. 'You, too, Miss Skye.'

I hesitate but stop short of saying I've got things to do. If I'm going to get to the bottom of it, then this is my chance. It's only going to get more awkward to raise the issue if I leave it to fester.

I beckon Skye and she jumps off the bottom stair and gallops across the hallway on the unicorn and into the Marsdens' apartment.

Inside, piped classical-piano music provides a calming back-drop. Audrey is waiting in the lounge as if she was somehow expecting us.

'Take a seat, dear, I'll make us some tea.' Audrey phrases it as a statement, not a question, and I don't feel I can decline even though I just want to get back upstairs and close the door.

She glides past me out of the room in that elegant way of hers. I inhale the cloud of Joy parfum she leaves in her wake. It feels almost like existing in a parallel universe in this house, a peaceful bubble compared to the outside world.

I perch on the end of one of the voluptuous sofas and fold my hands in my lap. Skye is about to sit down next to me when Audrey pops her head back around the door.

'Skye, would you like to come through for a moment? I've something very exciting to show you.'

Skye freezes and looks at me. I know she still feels a bit nervous around Audrey. I can't help but make a comparison of how relaxed she was around Lily Brockley yesterday.

I don't want her to feel pressured that she has to do what Audrey says. Besides, I can't get the picture out of my head of Audrey and that guy canoodling. She isn't all that she purports to be.

I put my arm around Skye and throw Audrey an apologetic look.

'She's been feeling a bit delicate today, haven't you, poppet?' I say lightly, although a few minutes alone with Dr Marsden would actually be useful under the circumstances. I don't want Skye hearing too much and getting worried, but neither do I want her feeling uncomfortable with Audrey.

'It's a very big secret,' Audrey adds cleverly, her deep voice swirling around the room so enticingly, I almost want to be let in on the secret, too. 'So if I *do* show you, you mustn't tell another soul. Promise?'

Curiosity wins out and Skye nods quickly, turning from me and heading for the door.

I reassure myself she'll be fine, it's not as if I'm leaving her here and going back upstairs.

'What is it with little ones and secrets?' Dr Marsden chuckles. 'They simply can't resist them.'

He sits down opposite me and crosses his legs. His feet are encased in regimental smoking slippers. Rich mulberry velvet with a gold insignia on the front.

'Now, there was something you wanted to speak to me about. Something that seems to be bothering you.' He gives me a small wry smile and reaches for a cut-glass tumbler from the side table that's filled with an amber liquid that looks suspiciously like whisky. Surely, at nine forty-five, it's a little early in the day?

He takes a sip and waits.

I listen to the reassuring tick of the regal mahogany grandfather clock. A car passes by outside the front bay window and I hear only the very faint whirr of it.

It feels like time runs at a far slower rate here inside Adder House. 'In your own time, Freya,' he gently prompts me.

This is my chance. I just have to jump in, I think.

'I – I know you said, when we first came to view, that we were the first tenants to live in our apartment?'

'Absolutely. And that remains the case,' he replies smoothly, replacing his glass on a brown leather coaster.

Somewhere else in the apartment, I hear Skye's tinkling laugh and I feel my shoulders drop a little. It sounds like she's warming to Audrey.

I swallow, wishing I had my tea to alleviate my dry mouth.

'It's just . . . well, there's a builder working on a house a few doors away.' I nod in the direction of the road. 'He told me that . . . he said . . .'

'Go on,' Dr Marsden says softly. He places his elbows on his knees and leans forward. His hair is mainly grey but odd patches are darker, a glimpse of the sandy brown colour he must have been when younger. 'What did the builder *out there* tell you?'

The way he says it makes me feel like I'm a fool for even listening to Mark.

But Mark had seemed so concerned. I've just met him but he just doesn't seem the type to enjoy peddling malicious gossip for the sake of it. And he'd even told me when his foreman was back, if I wanted to find out more.

I feel a conviction again. I want to know, I have a right to know.

'He told me there was a young woman living here, about eight months ago. And that . . .' I hesitate. I'm not sure how to say it, and yet I know there's only one way and that's to just come out with it. 'She had a small daughter and she killed herself. He said it happened here, at Adder House.'

The way the words came out like that feels more like I've phrased an accusation rather than a question. It hangs in the air, suspended above my head like an axe.

He doesn't react.

I can feel heat collect in my face and I press my hands into my thighs to still my twisting fingers.

I think we're going to have to leave Adder House. We can't stay here if it's unsafe.

We'll have to move back to a tiny bedsit even further out of London than Acton that costs double the rent of this place and Lewis's life-insurance money will run out in half the time. Skye will have even more massive upheaval and another change of school . . . and I won't even have Brenna nearby when I have a full-time job to support us.

I'll have failed myself and my daughter yet again.

26

After what seems like an age, Dr Marsden finally speaks.

'My goodness.' His bushy dark-grey eyebrows meet in the middle. 'That must have been quite a shock for you to hear. That's not good, not good at all.'

In the face of his calm reaction I feel myself relax just a touch. Could it be that Mark might have been mistaken after all?

'I should have perhaps mentioned there was indeed an incident late last year. Very tragic it was. Tragic.' He looks towards the window, his forehead creasing. 'But it didn't happen here at the house, my dear. And they weren't staying in your apartment.'

'Oh!' I'm unprepared for the wash of relief that comes with his words, and yet, the situation is still very unclear. 'Did . . . did they both *die*?'

'There was a tragic accident. We were all very shocked here.' His fingers drum the arm of the sofa and he shakes his head. 'It was a very sad business indeed.'

He hasn't answered my question.

Had their deaths left a vacancy at Adder House which Skye and I have now filled?

Even if we are in a different apartment, the very thought of it makes my flesh crawl.

I remember when I first met him at the coffee shop, he said someone had *let him down* so he was trying to fill the vacancy again. Surely he hadn't meant someone had died!

'What . . . what happened?' I ask him.

'Here we are, here's the tea!' Audrey announces brightly, walking in with a stacked tray. Skye bobs around behind her, scooting to sit next to me once she can overtake her.

I feel a bit out of breath. Shocked. But Dr Marsden smiles widely at his wife as if what we just spoke about means nothing at all.

'Audrey told me a secret, Mummy.' Skye's face is alight with excitement.

'That's nice of her.' My voice sounds flat, and my daughter's excitement immediately dampens a little.

I can't move past the fact that Mark was telling the truth after all. Dr Marsden is trying to talk around the terrible incident, but I can't just leave it hanging there, unresolved.

If there's nothing to hide, why didn't he just tell me exactly what happened instead of talking around it?

A vintage Royal Albert teacup and saucer appears in front of my face and I look up to see Audrey there. She looks at her husband and back at me. 'Milk, no sugar, I believe?'

'Thank you,' I manage, the china rattling in my hand.

'What's wrong, Mummy?' Skye reaches for my other hand and I squeeze hers. For a little one, she's so perceptive.

'Mummy's fine,' Dr Marsden answers for me. 'She's just had a little shock, that's all.' He looks at Audrey meaningfully. 'Local gossip-mongers at work again, I'm afraid.'

'Oh no.' Audrey puts down the tray and sits next to her husband. 'People exaggerate, Freya. Please don't take too much stock from idle gossip.'

'I'd like to know what happened, though. For my own peace of mind.' I look at Audrey, hoping to appeal to her woman to woman. 'I hope you understand.'

'It's perhaps not the best time to discuss it, dear.' She smiles at Skye, whose excitement has now disappeared and a worried frown has taken its place. 'Suffice to say, the child's mother was . . . very troubled.'

Dr Marsden nods sagely.

'We did what we could, of course,' Audrey offers. 'To support her, I mean, with the little information we had. But I'm afraid help can only be given if it's accepted.'

They're talking in riddles, but I can't do anything about that because I don't want to frighten Skye by asking them to clarify the details. They're admitting that something happened, but they've said it didn't happen here. At Adder House.

Dr Marsden categorically said that . . . didn't he? I fall silent. I don't know what else to say.

'Adder House is *your* home now, Freya,' Dr Marsden says softly. 'You mustn't allow some fellow you don't know to upset you in your own safe space.'

How can I just ignore it when someone as down to earth as Mark volunteers such shocking information with nothing to gain? And what about the woman's comments outside the café?

I desperately want Adder House to be our safe space, but I need to know exactly what happened here eight months ago. I just *do*.

Mindful that Skye is taking all this in, I choose my words carefully.

'So you're saying that *it* definitely didn't happen here at Adder House?'

'Definitely not. But perhaps this is not the right time to discuss such matters in front of this little one, who's all ears.'

Dr Marsden means well, but that way he's got, of telling me what I ought to be doing or not doing, like he's speaking to a child . . . it's irritating. Audrey does it, too.

I force my mouth into a tight smile. 'Perhaps we can talk about it again' – I glance at Skye – 'at a more appropriate time.'

'It's best not to trouble yourself with such thoughts.' Audrey's words sound clipped at the edges. 'We prefer not to revisit upsetting memories if we can. Far better to look to the future, I find.'

'True, true.' Dr Marsden echoes her thoughts.

Easy for them to say. They're not the ones in the dark here.

Audrey claps her hands. 'Speaking of which, it'll soon be time for our visit to St Benjamin Monks. Are you excited, Skye?'

Skye nods cautiously but doesn't say anything.

I finish my tea, the weight of what I wanted to discuss still hanging in the air.

Skye seems subdued and fidgets on the sofa next to me. I stand up and thank them for the tea and agree to meet Audrey in the foyer at 10.10 a.m. when we'll set off for the school visit.

The apartment door closes behind us with a dull thud and Skye runs ahead, skipping lightly up the stairs to the second floor. Her faint singing drifts down the stairs like a silver thread.

Sunlight dapples the polished wooden floor. I look around me and a warm, grateful feeling floods my chest, beating the worries back even if they don't dissolve completely.

Whatever happened to that poor woman, it didn't happen here. And it didn't happen in our apartment.

That's what I keep telling myself.

27

Back upstairs, we have about fifteen minutes until we have to leave for our visit to St Benjamin Monks.

I really didn't expect nor particularly want Audrey to accompany us to school, but I can't very well put her off when she's been so helpful. Besides, it might be a chance to talk more about what Mark the builder told me and what the woman at the café alluded to.

I let Skye watch *Beauty and the Beast* on my iPad for a little while as I sit on the sofa next to her with my laptop on my knee.

It's quite old now, as far as laptop models go, and the antivirus software is long out of date, but it will have to do.

When we were still together, Lewis used the laptop far more than me. I've never been that technologically savvy, never needed to be, save for my Facebook account, and I haven't logged into that for months.

I feel a bit guilty sitting next to my daughter, both of us not talking and glued to our separate screens. But it doesn't happen that often, and today, it's really important I get online and hopefully get this stuff straight before it grows bigger in my mind.

I might not use a computer much these days, but I'm pretty sure it takes about five times as long as usual to boot up. I open up Google and run a search for 'Adder House London death'. Lots of press stories come back, but they're all regarding people or animals who've been bitten by adders in London parks.

I tap in the actual address of Adder House and get back various nearby properties that have been listed on Rightmove for eye-watering sums in the last few years. None of them is this property.

I try: 'death of woman at Palace Gate'.

Incomplete search results boomerang back. Most featuring unexplained deaths of females in London, but missing various keywords in my original search query.

I try a whole host of other phrases – no joy – and finish with: 'Suicide of woman in Kensington'.

Unexplained deaths, murders, assisted suicides of the terminally ill, but that's it. According to the search results, almost no one has committed suicide in Kensington, or indeed the whole of London, in the last ten years. Which must be far from the truth.

It seems Mark was right. This stuff is not widely reported in the media, and that's something I never realised. It seems even journalists have their boundaries, and suicide is beyond what is deemed acceptable.

It occurs to me, in the tragic cases of young people who had been bullied, or university students who fell prey to depression and feelings of hopelessness, far more exposure is needed to shine a light and raise awareness and disrupt the taboo.

But in the case of a young mother who takes her life, leaving her young daughter behind, there is barely a whisper, online or otherwise.

The lack of information only serves to make me determined to find out more.

But for now, I close the laptop and snuggle up to my daughter, inhaling the scent of shampoo in her hair, my cheek resting on the soft skin of her upper arm.

Thinking about the as yet anonymous little girl who used to live somewhere in this house makes me feel very sad.

'You're missing it, Mummy!' She nudges me gently, thinking I'm falling asleep as I nuzzle close. 'Belle is about to fall in love with the beast!'

'Ooh, my favourite bit,' I say and sit up straight again. But watching Belle acting all coy gets my sleepy mind wandering.

Lewis and I met at a house party on Christmas Eve, thirteen years ago. We were both with other dates, and afterwards, we both said it was clear neither of us wanted to be there. I saw his bored face from across the room and felt vindicated that I wasn't the only party pooper present.

Later, when we bumped into each other at the drinks table, our dates appeared to have both drifted away somewhere.

'Where's your girlfriend?' I asked him boldly when he offered to pour me a wine.

Unsurprisingly, when I look back, our period of dating didn't consist of expensive meals out or romantic breaks away in boutique hotels. We couldn't afford that stuff, but truthfully, we never wanted it.

Our time getting to know each other was full of cycling, bowling, hiking, and sleeping. Lewis was the first man I'd met who relished an afternoon nap after a cheap lunch of cheese, crackers, and wine.

These were the precious moments we shared together. It gave me an intimacy, an acceptance I'd never known, and I thrived on it.

The happy times don't mean any less now because of what has happened since. It just means that mostly, I simply can't bear to think about how perfect everything seemed to be back then, our lives full of possibility and promise.

Of how being together was the singular, most important thing.

'Work to live, not the other way around.' That had always been Lewis's motto in the early days.

Given time, that had changed, too. And afternoon naps were looked upon as being a waste of time that could be spent working, not a luxury to share together.

Skye snuggles into me happily as we watch the film together. Except I am not watching the film at all. I'm bluffing. Laughing in all the right places because I know it off by heart.

It's a different story inside. I feel like I've swallowed a hard knot of rope; a lump in my stomach that ever can't be shifted.

We were close, Lewis and I. So close. We shared all our hopes and dreams. We shared our fears.

Once, we spent a long day hiking in the hills and when we got to the top, we sat and held hands to watch the sunset together.

'No secrets ever,' Lewis whispered in my ear before he gave me a long, lingering kiss. 'Promise me?'

'I promise,' I said, and I meant it.

I thought I would always be with Lewis, that he would always be in my life. My rock.

Now he's gone, not just out of our home but gone forever.

It brings up in me a feeling I want to hide from. A feeling I don't know how to deal with.

The feeling is *fear*.

Moving here amongst people I thought might become friends felt so good. But there are no people like us here . . . everyone is so much older and from a different life altogether. And now we're much further away from Brenna, and it feels like we're out on a bit of a limb.

Adder House might be a strange little bubble of privilege screened off from the world, but it's imperative that I feel sure my daughter is safe here.

28

You track the woman outside when you can, observe her and the child around the house and garden where possible.

Her mood is changing; her confidence is waning.

The fact the child will soon be starting at St Benjamin Monks is encouraging. This is where the fun really begins.

You reach for the cotton gloves and slip them on to your hot, moist hands.

◆　◆　◆

I carry Douglas through the spartan, echoing corridors towards Professor Watson's offices.

He will be one year old in just a month's time and he is getting heavy. He is not walking yet, but he is crawling. Sometimes, I feel as if my heart might burst with pride.

I glance at the signs for the scientific laboratories ahead of me and shudder.

Yesterday, I had taken a baby who was suffering from feeding problems up to the medical examination area for an appointment and I had to pass this turning.

On the way back down, I couldn't help myself. I peered in at those poor lab rats.

I had heard the scientists did not think of their small subjects as living creatures at all but viewed them merely as objects ... *things*, to be experimented on. That is how the doctors and scientists are able to distance themselves from the sheer horror of it all.

I would never agree to Douglas having an operation of any kind if he did not need it.

No matter what was offered to me.

But, as Rosalie assures me, Professor Watson is not that kind of scientist at all. I feel confident of that.

I have had a bad week with my boy. His calm, sunny nature has seemed to dissipate as the days go on. He has grumbled and whimpered, even after being fed and changed.

It isn't like him at all.

I spoke to Rosalie only yesterday and asked if the work Professor Watson is carrying out may be contributing to his distress.

Rosalie laughed. 'You have a healthy imagination, my dear. Has the professor ever touched a hair on the child's head? Has he struck him?'

'Of course not.'

'Then you must not worry, Beatrice. The professor operates within the highest ethical code and employs methods the likes of yourself, a mere wet nurse, cannot possibly contemplate. Only a few more sessions and dear Little Albert will simply forget everything that has happened.'

I nodded, feeling marginally better.

'And your position at the hospital will be secure, perhaps even a promotion on the cards if the professor is pleased with your efforts.'

A promotion will make life so much easier, particularly when my sister gives up working.

I turn left and walk a short way across a carpeted area that features plants and a large window overlooking the hospital gardens that lets in lots of natural light.

I knock on Professor Watson's office door and wait.

The door opens and the professor peers down at me through the wire-rimmed spectacles perched on the end of his narrow, bony nose. He has a very pale complexion as if he barely ventures out into the elements and thin, almost colourless lips that have now stopped smiling and returned to their customary flat line.

'Beatrice,' he says, matter-of-factly. 'Please come through.'

It is only afterwards it occurs to me that, as far as I know, Professor Watson has never uttered a word to, nor even smiled, at little Douglas at all.

◆　◆　◆

1920 Johns Hopkins University Hospital, Baltimore

Extract from the confidential case study diary of Professor J. Watson

OVERVIEW

The child does not want to leave his mother's arms today. He has cultivated a mistrust of the surroundings of my office in only two previous sessions.

The child is thinner and of a paler complexion.

Beatrice, the mother of the child, is to remain present during the sessions.

Session three takes place in a controlled environment, the private office of myself, Professor John B. Watson. Also present is Dr Rosalie Rayner and Beatrice, the subject's mother.

STAGE FOUR

A neutral stimulus is presented: Little Albert is given toy building blocks to play with for a period of five minutes. After a cautious start, the child appears to gather confidence and his interest in the bricks increases to normal levels.

Following this, the coloured bricks are removed and various other stimuli are presented to Albert with and without noise accompaniment: the rat, a rabbit, a Santa Claus mask, a seal fur coat, a dog.

BASELINE REACTIONS:

After a slow start, Little Albert played with the building blocks quite happily.

However, when the other stimuli were presented, they produced negative responses in the child including crying, moving away from the stimulus, and crawling away.

These responses remained with and without accompanying noise. End of session three.

Mother agrees to return with Albert in eight days.

29

As if to mark our departure from Adder House to visit St Benjamin Monks Primary, the sun comes out, bathing the foyer in a riot of colour from the stained-glass frontage.

The warm glow in here spreads through my bones and I'm a heartbeat from happiness, if only the weight on my chest would allow one. But that's not going to happen until I feel reassured about exactly what happened with the previous tenants.

While we wait downstairs for Audrey to come out of her apartment, I notice Skye is a bit quiet. I reach for her hand and give it a reassuring little squeeze.

'I wonder if your new school has this pretty glass in it, too? People seem to like it around here.'

'I liked my old school,' she says glumly, staring straight ahead. 'I don't want to go to a stinky new school.'

'Oh sweetie . . . sometimes new things can seem a bit daunting, I know.' I sit down on the bottom step and pull her towards me. 'But they can be exciting, too.'

She leans into me a little and sighs. Her small pale face looks troubled. 'Will Petra have already made some new friends at my old school?'

I do try not to lie to Skye if at all possible, but it's important to be kind, too.

'It's easier for Petra because she already knows the people in her class. I'm sure she'll find friends to play with, and you wouldn't want her to be lonely, would you?'

'No,' Skye says thoughtfully. 'But Martha Fox always tried to take her off me when we played tag on the field, and Petra used to say she was a show-off. And now Martha is going to be her new best friend.'

Skye folds her arms and stares at her feet.

'I think Petra will be just fine, as you will, too. And perhaps in the summer, Petra can come over and we can go for a nice picnic in Kensington Gardens.' I don't think there's any chance of this with Kat's current attitude, but I'm running out of things to say. 'In the meantime, you should put all your energy into finding some nice new friends for yourself at St Benjamin Monks.'

'I hope the other children like me.' Worry darkens her face again. 'I wonder if the little girl who lived in my room used to go to my new school, too?' she says in a small voice.

I pretend to look for something in my handbag to avoid having to answer. She's like a terrier clinging on to the idea of the girl.

It's completely natural that Skye is feeling apprehensive about her new school and mourning her friendship with Petra, terrified that her best friend is moving on without her.

But I don't quite know what to do about the 'little girl who lived here' thing. I'm not sure what else to call it.

Dr Marsden denies saying anything about it the day we moved in, and Skye insists that she overheard him. I have to believe that she did, now that other details have come to light.

I'm crossing my fingers that once her life is full of school and new friends, she'll forget all about it. I only wish *I* could.

There's a flurry of noise and the sound of a door opening and closing and Audrey appears out of the shadows, dressed in a black trouser suit, as if she's going to sit on an interview panel.

Her white, starchy quiff gleams in the filtered sunlight and her powdered skin looks heavily made-up this close.

'Ready?' she asks.

I nod and Skye grabs my hand and steps closer as we move towards the front door. A few minutes later, we're negotiating a labyrinth of back streets lined with white stucco houses that I can only imagine the cost of.

'I thought it would be nicer for you to see the hidden parts of Kensington, rather than we run the gauntlet of the high street,' Audrey says.

I appreciate the gesture, but today I'd have preferred the diversionary bustle of the traffic and shops.

'I'm glad you got the note yesterday letting you know the time to meet. I didn't realise you'd popped out, usually I hear the front door.'

'We were just downstairs,' I tell her. 'Lily Brockley in apartment four invited us down for tea and cake.'

'Lemon drizzle,' Skye provides.

'I see.' Audrey gives me a strange look. 'I didn't realise you two knew each other.'

'We met her in the garden,' I explain. 'She and Skye share a love of birds.'

'I'm helping Lily to feed the birds every day,' Skye says.

'Fancy that,' Audrey murmurs, but her expression seems to sour a little.

We emerge from a side street and cross the busy Kensington High Street. Straight in front of us is the back of a very big, very old Gothic-style church.

'St Mary Abbots. It has the tallest spire in the whole of London,' Audrey remarks as we draw closer.

'Wow!' Skye is impressed with this fact and lags back a little, looking up in wonder.

146

I manage to get her moving again, and we pass a war memorial before making a sharp left underneath a quirky little bridge that seems to be part of the church itself. We emerge on to a short narrow road with the school on our right.

Audrey marches slightly ahead while we're like two little sheep following her around another corner, which leads us into a pleasant green space bordered by the school playground wall.

Skye and I slow to a stop at the glorious sight in front of us. It's the front of St Mary Abbots in all its splendour.

'Breathtaking, isn't it?' Audrey nods.

A wall of noise spills over the high stone wall around the playground. The children must be outside on their break.

As we enter the bright school reception, I feel Skye's fingers tighten anxiously around my own.

When she sees Audrey, the middle-aged receptionist sits bolt upright. 'Mrs Marsden! How nice to see you.'

Audrey indicates for us to sit down on the comfy visitor chairs while she speaks in a low voice at the reception hatch.

'The headteacher will be with you in just a moment,' the receptionist calls over to us before resuming her conversation with Audrey. I wonder if she realises I'm the person she told yesterday that the head had no space at all in her diary.

Skye gives me a little grin, but I can see the nerves in the twitching corners of her mouth.

30

After a minute or two, the double doors leading inside the school building open and a handsome woman dressed in a midi tweed skirt and simple knitted sweater appears. Her short, wavy hair is dark with stylish silver tinges at the temples.

'Audrey, how're things?' she says in a no-nonsense tone. One of the rare people I've seen so far who isn't nervous in Mrs Marsden's company.

'I'm well, thank you, Iris,' Audrey replies and looks over at us. 'This is Freya Miller and her delightful daughter, Skye.'

She walks over to us, shakes my hand and then Skye's.

'Welcome to St Benjamin Monks, Skye,' she addresses her. 'Your class teacher will be along very shortly to show you around.'

Skye nods at her with wide eyes.

'Thank you,' I say. Before I can speak again, the doors open and a woman in her early thirties enters reception. She has neat bobbed hair and wears a floral maxi dress. She nods to Audrey and walks over to us.

'Hello, Mrs Miller and Skye, is it?'

I nod and shake her hand. I feel Skye pressing into my side.

'I'm Miss Perkins, your class teacher.' She extends her hand to Skye, who shyly takes it. 'Hello, Skye, I'm so pleased to meet you at last.'

Skye glances at me and I give her a little nod. 'Hello,' she says quietly.

'I thought we might go through so I can show you the classroom where you'll be joining us. It's break time, so all the children are outside . . . Mum can come, too, if you like?'

Skye nods, her face straining with tension. Part of me wishes I could just cuddle her and take her back home, but of course that's not in her best interests.

We follow Miss Perkins down a short corridor, where she opens a brightly painted blue door with glass inserts at the end.

'This is Fern Class. All the classrooms at St Benjamin Monks are named after things in nature.'

'That's nice,' I say. 'Isn't it, Skye?'

She doesn't answer me. She's looking through the window at all the children dashing around in the playground.

The interior of the classroom is spacious and bright and the walls are covered with the children's artwork. Judging by the papier-mâché models on the tables, it looks as though they're in the middle of a project on birds.

'I thought it might be nice for you to sit here today,' Miss Perkins pulls out a chair at the table next to her desk. 'Next to your new classmates, Javeed and Hannah.'

The colour drains from Skye's face and I look at Miss Perkins, puzzled.

'I thought it was just a quick visit today,' I say lightly. 'I didn't realise Skye was going to be staying.'

'Yes. I believe Mrs Marsden has made arrangements for Skye to be admitted from today. But if that's not the case . . .'

Skye looks up at me fearfully, but I'm too flustered to speak.

Why would Audrey take it upon herself to do that? I made it perfectly clear we just wanted a visit and to begin admission arrangements for September.

Miss Perkins crouches down so she's on the same eye level as Skye. 'I mentioned Javeed and Hannah because they're both really looking forward to meeting you and they can help you with your papier-mâché model. Have you made papier-mâché before?'

Skye shakes her head and her forehead furrows. I hold my breath, certain she's on the brink of bursting into tears.

'She loves birds,' I hear myself say. 'She can identify all the popular types.'

I'm not going to leave Skye if she gets upset. She's had enough upheaval in one week with the move.

'I'm impressed!' Miss Perkins pulls an exaggerated face. 'If you stay today you could have your very own bird to take back to your new bedroom.'

Skye bites her bottom lip.

'It's very easy and lots of fun. What's your favourite bird?'

'I like owls,' Skye says, looking down at her hands.

'Oh, in that case, let me show you Oscar's model.' Miss Perkins holds her hand out to Skye, and after a moment's hesitation, Skye takes it. The teacher leads her over to the far side where she picks up an impressive painted model of a tawny owl. 'He based it on the owl in Harry Potter. What do you think?'

'It's very good.' Skye nods. 'The owl's name in Harry Potter is Hedwig.'

'Oh, well remembered!' Miss Perkins exclaims and Skye smiles for the first time. 'I always forget his name but he's very cute, isn't he?'

Skye nods. 'Owls have brilliant eyesight, it's so they can hunt their food at night.'

'Spot on. Well, you could make one just like this and then hang him from your bedroom ceiling. How about that?'

Skye's face brightens and I relax a touch as I see her confidence growing before my very eyes. Miss Perkins is quite obviously a complete genius when it comes to kids.

'Perhaps you could tell the class a few owl facts later . . . is that something you'd like to do?'

Skye nods, still a little unsure. But Miss Perkins is very good at putting her at ease. And if Skye is willing to stay, it would be a massive weight off my mind to put the whole changing-schools issue to bed.

'Let's say goodbye to Mum then, and you can help me tidy up the models before everyone comes in.'

Miss Perkins winks at me and I give Skye a little wave. 'See you later, sweetie, have a good day.'

She waves and smiles and then turns to take the owl model from Miss Perkins without looking back at me.

I sigh with relief and close the classroom door quietly behind me.

31

I walk back up the corridor towards reception when someone calls my name. I look to the left, into an open office, and see Mrs Grant and Audrey in there. Audrey waves me in.

'How is the little one?' she asks in her deep voice.

'Fine,' I say, glancing at Mrs Grant. 'She's absolutely fine. I didn't expect to leave her today, I thought we were here just to look around and complete some paperwork.'

'There's not a problem with her staying, I trust?' Mrs Grant asks.

'Oh no, it's very kind of you to arrange it at such short notice, and Miss Perkins has completely put Skye at ease.'

'We aim to please.' Mrs Grant nods. 'And as our esteemed chair of governors requested it, well . . . we had little choice in the matter.'

Both women laugh, but I'm sure I catch a thread of tension under the surface.

Audrey twists in her chair to look at me. 'I didn't want to mention in front of Skye that she'd be staying today as I could see she was a little anxious. But it's best to get these things done and dusted as soon as possible, I find.'

'Yes,' I say, pressing my lips together. Audrey has gone too far in her willingness to help, she should have at least mentioned it to me. Thankfully it has turned out for the best.

'Push the door to a moment and take a seat, Freya,' Mrs Grant says quietly.

I do as she asks, pulling out a chair next to Audrey. I feel slightly uncomfortable under their intense stares.

'Audrey has explained your recent personal problems, the death of your husband and the challenges you face as a single parent with meagre financial resources.'

I open my mouth and close it again, unable to respond. I'm literally flabbergasted.

How *dare* Audrey presume she can repeat such personal information? It's not down to her to discuss such matters with Skye's school.

I jut out my bottom lip and blow air up on to my hot cheeks.

'Hope you don't mind me mentioning it, far better out in the open from the off,' Audrey says briskly. 'Iris can offer you a lot of support, Freya, so I do hope you'll take it.'

'Actually, I do mind.' I'm struggling to keep my voice level. 'I would have preferred you to at least check with me, Audrey, before openly discussing my personal circumstances.'

The two women look at each other and I notice Mrs Grant looks mildly impressed with my obvious dig at Audrey.

'Oh! Well I – I only meant to help,' she blusters before setting her lips in a tight line. 'I'm sorry if you think I've overstepped the mark.'

I'm beginning to realise Audrey rarely utters the word 'sorry'.

'We can arrange for Skye to see the school counsellor, and we can also offer subsidised trips to support you.' Mrs Grant warily eyes my darkening expression. 'If, of course, you are open to such measures. I don't want to force anything on you.'

'Thank you,' I say carefully. 'I'm very happy to chat about it, but it's taken me by surprise on Skye's first day in school. Perhaps you and I can discuss it in a day or two?'

I feel Audrey bristle slightly beside me but I don't care. I can't shrug off my annoyance that she's overstepped the mark so casually.

Mrs Grant glances at Audrey and clears her throat.

'Of course, that's no problem at all.' She stands up. 'Now, I won't keep you any longer. Why don't you leave Skye for a couple of hours and then pop back to sign the admission forms and pick her up? We don't want to overwhelm her on her first day.'

I feel my shoulders relax a little. It's the perfect arrangement and it shows Audrey I have boundaries.

'Thank you,' I say, and look at the two women in turn. 'I appreciate both your help in sorting this out.'

'No problem.' Audrey stands up and brushes invisible creases out of her black trousers and sniffs. 'I thought we might take a little walk up the high street and have a spot of lunch . . . but far be it from me to impinge on your arrangements.'

Her tone is cool and there's no doubt I've offended her, but I think about catching her canoodling with that mystery man and wonder how she'd take to me spilling *her* embarrassing circumstances to all and sundry.

'Lunch would be nice,' I say quickly before I can tell her not to bother. Like it or not, I'm best keeping on the right side of her if possible. So long as she doesn't pull any more similar tricks.

'That's settled then.' She smiles tightly. 'I've already made a reservation at my favourite place.'

And just like that, I feel like I'm back where I started – in her firm grasp.

We carry on walking down Kensington High Street where we stopped to turn off for the school. Then we walk back up again on the other side towards the top of the street.

'What a brilliant selection of shops. I'd no idea there's such a variety here.'

Audrey nods. 'No need to go into central London if you don't want to, there's ample choice of shopping here and it's less busy.'

I'd never go into central London for shopping anyway. It confirms that although Audrey is aware of my financial situation on one hand, she simply hasn't grasped the limitations it exerts on everyday life.

Still, there are lots of chain shops on the high street within my budget.

'If you carry on walking for five minutes past where we turned around, there's a Waitrose where you can shop for your groceries.'

Waitrose! I'd managed so far with getting bits from small independent shops on Gloucester Road, but I've already got in mind to google the nearest Aldi or Lidl.

Audrey rummages in her handbag and hands me a small slip of paper. 'There we go, a money-off voucher for Waitrose.'

'Oh, thanks.' I don't look at it, just slip it inside my handbag. Ten per cent off at the checkout still won't bring the prices down to discount-supermarket level.

'Here we are. My favourite spot for a light lunch.'

We stop outside an expensive-looking, ornate café with a mouth-watering window display featuring pastries to die for.

'Café Musica,' I murmur. 'Looks lovely.'

I feel the tendons in my neck start to tighten as I wonder about the cost of having lunch in a place like this.

The waiter spots us as we enter and makes a big fuss of Audrey.

'I reserved your usual table, madam,' he simpers, leading us to a quiet spot at the rear and pulling out two chairs at a small table underneath an enormous crystal chandelier.

'I like the extra light for reading the menu.' Audrey winks at me. 'The three-cheese omelette is good here, as is the Welsh rarebit. And by the way, lunch is on me today. No arguments.'

'That's really not necessary,' I say quickly.

I can't afford to treat her in a place like this but I can pay my own way.

She waves my concern away. 'I insist. Call it a "welcome to Adder House" treat.'

I feel my eyebrows knit together. *Another* Adder House treat?

Our new apartment certainly comes with lots of added benefits: removals cost, help with school admission, an expensive soft toy for Skye . . . where will it end? And more importantly, what might be expected of us in return?

Audrey clears her throat and I realise she has been watching me.

'It's no big deal for me, but if it makes you feel uncomfortable, then we can split the bill if you'd prefer,' she remarks.

I feel my shoulders drop an inch. 'Yes, let's do that,' I say simply, picking up the menu. 'Thanks for the offer though.'

We choose our food and Audrey orders a big pot of tea for two.

She slips off her tailored jacket, tucks her Gucci handbag under the table and somehow looks suddenly lighter, as if she's shed a heavy, restrictive second skin.

'You know, you remind me of myself when I was younger,' Audrey says suddenly.

'I do?' She surprises me. I'm making assumptions, but if I were to hazard a guess, I reckon Audrey probably went to private school and grew up quite pampered. I doubt she's ever had to worry about money. Plus, the Marsdens obviously have a rather open marriage, it seems, when my union with Lewis meant everything to me at one time.

No matter how I try and engage my imagination, I can't draw a parallel between us.

'We're not similar in terms of our circumstances, of course, they're very different. I'm just talking about what's in here.' She taps her chest. 'Despite my privileged upbringing, I never felt . . . I don't know, as if I *belonged*. I always felt like the imposter, the one who didn't quite fit in.'

I look up sharply from stirring my tea. She's hit a nerve.

'My brother was so clever, you see, I never really matched up to him in my parents' eyes. In fact, I remember the day my father took me to one side and said the best I could do for myself was settle with a man who was willing to look after me, even if there was no romantic love there.'

'How awful.' I'm truly horrified. 'You're worth so much more than that, Audrey.'

I wonder if this is why she's seeking affection from the man she was embracing in the apartment? Maybe Dr Marsden isn't so hot on the emotional side of things.

For the first time, I notice that those same eyes I thought were so icy and incisive are actually quite twinkly beyond the dark liner and mascara she favours wearing.

Under the thick layer of powder and blusher, Audrey's skin is clear and she has smile lines around her eyes and mouth that soften the artificial, bold colours she always applies to her face and lips.

She'd look perfectly lovely without any make-up at all, just her real, soft self.

'I wish I could've found it in myself to tell my father where to get off, but of course, I didn't. Things were a lot different in those days, and young women often had to settle for less.'

Is she saying that *is* what she settled for? That her marriage to Dr Marsden is one of convenience? My first impression of them as a couple was that they appeared to be so close. He seemed to adore her, but that was before I saw her with the other man.

Audrey has obviously now found affection in other quarters.

I can't possibly pry by asking, so I simply nod and sip my scalding tea.

'When I look at you, I see a young woman who knows her own mind, as I wish I'd have done.'

'I don't know about that.' I laugh. 'Most of the time I feel as if I just plough through life hoping for the best. That's why Adder House is such a wonderful opportunity for us both, to make our fresh start.'

'And you must remember that, my dear,' she says thoughtfully, running a fingertip around the top of her china cup. 'This is your chance, your time to shine. You mustn't let anyone stop you.'

32

I would never have believed it, but Audrey and I had a perfectly lovely lunch.

She was right, the omelette was delicious, and actually, the prices weren't as astronomical at Café Musica as I'd imagined. Once I get back to work, I'll be able to bring Skye here occasionally for a shared treat of a light lunch.

We chatted and got to know each other like friends who'd just met. I really felt that I'd misjudged her entirely.

When we returned to school, Skye seemed subdued when Miss Perkins brought her through to reception.

'I think she's had a good day, haven't you, Skye?' Skye gives a faint nod but she won't meet my eyes.

'She played outside with the children and made a start on her papier-mâché owl,' Miss Perkins continues.

'I can't wait to see it.' I ruffle Skye's hair but she doesn't react.

When Miss Perkins returns to her class, Audrey says she has to pop over and see the headteacher about some governor business and will meet us outside in five.

'What's wrong, poppet?' I bend down in front of Skye when we get outside. 'Was everything OK today?'

'I don't think anyone likes me here,' she says in a small voice.

'I'm sure that's not the case.' I stroke her hair and put on a pantomime outraged voice. 'Who could possibly not like you?'

Her lips turn up very slightly at the edges at my fooling around, but I can see she's not happy.

'It's hard at first when you don't know anyone, but soon you'll have oodles of friends, just you wait and see.'

'I've had a good think and I've decided I want to go back to Grove Primary, Mummy,' she says firmly. 'Even if we have to get two buses, it's much nicer there than at St Benjamin Monks.'

'Has someone in class said something to upset you, Skye?'

She looks at me as if she's deciding whether to answer me.

'Is everything alright?' Audrey appears, taking in my worried expression. 'Did you have a good time today, Skye?'

'It was OK.' She shrugs.

'Why don't we go back and sit in the garden?' Audrey says brightly, shooting me a supportive look. 'I've got some homemade lemonade in the fridge . . . and some chocolate peanut cookies.'

'Sounds delicious!' I exclaim, but Skye remains silent.

As we walk up the street, Audrey falls quiet, tapping away on her phone as we walk.

After a few minutes, though, she lays her hand on my shoulder.

'She'll be fine,' she whispers. 'No need to worry. No need at all.' Easy for her to say.

When we get back to Adder House, Audrey is as good as her word. She insists we stay downstairs and enlists our help. We carry a jug of lemonade, glasses, and a plate full of biscuits out into the garden.

I'm overcome when we walk outside to see balloons and the small group of now-familiar faces who say in unison: 'Congratulations on your first day at school, Skye!'

Despite her earlier melancholic mood, my daughter's face breaks out into a wide smile. Susan Woodings rushes forward with a small gift wrapped in brightly coloured paper for Skye, and she asks me how I am, commenting how proud I must be.

I'm truly overwhelmed and Skye is in her element, enjoying all the fuss. Audrey must have arranged this impromptu little gathering via text as we walked back from school.

I glance through the throng and see Miss Brockley appear around the corner of the house, clutching her bag of bird seed. I wave to her, and Audrey, who's standing next to Skye, follows my gaze.

She unceremoniously plonks her glass down on the grass, turns and stalks over to Miss Brockley. Audrey has her back to me but I watch as Lily's face drops and she says something as if to defend herself, but Audrey folds her arms, all the time talking and jerking her head and then jabbing her finger, as if to make a point.

I can't help but wonder what might be being said and I'm concerned for Lily. I know Skye would love her to be part of the celebration.

After a few more obviously tense exchanges with Audrey, Lily shrugs and turns on her heel, disappearing back around the corner.

I push my curiosity aside because I don't want anything to spoil Skye's moment.

I know everyone looks happy to be here; there's just this discomforting feeling I have that niggles me. Something is slightly off, almost as if everyone is playing some kind of a role.

What I really want is for my daughter to have a sense of belonging, to know that she has people around her who care. Not just me. My greatest hope for us both is to have a happy family unit again.

Susan and Matthew Woodings want to know all about what Skye did in class this afternoon and Susan is animated and charming, far from the troubled soul she seemed to be in the garden.

After all this and a spot of hide-and-seek with Dr Marsden, Skye starts repeatedly yawning. After profusely thanking Audrey and the other residents, who've shown such thoughtfulness for Skye, we finally head back upstairs to the apartment.

We pass Lily Brockley's door and I'm tempted to knock, but I think Skye has had enough interaction for today and I don't want to dampen the mood of excitement for her if Lily seems upset.

Once we get to the top floor, I unlock our apartment door and Skye ambles in before me. When I step inside, my skin prickles and I immediately stop walking and stand stock still for a moment to identify exactly what has spooked me.

The air feels different in here since we left. And there's a smell – not unpleasant – just different to how it was.

I snap on the light in the dim hallway and look around. There are a few flakes of plaster on the wooden floor and when I look up and see the cause of it, I take a sharp breath. My face feels like it's on fire.

'What's that, Mummy?' Skye says in a small voice as she follows my stare to up above the doorway.

A small, unobtrusive camera is pointing down the hallway, a tiny red light flashing rhythmically on it like a watchful, blinking eye.

33

I beat back the feelings that are threatening to overwhelm me and settle Skye on the couch with her blanket. I start the latest *Boss Baby* movie on Netflix and kiss the top of her head.

'Back in five minutes, sweetie,' I whisper.

'Where are you going? Where has that camera come from?' She sits up on her elbows.

'I'm just going down to ask Audrey about it now. No need for you to worry, just relax and watch the movie.'

Reluctantly, she lies down again.

Downstairs I hammer on the door of apartment one.

Dr Marsden comes to the door. 'Freya! Wasn't that a lovely little gathering in—'

'Sorry. I've had to come straight back down because I'm angry. I'm so angry.' I'm panting and my voice is trembling.

'Whatever is wrong?' Dr Marsden looks genuinely concerned. 'Is it Skye? Has someone upset her?'

'Skye's fine. But there's a fu—' I manage to bite back the curse. 'There is a *camera* inside our apartment and that is not acceptable. It's a violation of our privacy.'

'I'm so sorry.' Dr Marsden frowns. 'Audrey told me she'd spoken to you about that.'

'She did speak to me about it and I told her I didn't like the idea.' I'm still battling to regulate my breaths. 'I said I'd let her know but I've decided I don't want it in there.' I press the soles of my feet down into my shoes to anchor me in the face of Dr Marsden's silence. 'I don't see why you've put it there. It's creepy and I—'

He holds up his hands. 'No need to say another word, Freya. I shall come up this second and dismantle it myself. We just wanted you to feel safe here but I can understand—'

'Mummyyyy!!' I whip round as Skye's voice screams from the top floor.

'It's OK, Skye,' I yell, my throat tightening so I have to squeeze out the words. 'I'm coming!'

I turn and belt back upstairs, my heart feeling like it's about to explode. When I get to the first-floor landing I see that Dr Marsden is rushing upstairs behind me.

I'm nearly on my knees when I reach the top floor. Skye is out on the landing, eyes wide and clutching her blanket to her chest. I shouldn't have left her alone.

'What's wrong, sweetie?' I pull her to me and I can feel she's trembling.

'I think there's someone in our apartment,' she whispers to me, looking away as Dr Marsden appears at the top of the stairs. 'I heard them talking.'

◆ ◆ ◆

The next morning, I feel a little sluggish after our restless night.

I couldn't get Skye settled until nearly midnight, and in the end, she slept in my bedroom.

There was nobody in the apartment, of course. I'd obviously rattled her with my reaction to the security camera and then I'd left her to go downstairs and she'd frightened herself silly.

Dr Marsden insisted on checking each and every room himself, and true to his word, in ten minutes, with the help of a stepladder he brought up with him, he unscrewed the camera and the bracket from the wall.

I just don't know what they were thinking, installing it without my express permission while we were out, but they'll be under no illusions how I feel about it now.

He was so contrite and apologetic, in true British fashion, I found myself assuring him that there was 'no harm done' before he left.

But that wasn't really a truthful response.

I've had rumbles of discontent over various things since we arrived here, but for the first time, as I lie awake in the early hours this morning, I've seriously started to consider whether Adder House is the right place for us to stay.

Skye scowls all the way to the ground floor and even resists my attempts to engage her in conversation about her feeding the birds with Lily later on.

I'd prepared her favourite cereal for when she came into the kitchen, sleepy eyed, still in her pyjamas.

'So, ready to work on your owl today?' I poured milk into her dish, and when I put it back in the fridge, she still hadn't answered me. 'Has Miss Perkins said when you might be able to bring it home? I can't wait to see it hanging in your bedroom, and I bet Brenna will love it.'

Skye prodded at her cereal with her spoon.

'Why can't I go back to Grove Primary?' she said flatly.

I sighed. 'We've been through all this, poppet. This is our fresh start, remember? Petra can still come over, but Grove is too far to go every day. Besides, St Benjamin Monks is a far better school.'

'It's *not* better,' she remarked crossly, letting her spoon clatter into the dish. 'It's the worst school *ever*.'

I guess good examination results and varied holiday activities are not top of the priority list for most five-year-olds.

'Did someone upset you yesterday?' I touched her arm gently. 'You must tell me if something happened.'

'Nothing happened!' She stood up, her little fists balling. 'I just don't want to go. So there!'

She stormed out of the kitchen and I let her go.

'Five more minutes, then it's time to get ready,' I called after her, clearing away her untouched breakfast and picking up a banana for her to eat on the way to school.

When we finally get downstairs, the front door is already wide open and Dr Marsden is talking to a workman on the step.

'I can take a look now, or I can come back later,' I hear the workman say gruffly. 'But if you send me away, it might be tomorrow morning or the next day before I can come back. So it's your call, mate.'

'In that case, you'd better come in,' Dr Marsden says curtly, clearly irritated.

The workman picks up a soft toolbag and steps inside the foyer. The embroidered badge on his overall says 'The Cable Company'.

Dr Marsden turns with a start when he spots us standing behind him.

'Freya! Sorry, dear, I had no idea you were waiting there. Good morning, Miss Skye.'

'Morning,' Skye mumbles without enthusiasm.

'So where are you two off to so bright and early?'

Skye plants her feet and folds her arms.

'Skye is at her new school for the morning and I'm off to the supermarket.'

'Ahh, I see. Well, have a good day.' He glances at the open entrance door. 'Lock up as you leave, will you? I'd better get inside.' He nods back to his apartment where the workman is currently unattended.

I step outside and I'm about to pull the door closed behind me when the postman appears at the bottom of the steps.

'Morning,' he calls cheerily and hands me a stack of mail with an elastic band securing it.

'Morning . . . and thank you!' I call as he retreats, heading next door.

I step back inside and walk over to the console table to leave the mail there, which is where everyone picks it up as they pass in and out of the building.

I leaf quickly through the stack and take the two letters belonging to apartment six. I push both letters into my handbag and leave the house, being sure to check that the door is locked securely after me.

Skye is quiet all the way to school. We walk by the church and under the bridge and join the parade of parents and children. I see Skye take in their green-and-red clothing and look down at her own leggings and floral top.

'Your new uniform will be here next week. I can't wait to see how smart you'll look in it,' I tell her, but she doesn't react with any interest.

As everything is so new, I don't leave her in the playground like the other parents do with their children, but take her into reception.

The office manager rings through to the staff room and Miss Perkins comes to collect Skye. She's bright and bubbly and Skye goes off with her without causing a scene, which I feel eternally grateful for.

Outside, I slip off my cardigan so the sun can kiss my pale arms and I pull out the voucher Audrey gave me. I can just buy something nice for tea and use the discount.

My mouth falls open when I see it's actually a credit for £25. I look at it, unsure whether to give it back. Yet another gift.

But I know £25 is nothing to Audrey. And I don't feel like going back to the apartment to do the jobs I should have really already done.

So I carry on walking up the high street to Waitrose.

I saunter up and down the aisles, marvelling at the range and choice of high-quality brands.

Unsurprisingly, I don't get much for my money. Amongst some staple items to get us through the next few days, I choose stuffed vine leaves and artichokes in oil for myself and some fresh-fruit kebabs and LOL unicorn-themed biscuits for Skye. Not the best use of the available funds, but still, it's a real treat to shop there.

Afterwards, walking back, I impulsively decide to prolong the luxury. I stop at a small café I spot up a side street and order a latte, which I drink sitting in the sunshine, nestled at a tiny table outside on the pavement.

I reach into my bag for my phone just in case the school has messaged about Skye. Despite enjoying a laid-back morning, I realise I'm still feeling tense underneath because of Skye's bad mood, and I find myself expecting the worst all the time.

I'm relieved to see there is no text, but I spot the two letters the postman gave me this morning. The first one is a letter from the bank confirming my change of address to Adder House.

I pick up the second letter and see that in my haste to get out of the house this morning, I neglected to notice that although the letter is addressed to apartment six, the name is a Miss Sophie Taylor.

It feels wrong opening a letter addressed to someone else, but Dr Marsden categorically said there had been nobody else in the flat before us. Could it be just a circular?

Sophie Taylor.

I whisper the name out loud to myself. Roll it around on my tongue. She sounds like a real person, if that makes sense.

A knot of discomfort sits on my chest as a thought looms large in my head.

The woman who died that the Marsdens don't want to talk about . . . could I have stumbled here on to something that would provide a bit more information?

I could write 'not at this address' on the mail and pop it back in the postbox, but I decide against that.

Right or wrong, I make a snap decision and open the letter.

Dear Ms Taylor,

It will soon be twelve months since you and your daughter, Melissa Taylor, had your eye tests. We are pleased to offer you another appointment at your convenience, please telephone . . .

The rest of the optician's letter blurs out as I try my hardest to convince myself it's a mistake, but my gut feeling is that Sophie and Melissa Taylor *were* tenants in apartment six after all.

This leads to another fundamental question that makes my head spin. Why would Dr Marsden lie about something like that?

34

It's a ten-minute brisk walk from the café back to Adder House. I don't look over at Kensington Gardens, nor pause to listen to the birdsong when I turn into Palace Gate.

I zap my key card at the door and enter the house, silently praying Dr Marsden isn't lurking around to ask me inane questions about where I've been this morning. I just feel like I need a bit of quiet thinking time.

My prayers are answered. The entrance is empty and I'm able to head straight upstairs.

I stop outside the door next to our apartment and press down on the handle. Of course it's locked.

It's time to ask Dr Marsden why this apartment is vacant and who were the last people to live there.

Once inside, I shrug off my coat, slip off my shoes, and sit down on the sofa. I reach inside my handbag, pull out the letter to Sophie Taylor and read it again. Then I start to formulate a plan of things I need to do.

A few minutes in the calm, quiet atmosphere, and I feel the tension finally begin to seep out of my body.

A few minutes later, though, I'm roused by the sound of someone walking around.

Not above me, because we're on the top floor. Not below me, either. Oddly, it sounds like it's coming from the other side of the wall.

I jump up and press my ear against the wall that adjoins the empty apartment next door. At first there's nothing, then I hear the soft thud of footsteps again.

I creep down the hallway and out of my apartment door, listening to the house in general, but the landing is deathly quiet. I tiptoe next door and try the handle again. It's still locked.

When I press my ear to the door, there's nothing to hear. A crazy thought occurs to me. Could someone be secretly living in there?

I decide to go downstairs to see Lily Brockley. She's made it clear we are always welcome, so I'll see if she has time for a chat and a cuppa.

She's already said she's not sure what's happening to the apartment next to ours, but perhaps I can bring Sophie Taylor's name into the conversation and see if I get a reaction.

But I'm disappointed. There's no answer from Lily's flat.

I go back upstairs and busy myself unpacking a couple more boxes. There are no more sounds from next door.

I have to be back at school at one o'clock to pick up Skye, so I nibble at the Waitrose goodies in the fridge and scoff a chunk of freshly baked bread and cheese.

I'm hit by a wave of lethargy where I literally can't keep my eyes open. I lie back on the couch to rest my eyes for a few minutes.

At the sound of the shrill ring of my phone on the floor next to me, I spring awake and sit bolt upright, my heart racing. My mouth is dry and I have that horrible panicky feeling you get when you sleep too deep and too long during the day.

I snatch up my phone and answer without even looking at the screen. 'Hello?'

'Miss Miller?' a voice says curtly. 'St Benjamin Monks here. I'm afraid nobody has come to collect Skye and she's getting quite upset.'

'Oh God! What time is it . . . sorry. Sorry, I fell asleep, I'm on my way.'

I end the call before she can answer and rush to the door, slipping on my shoes and belting downstairs. I can't believe I let this happen, school was out ten minutes ago.

I run. Up Palace Gate, down Kensington High Street, dodging pedestrians and pushchairs, drawing irritated stares as I plough my way through shoppers. My chest burns with exertion but I don't stop until I get to the church and dash around the back to the school.

I get to the gate just as Miss Perkins and Skye appear at the main door, looking out for me. Gasping for breath, I wave and Skye breaks away from her teacher's hand and runs to me, her face tear-streaked.

'I'm sorry, sweetie. I'm so sorry.' I pull her to me and she buries her head in my middle.

'Why didn't you come, Mummy?'

Miss Perkins reaches us. She's holding a large piece of cream paper in one hand. She doesn't look angry at my late arrival, merely impassive.

'I can't apologise enough,' I tell her, still out of breath. 'I fell asleep! I can't believe I did it, I was just so tired and I lay down just for a few minutes and then the phone rang and . . . anyway, I'm so sorry.'

Miss Perkins nods without comment, and I feel bad that she's been working all day in a busy classroom and *I'm* the one complaining of feeling tired.

Skye looks at her teacher and then back down at the ground.

'No harm done,' Miss Perkins says, and I think how kind it is of her to let me off the hook so readily. 'We had . . . let's just say, a little misunderstanding this morning, didn't we Skye? But I think that's been sorted out now.'

'Javeed said I broke the wing off his papier-mâché owl, Mummy, but I didn't!'

'Oh dear.' I turn to the teacher, a bit nonplussed by Skye's sudden outburst. 'What happened?'

'We put the bird sculptures outside the classroom to dry in the sun while we did PE in the hall, and when we came out, Javeed's owl had been damaged.'

'But why did he think it was you, Skye?'

She doesn't answer but wipes tears away roughly with the back of her hand.

'Skye went out in the middle of the lesson to use the bathroom and Javeed was convinced that's when the damage was done,' Miss Perkins says regretfully. 'I've had a chat with Skye and she's adamant she didn't go near the artwork at all. Please don't worry, I'm sure it'll be forgotten tomorrow, but I thought it was best I mention it as she's bound to be upset.'

'Yes, of course. Thank you.' This is not the start I'd hoped for, for Skye. I haven't helped the situation in turning up late to collect her, either.

We wave goodbye to Miss Perkins and she hands Skye what I can now see is a painting. I take her rucksack and we walk out of the school grounds together.

'I painted us at the park,' she says glumly, holding up a painting. The paper is mainly bright green with daubed figures dotted here and there.

'Oh, I see us! There we are, sitting on the blanket eating our sandwiches,' I say. 'Lovely. And who's that?' I point to two dark, featureless shapes standing under a nearby tree.

'That's Daddy and Janine,' Skye says matter-of-factly. 'And this one here' – she indicates a small black figure lying prostrate on the ground nearby – 'this is the little girl who used to live in my bedroom.'

35

When we get back to Adder House, I press the keypad and Skye rushes in, ploughing straight into a surprised Miss Lilian Brockley.

'Ooh, sorry!' Skye gasps, backing away.

'So sorry,' I say, rolling my eyes. 'I hope she didn't hurt you, Lily?'

'Hurt me? Nonsense. I'm made of sterner stuff than that, my dear.' She smiles at Skye and holds up her seed bag. 'I'm just off round to the garden to feed the birds. Would you care to help me?'

'Yes please! Can I, Mummy?'

'Of course,' I say, feeling relieved that Skye has perked up at last and I'll have a few minutes to settle my thoughts down.

'I'll bring her back upstairs when we're finished,' Miss Brockley says, and the two of them walk out of the entrance together and head for the garden.

I get into the apartment and pour two glasses of orange juice, one for Skye when she returns. I drink it standing at the window, looking down on my daughter, who is chatting Miss Brockley's ears off by the looks of it.

I've detected a bit of frostiness from other people here towards Lily on a couple of occasions now.

Lily told me she hasn't got grandchildren, and Skye is bound to get a bit lonely at times as an only child moving into a new area.

So theirs is an unlikely friendship that works well for both of them, I think.

I smile as I watch them and then my attention switches to something else. There's a very faint buzzing noise that's quite irritating.

I look up, but the top windows that I usually open in the morning are closed now, so it isn't coming from outside.

I take another sip of juice and listen. The noise is barely there, but now that I've heard it, I can't ignore it and it's annoying me.

I look around the room but there's nothing obvious here, unless Skye has left something turned on and it's pushed down the side of a seat cushion.

I walk across the room and stand in the doorway, and here, the noise is definitely louder, although you could easily not notice it if the television was on.

A few steps back towards the middle of the hallway, it's louder still. I open the door to Skye's bedroom and instantly recoil at the sight of the window, buzzing with what seems like a million flies. The room is full of them.

I scream and jump back outside the room, slamming the door behind me and running into the lounge. I've never been flaky about much in my life, but ever since learning at school all about the disgusting habits of the housefly – *Musca domestica* – I've hated being near the vile creatures.

And there's something else, too. The furniture has been moved. Her toy box and the pink wooden chair under the window . . . they're at the opposite end of the room.

I bang on the window, but Skye and Miss Brockley don't look up.

My heart is pounding on my chest wall and I feel as if I'm going to be sick, but I dash out of the apartment, not bothering to lock the door. I hurtle down the stairs and hammer on Dr Marsden's apartment door, stooped over, trying to get my breath back.

There's no answer, so I burst out of the front door, leaving it wide open and run around to the garden, calling for help.

'Heavens, whatever's wrong, Freya?' Lilian Brockley clutches at her throat, startled.

'Flies . . . millions of flies . . . in Skye's room,' I manage.

'In *my* room?' Skye looks alarmed.

'Come on, we'd better have a look.' Lily leads the way, striding back down the side of the house and in through the front door where Dr Marsden suddenly appears.

'Does anyone know who has left this door wide open?' His voice thunders.

Skye flutters around me like a distressed butterfly.

'Sorry . . . it was me. There are flies . . . upstairs . . .' I start coughing, my throat is so hoarse and dry and I feel as if I might be sick. I haven't got a phobia exactly, but if there's one insect I can't bear near me, it's flies.

'Apparently there are hordes of them, in the child's room,' I hear Miss Brockley say.

'I'll go up there with you now,' Dr Marsden tells me calmly. 'This sort of thing is easily dealt with.' He looks pointedly at Miss Brockley. 'I'll take it from here, Lilian.' But Lily doesn't move, she stands there almost protectively.

'You haven't seen them,' I say, my voice still slightly manic. 'I've never seen so many. Where can they have all come from?'

'Were there any on my toys . . . and my bed, Mummy?' Skye looks close to tears and I regret blurting everything out in front of her.

'Don't worry, sweetie, we'll sort it out,' I say hastily before remembering something else and stepping towards Dr Marsden. 'And the furniture's been moved in there!'

He glances at me, his lips pressed into a tight line. He doesn't comment.

We're all huffing and puffing by the time we get up to the third floor.

'You really need to start locking doors around here.' Dr Marsden frowns when he spots the apartment door is wide open.

He walks in first, followed by Miss Brockley and then me and Skye. I brace myself as he opens her bedroom door.

'Hardly millions,' he remarks with a wry smile.

I walk into the room and count five dozy flies on the glass and windowsill.

'Yuk, can we still get rid of them?' Skye screws up her nose.

'They've all gone,' I say faintly. 'The room was full of them, the glass thick with them. I—'

I walk up to the window and stare through it blankly. Then I look around the room. Only minutes ago, it was a swarming black mass of tiny buzzing bodies in here.

'Come downstairs,' Miss Brockley says kindly, giving Dr Marsden a look. 'Moving can be very stressful, one might exaggerate all manner of things in one's mind and—'

'I didn't imagine it!' I instantly restrain myself. 'I'm sorry but they *were* here . . . I swear. And the furniture has definitely been moved. Skye, did you move your toy box and your chair?'

I look down and see my daughter's big blue eyes looking up, confused and fearful as she shakes her head.

'I thought *you'd* done it, Mummy,' she says.

36

The backdrop of squealing, laughter, and shouting in the playground merges into one sound, but sitting here in your secret place, you can still hear birdsong.

Wait . . . wait . . . there she is!

She walks out slowly. Alone. Her eyes rolling around the playground furtively. Her little hands are in fists and her arms are close to her sides. She is distrusting, expecting the worst from her peers, no doubt.

Click . . . click . . . click goes your camera.

A boy and girl run up to her. The girl takes her hand and drags her over to the lowest part of the wall, close to where you are sitting.

Three other children join the group; two girls and a boy. The child's shoulders hunch up underneath her ears. 'What's your name?' the tallest boy asks.

She replies in a voice so soft you can't hear her, but by his reply, you know she's told him.

'Sky? That's stupid. That's like your name being grass or soil or something.'

'Or mud!' the girl says in delight. 'Let's call her Mud!'

'You're supposed to call people by their proper name.' Skye frowns at them in turn. 'If you don't, I'll tell on you.'

'If you tell the teacher, nobody will ever speak to you again.' One of the other girls presses her face closer and Skye takes a step back.

'We'll play chase,' Javeed announces. 'And I say there's no stinky thick MUD allowed.'

The children laugh and organise themselves for the game. Skye is still part of the group but an outsider, standing apart.

You note the determined set of her jaw, her shoulders square and head held high. She has her mother's attitude. She won't be beaten down lightly.

It will take skill to break them both.

When the children go inside, you put on your gloves and pick up the journal.

◆ ◆ ◆

Little Douglas barely sleeps all week, waking this very morning at 2 a.m. for no apparent reason. He refuses to go back to sleep and clings to me so tightly I can barely move an inch.

I conclude he has probably had a nightmare but I eventually settle him again by stroking his feather-soft hair and murmuring assurances. Soon, he nuzzles into my side and grips my finger with one chubby hand as if to reassure himself I won't slip away.

Today is the fourth and, I very much hope, the final session with Professor Watson.

He intimated last time that he has almost concluded his work with Dougie.

Working on the maternity ward yesterday, Rosalie mentioned a welcome bonus that I hadn't been expecting.

'Professor Watson is going to pay you an amount to cover your expenses in taking part in his study. We don't pay a fee exactly, but I think you'll find his contribution quite generous.'

I did not protest, despite it being the courteous thing to do. With my sister's illness worsening by the day, I am hardly in a position to turn down the offer.

Instead, I smiled and thanked Rosalie. Money is always so tight and any extra will be a tremendous help.

'The next session is very important,' Rosalie continued. 'Please be prompt and do all you can to keep the baby relaxed prior to your arrival.'

I mentioned Dougie's disturbed sleep and Rosalie swiftly dispersed my concerns with the waft of a hand.

'It is completely normal for a child of this age to have trouble sleeping. He is probably teething, too. Rest assured it can have nothing to do with the work the professor is doing,' Rosalie insisted. 'Why, the child will have forgotten any distress by the time you step out into the corridor after each session.'

So when the time comes to visit Professor Watson for possibly the last session, I take care to dress a fractious Douglas in his one best outfit: a cream shirt and a pair of brown moleskin shorts with braces.

'My goodness, don't you look smart!' I coo, and he gurgles and kicks his chubby legs with pleasure, his earlier irritation forgotten.

I follow Rosalie through the familiar warren of the near-identical corridors featuring pale-green glossed walls and echoing concrete floors, until the turning for Professor Watson's wing appears.

To my surprise, Rosalie turns in the opposite direction and leads us into an unfamiliar wing of the hospital.

As we walk without speaking, only our heels clicking on the floor make a sound. I notice how the walls soon merge into a softer cream shade and a quality woven carpet appears underfoot, muting the harsh clack of our shoes.

'Ahh, there you are.' Professor Watson appears at the end of the corridor, his long, lean frame disguised by a voluminous white coat. 'This way, please.'

We walk a little further, make a sharp right turn, and Professor Watson stops at a set of double doors.

'We're going to be working in here today,' he says, watching Dougie, who keeps peeking at the professor and then burying his head back into my shoulder, whimpering. 'The main lecture theatre.'

I shiver. I know this theatre is used regularly for specialist post-mortem lectures. I hope Dougie won't have to sit on the steel table used at such events, but before I can comment, the professor pushes open the doors and Rosalie ushers us through.

As soon as I enter, bright lights hit me, momentarily blinding me. When my disorientation passes, I look around and gasp. The surrounding tiered wooden benches are packed to the brim with both medics and academics.

Rosalie leads us to the staged area in front of the tiered seating where the dreaded steel table sits waiting and the chatter and obvious excitement die down, fading away to silence.

'Professor, are all these people here to see Dougie?' I whisper. 'Your study is *that* important?'

'Immeasurably so,' Professor Watson remarks. 'Nobody has carried out an experiment remotely like this one.' I flinch at his use of the word *experiment*, but he doesn't appear to notice. 'It will shed light on one of the most mysterious areas of psychiatry. That is, whether selected behavioural responses are innate or can be learned. I hope that people will be talking about it for years to come.'

'I see,' I murmur, but I don't see at all. Better to just let him get on with it, I decide. Soon Professor Watson's study will be concluded. I have the whole day off and plan to take Douglas to the park later.

'If you're happy, then let's begin.' The professor turns to his assistant. 'Let's start with the baseline reactions, Rosalie.'

I stand next to the raised platform, clutching my son. In the spotlight, I feel like a bug under a microscope. Blinded by the light, I can hear Professor Watson and Rosalie busying themselves with preparations behind us, and I can feel the weight of expectation amongst the now silent spectators occupying the tiered seating.

Douglas shies away from the spotlight and whimpers. I struggle to contain him as he wriggles.

Professor Watson begins to speak in a booming voice, powerful enough to reach the back rows of the lecture theatre and those people standing in the balconied floor above.

He introduces himself, gives a brief account of his work so far, and then begins a detailed description of his experiment which I confess I struggle to understand.

'You can put the baby down now,' Rosalie whispers to me, patting the metal table. 'And then step back out of the light, please.'

I try to sit Dougie on the table, but his legs become rigid as he whimpers louder and clings to me. He doesn't want to let go. I am just about to ask if we could try again another day, when Dougie is in better spirits, when Rosalie steps forward and pulls him away from me, setting him down, startled and alone on the sterile-looking surface.

Just as Dougie opens his mouth to wail, Rosalie produces a small cage containing a white rat. She slides up the side and removes the wriggling rodent, handing it to Professor Watson.

Dougie falls quiet and watches the animal with wide eyes. I watch as my son reaches out to touch its warm, soft fur. He is OK. Dougie is going to be fine, I tell myself silently.

I am getting the whole day off and will be receiving an expense payment, and my son is to become part of a very important study in the area of psychology.

Everything seems to be going quite well until Dougie lets out a blood-curdling scream.

◆ ◆ ◆

1920 Johns Hopkins University Hospital, Baltimore

Extract from the confidential case study diary of Professor J. Watson

OVERVIEW

Session five, the final stage, takes place in the hospital's private lecture theatre in front of a carefully selected audience of esteemed academics. The presentation is made by myself, Professor John B. Watson. Also present is Dr Rosalie Rayner and Beatrice, the subject's mother.

STAGE FIVE

Albert is taken to a well-lit lecture theatre to allow me to present my findings so far and to demonstrate the effects of the conditioning on Little Albert.

Child is initially presented with the white rat without accompanying noise. There is an extreme negative reaction. The child becomes very anxious and distressed within seconds.

When calmed by his mother, all the other stimuli are presented, and the steel bar is hit each time.

The child is clearly terrified of anything resembling the white rat.

The conditioning is judged to be a success by all who are present.

BASELINE REACTIONS:

Child appears traumatised.

Child distressed at mere sight of stimuli and refuses to touch or remain close to them. At the sight of the white rat, Little Albert turns sharply and falls over on his left side.

He raises himself on all fours and proceeds to crawl away so rapidly, Dr Rayner is just able to catch him before he reaches the edge of the table.

Little Albert displays worsening fear reactions and we are unable to continue with the session.

CONCLUSIONS:

My interest in the Little Albert experiment first began because I wanted to develop and take the great Ivan Pavlov's research with dogs a step further.

Pavlov noticed the dog would salivate when its food appeared. In his controlled studies, he showed, in a few sessions, that by ringing a bell when the dog's food appeared, he could easily condition the animal to salivate *without* the food, simply at the sound of the bell ringing.

I pondered then; could certain emotional reactions not be classically conditioned in people? Could an ordinary child, showing no fear, be conditioned with a fear response in just a few sessions?

I have today successfully proven that this indeed can be done.

The boy initially showed no fear and is now terrified merely at the sight of the white rat, in fact, of all white objects.

Give me a dozen healthy infants, well formed, and I will guarantee to take any one at random and train him to be any type of specialist I might select – a doctor, lawyer, artist, merchant, and yes, even a beggar or a thief.

This is the power of my revolutionary study.

37

Viv is away on business, so I call Brenna and ask if she'd like to come over for a glass of wine and a chat later.

'Now there's an offer I can't refuse,' she says before hesitating. 'Are you OK, Freya? You sound a bit, I don't know, *weird*.'

'I'm OK now, but we had a bit of an upset here earlier and there are one or two things on my mind. I'll explain everything later, shall we say about seven? Then you can have half an hour with Skye before she goes to bed.'

I know I'll have a hellish job to get Skye to sleep when she knows her aunt Brenna is around, but that's the least of my worries. Having someone to talk to who knows me well . . . who knows I'm not crazy, is what I need right now to help me make sense of things.

I make Skye something to eat and tidy around a bit. Lily Brockley insisted on cleaning the window and windowsill in Skye's bedroom. She even vacuumed in there, too, so we could be sure not one dead fly remained. I felt so grateful.

Dr Marsden had me doubting myself in the end but now I've calmed down; I know what I saw in there and that was a black wall of flies. I don't know where they came from and where they went, but they *were* there. I was *not* imagining it.

If there's some kind of hidden infestation in the house and the flies are coming through vents or pipes, it will only be a matter of time before they turn up in someone else's apartment and then I'll be vindicated.

I tidy our shoes near the door and think about the camera that was installed there. I've told Brenna to text me when she arrives so I can pop downstairs to let her in.

Strangely, I've only just noticed there's no door intercom system here like most apartment buildings, where each tenant has the ability to buzz someone inside from the front door. I need to ask Dr Marsden what the process is for my visitors, too.

Just before seven, I'm in the bathroom and I hear a sharp rap on the door. Skye gets there before me and I hear voices in the hallway, including a man's voice.

I wash my hands quickly and when I come out of the bathroom, Skye has taken Brenna into the lounge and our front door is closed again.

I hug and kiss Brenna. 'I'm so pleased to see you,' I squeal, and I really am. In fact, ridiculously, I feel like I might burst into tears. 'Did I hear a man's voice out there?'

'Yeah, the creepy doctor let me in.' Brenna pulls a face and Skye giggles.

'Bren!' I look meaningfully at Skye and back at her. 'We don't want anything repeated!'

'Sorry.' She grins. 'I forgot I was supposed to text you, so I just knocked because there's no buzzer, and he suddenly appeared there, just like Count Dracula.'

Skye snorted. 'You mean *Count Duckula*, Aunt Bren, like the cartoon.'

'Yeah, that's what I meant, Skye. He appeared at the door like Count Duckula.'

'Bren!'

'Sorry! Anyway, Skye mentioned there was a problem with flies in her bedroom. Sounds nasty.'

The image of a swarm of buzzing black bodies fills my head for a second, like they're all still there inside my skull. I shudder.

'It's . . . been sorted now,' I say hesitantly.

'Skye said you thought there were *millions* of them, apparently.' She grins. 'But then when the doc came up, they'd all gone.'

She's looking at me with 1 per cent pity and 99 per cent amusement. I know exactly what she's thinking.

'They must've found a way to get outside again,' I say. 'It's the only explanation.'

'That's strange because Skye said the windows were all closed when she got up here.'

I put my hands on my hips and shake my head at Skye, smiling. She's managed to tell Brenna every single gory detail and she was only alone with her a couple of minutes! 'Hmm, well let's just drop the whole nasty subject. Sauvignon blanc OK for you?'

'Lovely.'

Skye picks up her colouring book and Brenna follows me into the kitchen.

'I take it you'd rather not talk about it?' She leans against the counter, watching me.

'I don't want Skye getting worried, that's all.' I sigh. 'I admit I did get a panic on. There's been a lot of change in her life lately, we can do without more trouble.'

'That's my concern, too,' she says lightly.

I take out two glasses and put them on the worktop. 'What do you mean?'

'Well, I'd hate to think of Skye getting worried because you're stressed out and imagining stuff is happening.' She keeps her tone light but the words still sting. 'I just mean that you've had a lot on, too, Freya. It's easy to get overwhelmed and start to—'

'I did not imagine those flies, Bren.' I enunciate every word.

'Maybe. But Skye said you moved the furniture and then forgot you did it?'

'I didn't! I didn't move the furniture; Skye must've done it. Look. I'm not going into all this with you, it's not important in the scheme of things.' I had wanted to discuss my worries with Brenna, but her continued assumption that I'm imagining stuff is starting to annoy me. I'm now in two minds whether to speak to her about what else is bothering me.

When I walk past her to get the wine out of the fridge, she lays a hand on my arm and speaks in a soft voice. Her *psychologist's voice*, as Viv laughingly calls it.

'If things are getting on top of you again, then you need to tell someone. There's nothing to be ashamed of, but we have to make sure you get the help you need like you did before.'

I might have known she'd bring *that* up. I've suffered quite badly with depression and anxiety in the past, before I'd even met Brenna. Lewis was supportive and I sought help, but in the early days of our friendship, I told Brenna all about those dark, desolate times and now I wish I hadn't.

'We have to think about Skye's wellbeing.'

'I do realise that,' I say curtly, noticing my hands are trembling a little. As I pour the wine with Brenna watching, I have to really focus so I don't spill it.

Why is it that everyone can forget about physical ailments quite easily, but when it comes to mental illness, it sticks to you like glue for the rest of your life?

Everyone remembers your *difficult time* in glorious Technicolor, and it lives on, rearing its ugly head periodically just to remind you that even the people nearest and dearest are forever on full alert for any signs of a relapse.

'Seriously, I'm fine.' I hand her a glass. 'I'm just a bit unnerved, like anyone would be in that situation.'

I make a snap decision not to speak to her about my other big worry. I've always managed to deal with most stuff alone in my life, and that's what I'll need to do in this instance.

Brenna takes our wine through to the lounge, and I open a bag of corn chips and empty them into a bowl. I grab the dips I bought earlier from the fridge, and as I close the door, I hear something click behind me.

I turn, expecting to see Skye or Brenna in the doorway, but I'm alone. I wait a few moments, frozen completely still.

There – the clicking noise again. It seems to be coming from the inside wall.

I walk closer to the wall and then stop, pressing my ear to the narrow space between the corner and the first cupboard. Behind this wall is the vacant apartment next door.

I wait, listening for the noise again, but there is nothing. Just silence.

38

One thing I seem to have forgotten about Brenna, is that you can't keep deep-seated worries from her for very long.

Relaxed from the wine, I answer Brenna's clever probing questions easily, and by the time I realise her motive, she's already picked up on something I said.

'What do you mean by that?' Brenna stops me. 'You said earlier, *I think we could be really happy here.*'

'Yes.' I shrug. 'I think we will.'

'But you subconsciously used the word *could*, which hints there's a condition to be met in order for that to happen.'

I laugh to cover up my irritation. 'Give it a rest, Bren, you're not at work now.'

'Maybe not, but you might as well just tell me what's bothering you to save time.' She looks at me over the top of her glass. 'I know something *is* bothering you.'

I try and use Skye as a diversionary tactic. 'Come on, poppet, bedtime. Say goodnight to Auntie Brenna.'

'Nooo!' Skye wails, throwing herself at Brenna's feet. 'I don't want to go to bed. Please, Auntie Brenna, tell her!'

'Tell you what, go clean your teeth and get into bed and I'll read you a story.' Brenna winks at me. 'How about that?'

'Yesss!' Skye punches the air before scampering off to the bathroom.

'So' – Brenna looks at me – 'spill the beans.'

And so I tell her what I know about the mystery woman and her daughter.

'And a local builder told you this?' She tips her head to one side and looks at me.

'His name is Mark Sutton and it was something he heard, working in the area. We also met a woman in a café who seemed spooked when I mentioned Adder House.' Brenna watches me. 'But creepily, when we first moved in, Skye talked about the little girl who used to be in her room.' I sigh, thinking how silly it all sounds, hearing myself say it out loud. 'She said she'd overheard Dr Marsden and Audrey talking about a little girl who used to live here.' I shrug. 'I did ask him about it, but he said he didn't say anything of the sort and Skye must've got confused.'

'And now Dr Marsden has categorically said a woman and her child didn't live in this apartment before you?'

'Yes. But he has now admitted there was some kind of an incident, a tragedy. Although it didn't happen here in the house, he said, but neither he nor his wife would elaborate. Then earlier today, I got this in the post.'

I hand her the letter from the optician. She reads it and frowns. 'I don't get it.'

'That's obviously the name of the woman who was here. Sophie Taylor and her daughter, Melissa.'

'I see where you're coming from,' Brenna says slowly, handing me the letter back. 'But opticians do get people's details wrong all the time. Still, you need to get this sorted once and for all. Let's have another glass of wine when I've completed my aunt duties and we'll come up with a plan.'

Brenna gets up to read Skye her story and I sit alone in the silence of the lounge. Nobody seems to think this is a problem except me. And Mark.

Mark seemed to understand.

I read somewhere that moving house was in the top ten most stressful life events.

Maybe that's it; I'm just feeling the stress. Placing more importance and relevance on various things than I would've done back in my old house.

I don't know whether that's the truth of it, but I guess I'm willing to keep an open mind. Everything here is new and strange and I *so* want it to work out, maybe I'm just on high alert watching for anything that could potentially cause a problem.

'Oh!' I jump up, spilling the last drops of my wine when a loud buzzing noise sounds close to me. I look around wildly at the windows but can't spot any more flies.

There it is again . . . a definite buzzing noise!

I look down and see Brenna's phone moving slightly, half-covered by a cushion.

I dash to pick it up in case it's Viv, but when I look at the screen, I see it isn't Viv at all.

The name on the screen reads: *Audrey Marsden*.

Fifteen minutes later, Brenna is back from her bedtime story. 'Your phone rang,' I say.

My throat is so tight I'm surprised the words manage to get out at all.

'I meant to turn the damn thing off.' She picks it up and taps the screen, viewing the details of her missed call. Her face doesn't change, doesn't even miss a beat. 'It's nothing that can't wait,' she says simply. 'Now, where were we?'

But I don't want to talk to Brenna about my problems now. I want to talk about why Audrey Marsden has her number.

'I saw who it was, Bren,' I say, hearing a little tremor in my voice. 'It was Audrey Marsden calling.'

Her face and body freeze. Her expression and posture stay the same for a couple of seconds until she deflates.

'It's nothing, honestly . . . not what you think, anyway.'

'What *should* I think?' I bite down on my tongue. 'You know Audrey?'

'I know her *now*,' Brenna says easily, but her face is turning a telling shade of scarlet. 'I didn't know her before you moved in here.'

'I'm sorry, Bren, but something isn't quite adding up. You've made no secret of the fact you can't stand Audrey, so why the hell is she calling you?'

Brenna sighs. 'It's only the second time she's rung. The first time it was to ask me to keep an eye on you because you seemed very stressed. I don't know why she's called this time.'

If she's telling the truth, Audrey might be ringing regarding our conversation about the previous tenants.

'But why wouldn't you tell me she called you?'

Brenna's hands wave in front of her. 'She asked me not to, and I didn't see the harm in keeping it to myself, really, with you being stressed out and all. She seemed genuinely concerned and said they wanted you to feel safe and happy here.'

Something twists inside me. I'm not a ten-year-old child who needs an adult to supervise me. Both Audrey and Brenna obviously think me incapable of withstanding difficulties without their assistance.

'I'm really tired,' I say quietly, and Brenna stands up a bit too willingly.

'Hey, no worries, I'll get going. I know how much you've got on right now.' *Courtesy of Audrey Marsden*, I think, a little spitefully.

She slips her phone into her jeans. Then she picks up our empty wine glasses and takes them into the kitchen. I follow her.

'I'll speak to Viv and sort out a date for you and Skye to come over. We're well overdue for one of her Hungarian goulash feeds.'

She wants to pretend this never happened but I still feel peeved, so I don't say anything.

In the hallway, I pop my head around Skye's door. She's supposed to be asleep now but she's sitting up in bed with her lamp on, looking at a picture book.

'Just seeing Aunt Brenna out. Be back in two minutes.'

She nods, pointing at the words on the page and whispering them to herself.

'Quiet here, isn't it?' Brenna says as we pad downstairs. I've been careful to lock the apartment door behind me even though I'll be no time at all. 'I've never been in a converted house where you can't hear a squeak from the other residents. Usually, there's a lot more noise than in soundproofed purpose-built apartment buildings.'

I can't even recall what I say. I think I just make an agreeable sound. I can't stop thinking about why Audrey Marsden has taken to calling Brenna if they barely know each other. Her explanation doesn't really stack up.

As we descend the last flight of stairs, an old familiar weight settles on my chest. The realisation dawns that people are talking behind my back, sidelining me. People I thought I could trust and had a solid rapport with.

I honestly felt like I had a deeper understanding of Audrey after our lunch together.

She'd tried to make me feel as though I was a part of the Adder House family by getting involved in Skye's school arrangements as she had. Even though she obviously has her own secrets to hide.

But now . . . now all my old imposter insecurities are flooding back. Just as we get to the front door, something occurs to me.

'When did you give Audrey your phone number?' I keep my voice down, mindful of the echoing entrance hall.

Brenna frowns. 'I didn't. It never occurred to me to wonder how she got it. It's not online, I know that.'

Brenna has online profiles pertaining to her research work, but I've looked before and only her work email and the university's general landline number with her extension appear there.

But there's an old-fashioned contacts book on our hall table that I've had since being a child. It has A-Z indexed pages and the cover is frayed and loose, but I'm very fond of it.

I write everyone's address and phone number in there just in case my phone dies and I need to make a call.

It's the only possible place that Audrey could have obtained Brenna's number.

◆ ◆ ◆

When Brenna has left, I go upstairs, kiss a sleepy Skye goodnight, and then go back into the kitchen. I pour another glass of wine for myself and sit at the breakfast bar with my laptop to google search 'Sophie Taylor'.

The search page informs me that Google has found 114 million results. I scan through the first five pages but find nothing that looks remotely relevant.

I try searching other word combinations:

'Sophie Taylor, Melissa Taylor Adder House'.

'Sophie Taylor death'.

I try one awful combination after another, but there's nothing conclusive.

I know that everyone has the right to be 'forgotten' online these days, that it's possible to remove historical information.

What if someone had wanted references to the death of Sophie Taylor to disappear?

It's so utterly frustrating, like searching for a needle in a haystack. And then I have a brainwave.

39

The next morning, I don't have to wake Skye. She comes into my bedroom as I'm pulling up the blind.

'Mummy, why have you moved my toys around?'

I turn to look at her. 'I haven't, poppet. Show me.'

I follow her into her room, a creeping unease stirring in my abdomen. She points to the floor.

'My Sylvanian Family house was over there last night.' She points in front of the wardrobe. 'But when I woke up, it was over here *and* the mummy rabbit is completely missing.' She scowls up at me. 'I've looked but I can't find her anywhere.'

I sit on the edge of the bed, my heart racing. Nothing makes sense.

'The voice in my dream told me you have it,' Skye adds and I breathe a sigh of relief.

She's just dreaming they moved!

'Mummy rabbit will turn up, sweetie, don't worry. You probably moved the house when you were tired and just forgot.'

'I DIDN'T!' She stamps her foot.

'Hey, madam! Remember Lily lives underneath us and it's still early.'

Skye follows me into the kitchen, her face surly. She looks tired, as if she hasn't slept that well.

I'm reaching for the breakfast dishes when I hear her gasp. 'Mummy, my painting!'

I look at the wall next to the fridge and see the last painting she did at Grove Primary is still there but it's been torn right up the middle.

'Oh!' The unsettled feeling is back and Skye looks alarmed. 'Maybe I caught it as I walked by and didn't notice. Sorry, poppet.'

She's not impressed and stalks out of the room.

Was it torn last night when Bren came over? I can't remember looking at it, even when I got the wine out of the fridge.

I lean on the worktop for a moment, staring at the painting. It's not in a position where I could damage it without noticing and I know Brenna would have said right away if she'd done it by mistake.

Besides, it looks cleanly torn. As if someone has done it on purpose.

◆ ◆ ◆

When I take Skye to school, she's quieter than usual. I hate the thought that she's unsettled because of unexplained things at the apartment.

I think we're both nervous. If someone had managed to break in without leaving a trace of entry and not waking either of us, I think they'd be after more than pocketing a toy rabbit and tearing up a child's artwork.

I feel better for this thought. Put things into perspective, that's what I need to do.

'Mummy, what shall I do if Javeed is mean to me today?' Skye asks quietly.

'Why would Javeed be mean?'

'Because of the *owl*.'

I'd completely forgotten about the owl trouble Miss Perkins mentioned yesterday. A bit of damage to a papier-mâché bird isn't exactly the crime of the century, and anyway, I think if Skye had accidentally damaged it, she would have owned up to that.

I really ought to have talked this all through with Skye last night, but time ran away with me in the end.

'Don't worry about the owl, sweetie. Miss Perkins knows you didn't do anything wrong, and she said it would all be forgotten about by today, remember?'

Skye doesn't look convinced. 'Javeed has lots of friends.'

'Well, so will you have soon. Now, how about I make a macaroni cheese for tea and we watch a Disney classic together . . . *The Little Mermaid*? How's that sound?'

She nods in agreement but still looks distracted. I feel a twinge of guilt because I can't seem to focus on our conversation like I usually would. It occurs to me that I seem to be fending off all her concerns lately and distracting her with something else.

This morning I can't stop thinking about what it is I've decided I'm going to do after I drop Skye off at school.

The high street is busy with pedestrians, mostly commuters judging by the purposeful way they're walking, some talking into their phones or clutching take-out coffee as they stride towards the Underground station.

In the sea of people, I spot a familiar face. The hair, the set of the mouth, the cold eyes . . . Janine! I knew it. I knew she hadn't just disappeared from our lives, she's been watching us, following us.

I position myself in her path as she strides towards me. She seems distracted and then her eyes widen, her step falters and she puts on an Oscar-worthy performance, pretending she's shocked.

She tries to veer around me but I grab her arm and pull her to the side of the moving crowd. I feel sweat rolling down the middle of my back.

'Get off me!' She struggles to break free of my hold.

'I know what you've been doing.' My voice sounds strangely calm, menacing, even. Inside, I'm a shaking mess. 'Following us, sending messages to the school. I know it's you.'

She takes a step back, actually looks unnerved. 'What are you talking about?'

I smile. 'I think you know exactly what I'm talking about. Why else would you be here? If it continues I'm going to the police. I—'

'I'm here to meet a friend, although it's got nothing to do with you.' She looks over my shoulder and waves. 'I could ask what you're doing here, too. I hoped never to set eyes on you again.'

A woman appears from behind me. 'Janine, is everything alright?'

The friend she is meeting.

'So you haven't been following me, or—'

'You need to see a doctor,' Janine snaps scathingly as her friend's mouth falls open. 'You have seriously lost it, you sad cow.'

And then they're gone. Shaking their heads together, laughing, as they disappear into the throng of people.

I'm shaken. I press up against the shop window behind me and breathe deeply for a few moments.

The noise level is high, people talking to each other, chatting on phones. Horns beeping, engines revving . . . I need to get away from this.

I start walking again, feeling even worse since Janine has gone. If she's not responsible for some of the strange things that have been happening . . . then who is?

Once I get clear of the Underground station, the people thin out a little. My heart rate has slowed a little and I don't feel as overheated.

About halfway down the high street, I spot a sign with an arrow indicating a shop down a little snicket off the main street.

I open my bag to fish out the letter I put in there yesterday, so I can check this is the right place, and my hand flies up to my mouth. The little mother rabbit Skye was looking for earlier is in here, tucked behind my purse.

I stand still for a moment. I haven't touched her little figurines since we moved in, except to tidy them now and again. And yet here it is. If Skye didn't put it here then *I* must have!

I'm either losing my mind, or I'm so distracted with everything going on that I slipped it into my bag by mistake without it registering. That must be it. I've got to sort myself out; it could've been something really important I misplaced.

I push the toy rabbit further down in my bag and take out the letter to double-check.

Crystal Clear Opticians. This is definitely the right one.

I walk down the dim little alleyway, which opens out into a sort of quaint cobbled yard, and there the shop is, in front of me.

I'm relieved to see it looks like a small family-run business, rather than one of the big chains. Hopefully, it will be missing some of the hefty policy documents that force staff to follow a strict data-protection procedure when it comes to giving out information.

'Morning!' A lady in her sixties with grey, wiry hair and zany cerise-pink glasses smiles at me as I walk in the shop, activating an old-fashioned bell above the door. 'I'm afraid Mr Frazer, the optician, is running a little late and isn't in yet. Are you here for an appointment?'

This is looking more promising by the second.

'No, I wanted to *make* an appointment actually, for my sister. She's not able to get in herself.'

'Ahh, well we can do that no problem at all.' She walks over to a desk and sits down, pressing a couple of buttons and peering at a monitor. 'Has she been here before?'

'She has.' I smile, ignoring the thumping in my chest. 'And she was quite insistent I had to make the appointment here, as Mr Frazer did such a good job a year ago.'

I'm pushing my luck here making some assumptions, but it's my only chance to get her onside.

'Well, that's nice to know. What's your sister's name?'

'Her name is Sophie Taylor,' I say, pleased she isn't looking at me.

'Here we are, I have her right here. 6 Adder House.' She frowns. 'I see we've just issued her an appointment reminder. How is she getting on with her glasses?'

'I think she might need them adjusted. I've been telling her to come back in for a while.'

'Tell me about it!' She takes off her spectacles and pinches the top of her nose. 'I have three adult children and all of them wear glasses. And can I persuade them to come in to see Mr Frazer without a fight? I cannot!'

We share a smile, but I'm willing her to get a move on before I trip myself up somehow.

'I'll just get Mr Frazer's diary up.'

I make an appointment for a week from now and then I take a breath. Here goes. 'Could I ask a big favour? Could you possibly print off my sister's details, so she can check them over?'

She looks blankly at me.

'It's just that she's already moved from Adder House, she got your letter via the mail redirection service. She's recently changed her phone number, too, and she wants to write her new details down for me to pop back to you.' The woman's eyes narrow. She's not falling for it. 'It's fine if not, I just thought it would save time when she comes in next—'

'Good idea!' she says as the printer starts whirring. 'We're not supposed to give out customer details, of course, but I can see you're only trying to help, which makes a change from some of the awkward so-and-so's we have to deal with around here.'

She hands me the sheet and I take it, willing my hand not to shake for just a few more seconds. Outside, I rush back on to the high street and quickly read the details . . . there's a next of kin on there with an email address and phone number. Also a date of birth and previous address.

I feel dizzy and elated.

At last it looks like I might have a chance to find out who Sophie Taylor is.

40

Back at the apartment, I sit and comb through the personal details on the optician's form.

Aside from Sophie Taylor's own details, it's the next of kin I'm really interested in.

She's named as Linda Gent, relationship: sister.

Before I can get cold feet I rattle off a short email.

Dear Linda,

I'm so sorry to send this unsolicited email but I am an old friend of your sister's, Sophie.

Would it be possible to meet for a coffee or have a chat? I'm sorry to intrude but it's really important to me that we speak.

Best wishes, Freya Miller

There's only a little fib in there, that I'm an old friend of Sophie's. If she agrees to meet me or chat on the phone, I'll come clean right away and hope she'll understand why I've had to stretch the truth to find a way forward.

I feel so desperate to speak to Linda right now. Email is less intrusive than a phone call, but perhaps if I texted . . .

I pick up my phone and fire off a brief text explaining I've sent her a longer email, but asking if she could meet me ASAP as I've just found out about Sophie.

I don't know where the rest of the morning goes. I feel lethargic and out of sorts and I just lie on the couch, unable to rest, unable to get anything done in the apartment.

When my phone dings signalling a text message, I grab it and see it's a text from Linda Gent.

She's agreed to meet me at 1 p.m. at a café just two Tube stops away.

◆ ◆ ◆

The door of the café opens and a short, thin woman stands dithering there before stepping inside.

She reminds me of a frightened bird, the way her head is jerking this way and that as if she's looking for danger nearby before she is willing to hedge her bets and step fully into the café.

She looks like I have started to feel myself.

I just know that this woman is *her*. This is Linda Gent, Sophie's sister. She sees me looking and tentatively approaches my table.

'Hi, is it Linda?' She nods, relieved. 'I'm Freya. Thanks so much for coming.' I offer to get her a coffee, but she's in no mood for small talk.

'Not for me, thanks. How do you know Sophie?'

I can tell that if I admit to blurring the truth too early on in our conversation, Linda is nervous enough to walk away.

'I *think* she's the Sophie I knew a few years back but what's reminded me, is that I think I might have moved into her old apartment on Palace Gate.'

207

Linda frowns. She's going to stand up and walk out any second, I can feel it.

'A letter came for her from an optician and your name and phone number was on there as next of kin. I just—'

'I need to check if it's the same place. You said you're living on Palace Gate. Is the building called Adder House?'

'That's right.' I swallow hard. 'I live in a small top-floor apartment with my daughter, Skye.'

'Oh God.' Linda's hand flies to her mouth and she squeezes her eyes shut as if she can't bear the pictures that are flooding in. 'This is important, Freya. How did you find out about it, the apartment? How did you know it was up for rent?'

'It was totally by chance. I was in—'

'A coffee shop? And Marsden happened to sit at your table by chance? Showed you his rental flyers? Asked if you wanted to view the apartment, despite it being something you could never afford to rent in a million years?'

'Something like that, yes.' I swallow again, wiping my damp palms on my jeans.

'That's exactly what happened to Sophie, and I can assure you that chance had nothing to do with it. Every single word he uttered to you was planned.'

41

This is all just starting to feel more than a bit paranoid now. Had Brenna been right about Dr Marsden all along? Linda has obviously had the most terrible experience involving her sister and young niece.

'I'm Melissa's legal guardian now. She's still not sleeping through the night, still having the most awful nightmares.' Linda stands up, wringing her hands and scanning the windows of the café. 'Do they know you're here? You might have been followed.'

'It's OK, Linda, please relax,' I say as calmly as I can while my own heart gallops. 'We're quite safe, nobody knows I'm here.'

She sits but slides further down her chair as if she's trying to hide from something . . . or someone.

I'm totally committed to finding out exactly what happened to Sophie so I can feel secure in my own home and be reassured my own daughter is safe, but now I'm thinking poor Linda seems to be more than distraught.

She seems to be *unhinged*, for want of a better word. I'm not judging her; tragedy can do that to a person. I'd managed to convince myself that Janine Harworth was stalking us and honestly, when I confronted her, the reaction was so genuine, I'm now pretty sure it's all been in my head.

I don't want to end up like Linda.

'I changed my own name after it happened so they didn't come after me, too,' she says a little breathlessly. 'I only got your email because you sent it to my old workplace and an ex-colleague forwarded it on to me. I've tried everything to put that place . . . *Adder House* . . . behind me.'

Her fear is palpable. It's a clammy sheen on her face, a wild look in her darting eyes.

'What happened?' I say, suddenly desperate for some closure on the issue. 'How did Adder House have anything to do with what happened to your sister?'

'It had everything to do with it.'

She lets out a sad little sound. A couple at the next table glance over, but Linda makes no attempt to cover up her distress. I think she's past controlling it at all.

'They were so happy there at first, Sophie couldn't believe she'd been given this amazing chance.' I squirm a bit in my seat. 'Truthfully, we were all very sceptical when she told us about Marsden's offer. Until we saw the place, that is, then we were as smitten as she was.'

'Did you visit her often there?'

'Oh no! The landlord hates visitors, haven't you come across that, too?' I nod. 'He'll go to any lengths to make it uncomfortable for family or friends to drop by. We helped her move in, and I went over once after that when Marsden himself called me because Sophie was clearly unwell.'

So Dr Marsden *had* shown some concern for Sophie. Was Audrey just concerned about me, too?

Linda looks at her hands on the table and links her fingers together as if she's trying to find the strength to carry on.

'Anyway, Sophie was really happy for a while. I'd never seen her so bright and full of optimism for the future.' Her face clouds over. 'That was before things started happening there.'

'What things?'

'She called me a couple of times, thought she'd heard noises, knocks at the door and nobody there. Stuff that sounds like nothing, but when it's constant, it can drive you crazy.' Linda's eyes are swimming and my heart is hammering. 'I just batted away her concerns. "Who cares if someone played knock-a-door-run?" I asked her once. "You live in Kensington for a peppercorn rent, for God's sake. Just put up with it." I think about how I dismissed her every day. Every single day.'

'Don't be too hard on yourself,' I manage to say. 'It wouldn't have seemed much to complain about at the time.'

'She stopped calling me and popping around to the house as much after that.' Linda rubbed her eyes. 'When I bumped into her at the dental surgery, I was shocked. Sophie had always been slim, but that day she looked skeletal with these deep, dark shadows here, under her eyes.'

She touches the top of her cheeks lightly with her fingertips.

'Her hands shook, even her voice sounded different, as if someone had sucked the very life spirit out of it. I told her to get out. I said, if this is what the place is doing to you then you need to get away from it.' Her voice grows faint. 'She said she'd think about it and promised to come over to my house later in the week with Melissa.'

Something about the way she says it makes my stomach curdle. 'And did she come over, like you arranged?'

Linda's head drops forward and I can see she's biting back tears.

'What happened?'

She takes a few more moments then looks straight at me.

'She "fell" down the stairs, apparently. That's what they told the police, anyhow. Cracked her head on the sharp edge of some metal filigree work.'

'She . . . did she . . .'

'Die? Yes, she died. But the fall didn't kill her. She sustained a head injury but didn't die in the house. She refused medical attention and went back upstairs for a few hours and then fled in the middle of the night, leaving Melissa asleep in bed. She was mowed down by a big overnight freight truck on the top road. The Dutch driver said she just jumped out in front of the lorry.' A salty track forges its way down Linda's face. 'She changed so much in a short time while she was living there, but I was too blind, too absorbed in my own life to fully notice. That place turned her from a gutsy young woman into a bag of nerves in record time. She must have been so low and desperate to leave Melissa alone in that house after sending me a text and asking me to look after her when she's gone.' She presses her phone so it lights up and a dark-haired child with ruddy cheeks and a lovely dimpled smile fills the screen. 'This is little Melissa,' she says, her voice full of regret. 'Our little star.'

I look at her, wanting more, but it feels disrespectful to question her when she's obviously still grieving and so upset.

'She's beautiful,' I say softly. 'She's very lucky to have you.'

My stomach turns when I think what would happen to Skye if I died. She'd have Brenna and that's it.

Linda looks at me, her bloodshot eyes pinning me down.

'The police investigated briefly, spoke to Dr Marsden and the other residents. They said that, possibly, the head injury sustained at the house may have caused massive confusion and that's why she ran out into the road.' Linda wrings her hands and her voice grows louder in her desperation to make me understand. 'I tried to tell them about the stuff that had unnerved her, the effect living there had on her, but they wouldn't listen. The coroner reported her death as sudden and most probably suicide. Thank goodness our mum was no longer here to read it.'

'I'm so sorry, Linda.' I reach for her hands and hold them in my own. 'It's just awful, all of it. I don't know what to say.'

'I have no hard evidence but I know in my heart it wasn't suicide in the truest sense of the word, Freya. Sophie didn't plan her own death, she loved her daughter too much. She was terrified for Melissa's safety more than for her own, and she died because she was desperately fleeing something. Sophie was driven by something or someone to take her own life.'

Up until this point Linda had really unnerved me with her descriptions of weird happenings at Adder House. I'd started to draw parallels to the incident with the flies, furniture and belongings apparently moving.

I thought she was going to say that Sophie had died in our apartment. Linda's voice breaks my thoughts.

'You're probably being brainwashed, too.' She pulls her hands gently away and takes a tissue from her sleeve. 'You need to get out of that place as soon as you can.'

I know she's right. We have to leave.

'I have to go,' I say faintly. 'I have to think about what we need to do.'

'That's the easy bit, Freya. You need to *get out*,' Linda says emphatically. 'You know, I visited Sophie there once or twice. It was like Fort Knox trying to get in, that creepy landlord insisting he should know if someone so much as sneezes in there. It's not healthy. It's not appropriate.'

She's right. And that sounds just like Dr Marsden.

'Sophie and Melissa had the big apartment on the top floor. It's the only one up there.'

'We're in number six on the top floor.' I frown. 'It's a small apartment next to an empty one that's being refurbished. That must have been their apartment.'

Linda frowns too. 'There was only one door up there and you couldn't accurately describe Sophie's apartment as small.'

213

I think about the new plaster on the outside wall and the fact that our doorframe looks newer, somehow. *Surely not.* Surely our small apartment hasn't been created to make two residences out of what used to be Sophie's bigger apartment . . . that would make Dr Marsden technically right when he said we're the first tenants to move in.

Linda stares at me for a moment and then shakes her head, as if I'm a lost cause. 'There's something about that place that's just not right. I know you must feel it, too.'

I push away my latte. I can't face its creamy sickliness any more.

42

When I get back to the house, I rush upstairs. My mouth is dry.

When I get up to the top floor, I swipe my key card at the door and step inside, relieved to be alone at last.

I'm trying to run through everything Linda has told me, to untangle the threads and make some sense of it all.

Something made Sophie turn from being a loving mother into someone who'd leave her child behind and take her own life. I have this rising panic inside that comes from our association by default with Sophie and Melissa. By choosing to live at Adder House, it's as if their tragedy could be duplicated in our lives, too.

That by staying here, I'm sending the universe a message that I also accept a terrible fate. It might not be logical but it feels very, very real, like the inevitability of something bad happening is a real thing. My overwhelming instinct right now is that we have to get away from here.

Inside, the apartment is cool and quiet without Skye here. I'm so used to the backdrop of television or her playing a game on my iPad.

My old life feels a million miles away already. I think how Skye cried when I snapped at her this morning when she left for school.

The way she looked at me when I swore to her that I hadn't moved her toys, or ripped her painting.

I flop down on the couch, exhausted but racked with a nervous energy that refuses to let me rest. Did Sophie feel this way, too?

I'm not Sophie, I remind myself. I have a choice to get out before things get worse here. For once, I'm pleased I've still got so much stuff in bags and boxes. That will save us time.

I will myself to just calm down and breathe. There are decisions to make about our future, but I have a few hours to get my head straight before Skye comes home, and my body feels so worn.

At last my breathing calms, my limbs feel heavy. Blissful peace settles over me like a feather-light blanket.

I'm drifting off, floating somewhere between wakefulness and sleep, when I first hear it. The faintest wailing noise. I'm not sure if I've dreamed it, but it's alarming enough for me to sit up and listen.

There's nothing for a few minutes. I have the window open, and every now and again, I hear the faraway rumble of a big lorry passing through Palace Gate from the busy top road.

Skye's face flits into my mind's eye.

I sit bolt upright. There it is again . . . louder this time. A wail . . . a howl. It's a child crying, a girl.

I jump up and run to the doorway, convinced for a moment that Skye is back, hurt or injured and crying for me outside the apartment door. But when I reach her bedroom, I stop dead, a tendril of pure dread snaking down from my scalp, all the way down my back.

The sound is coming from behind Skye's bedroom door.

For a moment or two, I literally can't move. My whole body feels frozen to the spot. Thoughts and possibilities zap through my mind, so quickly I can barely keep track of them.

I feel a little disorientated from my nap.

216

Is Skye here? Did I get confused again and she hasn't gone to school today? Did she return while I was out? Is she hurt . . . in pain?

My hand slowly reaches for the door handle and I push down and throw the door wide open.

But Skye's room is empty. And completely silent.

43

I stand at the bedroom door, trying to work through where else the noise could have come from, when the doorbell rings.

I rush down the hallway and fling open the door, expecting Dr Marsden to explain about the noise.

'Freya! What's wrong?' It's Lily from downstairs.

'I'll be fine in a minute,' I say, relieved it's her. 'I just had a bit of a shock. I'm OK.'

I'd really like to confide in her, but I don't want her to think I'm crazy and tell the other residents. I take a step back inside my apartment.

'You don't look OK,' she says, laying a hand on my arm. 'Why don't I come in and make you a nice cup of tea?'

I haven't got the energy to fight. Part of me wants to hide away and not come out for the rest of the day. The other part of me feels like I don't want to be alone up here.

In the end, Lilian makes the decision for me.

'Come on, let's get you back inside.' She walks ahead of me, and when I've shuffled past her, she closes the door behind me. 'Sit yourself down in the lounge, dear, and I'll put the kettle on.'

She strides ahead into the kitchen and I rush past Skye's bedroom without glancing in. I sit down on the sofa as instructed, zombie-like. A few seconds later, Lily joins me.

She perches on the edge of the cushion and turns in a little to look at me.

'I don't want to pry, Freya, but I can see something has upset you. The last couple of times I've seen you, you've seemed . . . a little stressed, for want of a better phrase. Don't feel you have to tell me anything too personal but . . . are you alright?'

'Yes!' I say, my voice sounding slightly manic. 'I'm fine. I just—' Here it comes. The emotion I've been trying to keep down for the last few days. 'I just . . . things are getting on top of me a bit. I don't think we're going to stay here, Lily,' I splutter between sobs.

'Oh no, come here.' Lilian cradles her arm around my head and I just let go. I can't stop myself. 'That's it, dear, let it all out. Holding stuff in never did anyone any good at all. I should know.'

Something about the kind tone of her voice gives me licence to let go. I override the feelings of shame and embarrassment and instead, I just release all the tension I've kept bottled up.

It goes on for a while. I hear the kettle click off in the kitchen and still Lily holds me and still the emotion comes.

Lily loosens her comforting hold and I pull gently away. 'Better?'

I nod. 'Thank you. I don't know what came over me. This is not like me at all.'

'You said you might not stay here,' Lily says, her gentle eyes creasing with concern. 'Why is that?'

'I'm living on my nerves with the odd things that keep happening and . . .'

'Yes?'

'I met with Sophie's sister, the woman who lived here with her daughter. She's convinced Dr Marsden drove her to the brink of insanity.'

I bite my lip. I've probably said too much, after all Lily has lived here for many years and I don't want her to think it's a reflection on her.

'The poor woman sounds distressed. I didn't have much to do with the young woman and her child but I got the impression, and please don't think ill of me for saying so, that she was troubled before she even arrived here.'

I nod, wanting to believe Linda is wrong in her assumptions, but I can't do that. My own experiences here correlate with a lot of what Linda says happened to Sophie.

'It's fine you know, to say you're not coping too well. I've been there.'

The inference of her words isn't lost on me. Lily obviously thinks I'm struggling mentally.

'I recognise the signs of anxiety,' she says softly. 'I've been there, too.'

'You have?' Lily seems so confident, so level-headed and sorted.

'Oh yes. There was a time a few years ago, when my husband left me and – I still feel awkward about saying this but I will because it's true – I fell apart; lost my job, my home, and I very nearly lost my mind.'

'No!' I whisper.

'I know what it's like to live on the edge of paranoia and fear. It's not a nice place to be.'

I glance at her face and for the briefest moment I see the wound of her hurt laid bare, like cutting into a cooked piece of meat to find it's still raw inside.

I sit quietly, unsure what to say. She seems to think the problem here lies with me, not with the Marsdens.

'You look so . . . afraid. Actually you look terrified. I don't want to intrude, but is there anything you want to talk about?' She lowers her eyes and touches me lightly on the shoulder. 'This place can

220

get you down. I'm more aware of the influence of certain people than you think.'

She means the Marsdens now, she must do. It's painfully obvious they don't like having her around and now I'm beginning to see why. She's unimpressed by Dr Marsden and Audrey when everyone else here seems to look up to them.

She folds her hands in her lap and looks at me. 'Tell me what you were like as a child, growing up.'

'Quiet but confident, I suppose,' I say, thinking back. 'I had . . . a difficult time, but I always remember a sort of strength inside that got me through.'

Lily nods. 'And you stayed that way throughout adulthood?'

'Basically, yes. I've always tried to tackle any problems head on, look at things logically. Until now.'

'What about *now*? What's bothering you, Freya?'

I hesitate. What if I open up to Lily and she tells Dr Marsden and Audrey? Despite what he's done for me, I just don't know if I trust him any more. The irony is that I still can't put my finger on exactly why. But he holds the power over my tenancy here.

She looks at me, seeming to read my mind. 'Whatever you say is strictly just between us.' She smiles, holding up her little finger. 'Pinky promise. I don't know if you've noticed but I'm not really flavour of the month around here anyway.'

Of course, I had noticed the way the other residents don't seem to want Lily around, how Audrey reacted a touch frostily when I said we were going downstairs to Lily's for tea and cake. And even how they all went quiet that day in the garden when Lily came down to join us.

So I tell her. I tell her about the noises I hear when I'm alone, the feeling that someone has been in the apartment, and I tell her about just now how sure I was that I heard a little girl crying in Skye's room.

And then I ask her point-blank about Sophie and Melissa.

'I was abroad for the whole time they were here. I did hear talk about it from the residents, but they don't include me in their little gatherings.' Lily sighs. 'All I know is that there was an accident . . . but I don't think it happened here at Adder House. Michael is an interfering old so-and-so, but I can assure you, Freya, he is quite harmless, as is Audrey.' She looks me straight in the eye. 'I think someone has spun you quite a tale.'

I let out a long sigh, unable to contain the relief that floods through me. I don't know why I didn't just confide in Lily in the first place.

Still, the mere thought of living in this apartment used to give me joy, but now I feel sick as soon as I approach the front door of Adder House. There's lots of stuff making me feel uncomfortable here, not just what Linda has told me.

'Listen. Why don't I look after Skye this evening? You can bring her to me when you pick her up from school and we might bake, or test each other on the names of garden birds while you run yourself a nice bath, light a scented candle.' Lily squeezes my hand. 'There's nothing wrong here, Freya, you're just a little stressed out. That's all.'

I open my mouth to say 'thanks, but no thanks' and then I stop. The thought of a few hours when I can just get my head together sounds wonderful. I can decide exactly when I'm going to speak to the Marsdens and leave with Skye.

'Well, only if you're sure,' I say. 'That would be perfect, thank you.'

'That's settled then.' She smiles. 'Oh, and keep away from the Marsdens, too. Those two should have a public health warning stamped on their foreheads. I don't even want to think what goes on in that apartment between them.'

I wonder if she knows about their obvious marital 'arrangements'.

'I suppose what they do in their own marriage is their business,' I say, hoping I'm conveying that I'm fully aware of their liberal arrangements.

'Heavens, I hope you're wrong, or it's even worse than I imagined!' Lily laughs out loud. 'The Marsdens aren't *married*, my dear . . . they're brother and sister.'

44

When Lily finally leaves my apartment, I can't stop her words echoing in my head.

They're brother and sister. Brother and sister!

But Dr Marsden had referred to Audrey as his wife on several occasions . . . hadn't he? When Skye and I arrived at Adder House for the very first viewing, he'd said, 'my wife isn't here'. Or had he said simply, 'Mrs Marsden isn't here', and I've happily filled in all the blanks myself?

Can I trust my judgement at all any more? Sometimes I wonder.

On the way out to pick Skye up from school, someone calls my name. I look across the road to see Mark Sutton waving at me.

'Don't suppose you fancy catching up over a drink tonight?' It's a casual-enough invite. He saunters out on to the pavement, his ripped jeans and tousled hair somehow looking fresh and attractive at the end of the day. 'I know a little pub ten minutes' walk away from here that's nice and quiet, if you could get someone to watch Skye for a couple of hours.'

I think about my bath and candle and the fact that I've already arranged for Lily to have Skye. But I think Mark's level-headed opinion on whether there's really anything to worry about here would be more valuable even than my planned relaxation.

'Thanks, I'd love to.' I smile.

'Call for you about seven then?' he says cheekily like we're still at school.

My day finally seems to have picked up, but then my heart sinks when Miss Perkins calls me over in the playground at the end of the day.

'Skye has unnerved one or two of her classmates by claiming she saw someone taking photographs from the school fence. Apparently, she said it just before home time yesterday. We've already had a few parents calling the school office, concerned if there is a prowler.'

'She hasn't mentioned it to me,' I say, genuinely shocked. 'I'll ask her about it.'

Miss Perkins nods. 'Thank you. When I asked her to describe what she'd seen, she denied saying anything and claimed the other children were telling lies.' The teacher pulls a little apologetic face for having said it. 'But it appears most of the class heard her saying it.'

I feel like I don't know what's got into my daughter, lately. She seems to be acting completely out of character.

I run Skye a quick bath before she goes down to Lily's and I jump in the separate shower. When I get out, she's singing and pouring water into plastic cups, pretending to make cocktails.

Just as I'd hoped, she's feeling more relaxed.

'Miss Perkins mentioned you'd seen someone taking photographs at the school fence, sweetie?'

Skye throws me a sly glance and nods. 'I did,' she says simply.

'Were they taking photographs of different children?'

'No, just of me and the children I was watching play.'

225

'You were *watching* them play?' I grin. 'I hope you were playing with them, too.' Skye shrugs and her expression darkens a touch. 'This person . . . what did they look like?'

'I couldn't see,' she says matter-of-factly. 'They had on a hat and coat and scarf . . . oh, and gloves, too.'

'Whoever it was must've been sweltering in July!' But Skye doesn't smile. 'Was it a man or woman?'

'I don't know,' she says quickly. 'I couldn't tell.'

I nod and hold up the towel so she can step out into it.

As I wrap her up and hold her close, I ask myself the question: could there have been someone taking photographs of my daughter outside school?

As with so many other things here, I just don't know what to believe.

◆　◆　◆

Mark takes me to a traditional pub called The Britannia, tucked away just off Kensington High Street, and about a fifteen-minute walk from Adder House. It's not busy and within a few minutes, he's back from the bar with our drinks and puts them on the table.

'OK, there's something I need to tell you first off,' he says, biting his bottom lip. 'Somebody's trying to cause trouble, get me off the job.'

'What?' I hold my breath, dreading what he's about to say.

'Someone's complained to the people who own the house I'm renovating.' He gives a bitter laugh. 'Apparently I've been slandering people, swearing in the street and throwing rubble in people's gardens.'

'Who's complained?' Even as I ask, I know the answer.

'Mr Hertz won't say but he's warned me he'll have to let me go if the complaints continue as he doesn't want any bad blood amongst his neighbours.'

'That's so unfair.' I can feel my face burning. 'Did you tell him it was all lies?'

'Course. He'd be a fool to put me off the job six weeks away from completion anyway, and he knows it. But I suppose he felt he had to say something.'

'Mark, I feel awful. It's obvious the Marsdens at Adder House are behind the complaint.'

He shrugs. 'I'm not losing sleep over it but I just wanted you to be aware.'

I'm mortified. I should never have mentioned my source to Dr Marsden when I first raised the subject of the previous tenants.

'Come on then, let's hear what else has been happening at the house of horrors.' Mark grins, upbeat again. Then he sees my serious expression. 'I'm sorry, Freya. I'm only trying to lighten things up, but I can tell you're worried.'

'You're going to think I'm crazy,' I say, taking a sip of the red wine and savouring its deep fruitiness on my tongue.

'Look, if *you're* crazy, then there's no hope for me either. Just tell me what's been happening and then I'll give you my honest opinion.'

Before I can think how to best phrase all the craziness, my worries and fears come tumbling out. I tell Mark about the flies, the repositioned furniture and toys, Skye's ripped painting, the noises, the child crying . . . when I've finished, it feels like I just had an hour's therapy session.

'Blimey.' Mark puts down his beer. 'I'd heard that place was creepy but some of this stuff is seriously messed up. No wonder you're worried.'

'But don't you see, it's also just small stuff that people can easily say I've imagined. And like Dr Marsden said, Sophie's death actually had nothing to do with Adder House.'

'They *lived* there, for God's sake!' Mark shakes his head.

He understands why I've been so worried. Maybe I'm not going crazy after all. I continue, eager to get his thoughts on the rest of it.

'There's other stuff that's spooked me that they just play down; the flies weren't there when Dr Marsden came upstairs, there was no crying child in Skye's room when I opened the door, so again, the implication is I must be imagining it. The only person who takes me seriously there is Lily downstairs, and nobody seems to like her. I'm worried all this is unnerving for Skye and that's why she's having problems at school.'

'Look, Freya, I'm no shrink but I can see you're absolutely not crazy. You're just not! It sounds to me like someone is taking the mickey and setting you up to *look* crazy.' He is angry and it gives me strength.

'But why? Why would anyone want to do this to us after inviting us to live there? It doesn't make sense.' I glance at him. 'And anyway, how could someone set up insects and kids crying and all the other stuff? It's like I'm channelling *The Amityville Horror.*'

Mark picks up his glass and takes a swig of beer, thinking for a moment. 'Look, I don't want to spook you, but there are ways and means of doing all sorts of covert stuff if you've got the right setup.'

I haven't a clue what he's talking about.

'Take that house I'm working on, it's one of four properties that stand together in a row, built at the same time. I've seen the original architectural plans and Adder House is one of those identical buildings. It's just the façades that give them their individuality.'

I recall that the house Mark is working on is redbrick with ornate pillars and wrought-iron Juliet balconies where Adder House features classic white stucco. They do look like completely different houses, but still, I don't see how it's relevant.

'As you know, I've been doing the refurb there for weeks, including all the structural alterations and a complete rewire. I know the fabric of that dwelling like the back of my hand which means I have the same detailed knowledge of all four properties.' He hesitates as if he's considering whether to say something.

'And?' I prompt him.

'Well, let's just say I know where I'd conceal certain covert devices if I needed to.'

Covert devices. He's talking about secret electrical spyware, invisible eyes you don't know are watching . . .

My blood runs icy in my veins as I'm hit with the full force of what he thinks might be happening inside our apartment . . . the camera above our door for starters. Thank goodness I got rid of it.

I look up, startled, aware he's been talking while I've been distracted by my thoughts. 'Sorry, what?'

'I said, "If you can smuggle me into Adder House, I can soon find out exactly what's happening in there."'

45

Back on Palace Gate, I tap the code into the keypad, open the front door of Adder House, and close it softly behind me.

The foyer is bathed in a soft glow that emits from the lamp on the hall table.

Instead of cutting across the middle of the floor to the stairs as I usually would, I stick closely to the walls, past the Marsdens' concealed apartment door, where I stop and root about in my bag, listening.

I can't hear anything from in there, indeed the whole house is just as silent as ever.

I'm an hour earlier than the time I told Lily I'd be back, and I need to use that time well before I collect Skye from her apartment.

I text Mark, who I know is waiting just a short distance away at the Albert Memorial for my 'all-clear' message, before turning off the hall lamp so the foyer is lit only by streetlights filtering in through the coloured glass.

Quietly as I can, I unlatch the front door. Mark must have jogged down, because only a few minutes later he appears at the bottom of the steps and I hold open the door as he slips silently into Adder House with a heavy cloth toolbag he picked up from the house he's working on a few doors down.

It occurs to me what a ridiculous situation I've inadvertently allowed here. Cheap rent or not, I'm a woman in my thirties, a mother, and I'm creeping about like a teenager to avoid being 'found out' for bringing a visitor back home!

Still, now is most definitely not the time to make a stand. It's more important that the other residents are not aware of Mark's presence while he carries out the various 'checks' we talked about in the pub.

I close the door softly behind him and click the latch, leading him to the stairs. We're halfway up to the first floor when I hear the sound of Dr Marsden's door unlocking.

I poke Mark to chivvy him faster up to the top of the stairs and then I grip his arm and press my finger to my lips.

Light floods down below us as the Marsdens' apartment door opens.

'Michael!' Audrey's irritated voice rings out. 'The lamp in the hall is out *again*.'

A shuffling sound and then Dr Marsden sighs. 'I only replaced the ruddy thing last week. I'll go and get another bulb from the drawer, now.'

'I'm sure I heard something out here.' Audrey's footfalls sound across the tiles in the foyer. Then a rattling. 'The door's secure. It must've been the wind.'

Her footsteps move back across and then stop at the bottom of the stairs.

'Hello?' Audrey calls out. I hear her step on to the first stair and my heartbeat jumps up into my throat, threatening to choke me. I take a step back and Mark's hand steadies me. 'Is anyone up there?' Audrey calls.

'Come back inside, dear, and I'll sort the bulb out when the film has finished.'

'I swear I can smell perfume in here,' Audrey grumbles as their apartment door closes again, and I curse myself for using a liberal spray of Thierry Mugler Angel before I left to meet Mark at The Britannia.

Once we're sure the Marsdens really are back inside, we continue tiptoeing up the stairs, past Lily's apartment and up to the top floor.

I wave my key card in front of the lock, and I hear the soft click that tells me the door is now open. Mark taps my arm and I look at his face, shadowed in the faint street light emanating from the landing window.

'Who lives here?' he whispers, jabbing a forefinger at next door.

'It's empty,' I hiss back.

I reach for the light switch and Mark moves to block my hand.

'Not yet.' He pushes me very gently back against the door and his fashionably stubbled cheek slightly grazes mine as I inhale the bergamot scent of his aftershave.

For one crazy second I think he's going to kiss me, but then I realise he's just being cautious until he's fully checked the place out.

'Wait here,' he says gruffly. 'Never know who might be watching.'

I shiver at the thought and slip off my shoes. I put down my handbag by the door and watch as Mark inches silently down the hall, close to the wall.

He slips inside Skye's room. 'Make us a drink and I'll knock on the wall when I want you to come in,' he whispers, pushing the bedroom door closed behind him.

I go to the kitchen and stick the kettle on. I'm not sure whether Mark is expecting a wine or a beer, but it's strong coffee I think we both need.

After about a minute, there's a soft tapping on the wall. I turn the kitchen light off and step into the hallway again. Skye's door opens and Mark beckons me in, signalling for me to stick close to the wall when I'm in there, which is strange.

I tiptoe inside the room in my sock feet, huddling close to the cool plaster.

I stand next to him, and weirdly, he doesn't move but stares at the wall at the bottom of Skye's bed. I open my mouth to ask what I should be looking at, but he's so focused I just follow his stare instead.

He seems to be interested in the bookshelves that run along the wall above Skye's toy box. She loves reading and was pleased when she saw the bookshelves already fitted there.

They're packed to the rafters with all her favourite books, different shapes and sizes and all well read.

It looks like any standard kid's bedroom; nice enough but not something I want to stare at for much longer.

Mark tugs at my elbow and I take one step to the right and he points at the bookshelves again. I sigh, shift my weight to the other foot, and just as I'm about to turn to him to ask what I'm supposed to be looking at, I see it.

The tiniest red flash, so minute and quick, it's almost invisible.

My mouth falls open and I stand staring until about five seconds later, when it flashes again. 'What the . . .'

I stagger back slightly and Mark steadies me, points at Skye's small painted chair that's directly behind me. I sit down heavily on it, trying to sort through the implications of what I'm seeing . . . what someone has done . . .

I feel as if I'm watching down a tunnel as Mark turns on the torch on his phone and lies sideways on the floor, sweeping the light underneath my daughter's bed and then up at the springs and the mattress.

The phone flashes and I realise he's taking pictures of something under there.

Still sitting on the chair, I lean back against the wall and close my eyes. I can't process the terrible thoughts filling my head.

Someone has been *spying* on my daughter?

Revulsion washes over me and I feel dirty on the inside. If I scrubbed myself from head to foot with bleach I still couldn't feel clean.

What is this place? How can I have put my daughter in so much danger? I should never have come back here. Brenna would have packed up our things.

I'm shivering and my skin feels clammy.

'I want to get Skye from downstairs and get out of here,' I whisper.

Mark clambers to his feet and helps me stand up, leading me out of the room without speaking. In the lounge, he sits me down. The room is still dark with the lights off and I can only see him when he comes really close. Close enough to feel his breath on my cheek.

'Sit here while I check out the other rooms and I'll do this one last,' Mark says gently. 'When I know exactly what we're up against, we'll call the police and get out of here.'

'Skye's with Lily,' I manage. 'I have to get her, have to know she's safe, before we do anything else.'

'Course.' He nods. 'We can get her back as soon as I've checked the other rooms.'

Mark leaves the lounge again and I sit in the silence, in the dark, trying to make sense of it all. I think about Audrey asking me, so matter-of-fact, if it was OK for the security camera to be installed. I hadn't been happy and said so, but I never, for a minute, suspected it would lead to any of *this*.

She must have arranged for all the other spy devices to be fitted at the same time . . . when we were in the garden, perhaps, and everyone was being so nice.

Maybe they're monitoring everyone who lives here. Even Lily, who's lived here for a long time. If she wants him to, Mark could check her place out, too, while he's here.

I really felt Audrey had let down her steely defences with me. And all the time, it must've been part of the act.

I've been naïve, a pushover. I've been such a trusting fool.

46

Mark comes back in the lounge and cases around the walls. I don't watch him, I feel if I move my head an inch, I'll be sick.

All I want now is to get Skye and get out of this hellhole. Mark sits down next to me on the couch and I open my eyes.

'OK, there's nothing in here, nothing in your bedroom. The only room that's been fitted out with surveillance is Skye's bedroom. So far as I can tell, there's nothing anywhere else.'

'Dear God.' I choke back tears. 'Spying on a tiny girl . . . Marsden must be a pervert . . . and Audrey knew about all this, I'm certain of it.'

'Only the worst kind of people could even think of doing this.' Mark shudders and falls silent for a second, his expression grim. 'Listen, Freya. I need to tell you exactly what I found. There's a camera fitted into a fake book casing on the shelves and . . .' His voice falters.

'Go on,' I say fearfully, steeling myself.

'There's a recording device secured under the bed.'

'What?' I clench my fist and bite my knuckle hard. 'What would they be recording, me reading her a bedtime story? It doesn't make sense.'

'You misunderstand me,' Mark says gently, shaking his head. 'It's the sort that plays recordings *into* the room.'

'Huh?' And then it hits me.

The voices, the crying child . . . Skye's troubling dreams.

I jump up and run over to the sink just in time, turning on the tap full pelt to wash down the vomit.

Mark hands me some kitchen roll.

'Let's leave it there, I can fill you in with the rest when you're—'

'No! I want to know everything right now. Tell me everything.'

'Well, from what I can tell by a quick survey of the wiring, it's clear that all the data is being beamed next door.'

'The empty apartment?'

He nods. 'Someone is using it as a kind of spy HQ. It's like you and Skye are part of someone's sick experiment.'

'We have to call the police.' My stomach is still churning, wanting to retch even though there's nothing left in there. 'I just need to know Skye is OK. Lily can keep her until we've told the police, but I want to see her first.'

Mark nods. 'Why don't you go downstairs now and get Skye? Act as normally as you can. I wouldn't say anything to Lily yet until I've got access to next door to see the full extent of it all before anyone else gets involved . . . We don't want to tip them off.'

I nod but don't know how calm I'll remain when Lily answers her door. I feel like screaming the place down right now, letting everyone know the full horror of Michael and Audrey Marsden's wicked existence.

I walk towards the door. My head is swimming, my heart feels raw.

'Freya?' I turn around to face Mark. 'When you get back up here after checking on Skye, we'll ring the police, OK? This will all soon be over.'

'OK,' I whisper, feeling so grateful I've got someone like Mark onside.

47

When I leave the apartment to walk down to Lily's, Mark takes a tool and starts prodding at the handle of the apartment door next to ours.

'Any luck, I'll have this open in no time,' he says as I pass him on the landing.

The thought of the Marsdens sitting in there watching my daughter makes me feel sick to my stomach. But I have to get past that and try to think clearly. I push the thoughts aside. My priority now is to get her back safely in my arms. Nothing else really matters.

Lily is perceptive. When she called earlier today, she could tell right away there was something wrong with me. It's going to be hard not to tell her the horror of what Mark has uncovered, but the time isn't right now. The main thing is to get Skye and then let the police know what's been happening here.

I knock on Lily's door and when there's no answer, I knock again and wait. Nothing. I knock harder.

No answer. I feel a heat rash break out around my collarbone.

Maybe they're out in the garden.

I rush downstairs and out of the front door, leaving it wide open behind me. I can hear the sound of traffic passing by on the top road. I'm in my own little bubble of horror just paces away from where people are leisurely driving home, taking a walk through the park, or just out for the evening.

And I can't find my daughter in a house I can never think of as home again. 'Skye!' I shout before I even round the corner of the building. 'Where are you?'

Birds whistle and the whisper of a warm breeze caresses my damp hands. But my daughter doesn't answer.

There's no one out there.

And then I hear a whimper. I rush down the garden. 'Skye! Where are you?'

A small white face appears from the bushes, and I gasp with relief that I've found her and then . . . I see it's not my daughter at all.

'Susan!'

Her face is tear-stained, her hair wild. She staggers towards me, her bony arms outstretched, the sleeveless cotton dress she's wearing hanging like a shroud on her skeletal body.

'Susan, have you seen Skye? She's missing . . . has she been out here in the garden?'

'Get away from this place, Freya. Take your daughter.' She wails. 'Get out now!'

'Come inside,' I tell her, backing away. 'Where's your husband? You shouldn't be out here alone.'

I turn on my heel and run back up to the house. I feel a twist of guilt but can't stop and talk to poor Susan, I have to carry on searching. My head is pounding now. Where is Skye? Where's Lily?

I know everyone dislikes Lily, but would the Marsdens be prepared to hurt her to get to Skye?

As I run back towards the entrance of the house, I think about Mark's words of advice: *act normally*. It's an impossible ask. What is he discovering this very second in the empty apartment next door to ours on the top floor? I want him down here, helping me find

Skye. I want to call the police right now but my phone is somewhere in the apartment.

Back inside I leave the front door open and run to the corner of the foyer, pushing away the potted ferns that hamper my progress. I hammer on the Marsdens' apartment door with both hands, I ring the doorbell and rattle the brass lion's head.

I listen. Silence.

'Mark!' I howl at the bottom of the stairs. 'Call the police.' Back at number one, I hammer again. I kick the door.

Nothing from Mark. Not a sound in the house. I might as well be alone in here. I'm thinking through fog, my whole body is trembling.

Run next door . . . get them to call the police.

I'm about to turn to dash out of the building again and then I hear it, a scuffling noise behind the door. The sound of bolts being slid back, and I take a step away as the door finally opens.

And suddenly, I'm face to face with Dr Michael Marsden.

'Where's my daughter? What have you done with her . . . and with Lily?' He doesn't respond, his face impassive.

'I know what you've been up to . . . it's illegal, what you're doing. You can't—'

'Please, Freya. Calm down.'

His manner both infuriates and terrifies me. I back away from the door.

'*Mark!*' I screech his name at the top of my voice and start to run upstairs. 'Mark, call the police!'

'Freya, stop!' Marsden finally calls to me. I ignore him and keep bounding upstairs, two steps at a time. Downstairs, I hear the front door I left wide open slam closed.

I stop outside Lily's door again.

Bang-bang-bang.

240

Nothing. Maybe she took her out for a walk . . . maybe they're at the park!

In the dark?

It could be an adventure. It's the sort of thing Lily would love to do, I'm sure. The fact this only just occurs to me slows me down. Skye could be perfectly safe with her and on her way back home right now.

Up on the top floor, I see the empty apartment door is still closed. It doesn't look like Mark managed to get in there after all.

I rush towards my open apartment door.

'Mark! Didn't you hear me shouting? Have you called the police? Skye's not there, but maybe she's at the park, we need to—'

He's not in the lounge or the bedrooms. My apartment is empty. Where the hell is Mark?

48

I turn my handbag upside down to save hunting through for my phone, but it's not there. I can't remember taking it out, but I rush into the kitchen and search the worktop.

It's not here either.

'This is crazy!' I yell out loud, thumping the work surface and hurting my hand. My voice seems to echo, magnifying the emptiness of the entire house.

Where's my phone? Where are Skye and Lily? Where the hell is Mark? Where is *everyone*?

It occurs to me that Mark himself suggested I go downstairs to pick up Skye from Lily's.

At the time, it seemed the sensible thing to do. I wanted her back with me where I knew she'd be safe, but now I can't help wondering, did Mark want to get rid of me for some reason? Or maybe he ran for help when I went out into the garden.

I don't know. I'm not thinking straight, suspecting everyone because my trust has been broken in so many ways.

The one thing I know for sure is that I just need to find my daughter. Nothing else matters.

I take off downstairs again, slipping and sliding down part of the flight. I bang on apartment five on the second floor and then on Lily's door again as I pass.

'Someone help me!' I yell out at the top of my voice into the silent building. 'Help!'

Downstairs in the foyer, I lurch at the door, aiming to pull it open like I did before. Except this time it doesn't open. I twist the latch and pull, but it's somehow locked fast and solid. It won't budge.

I howl like a trapped animal.

'Skye!' I scream to emptiness. 'Someone, call the police!'

You need to get out.

Linda's words reverberate around my skull. Oh God, now I wish with all my heart I'd listened to her and left immediately with Skye.

Everything that's happened . . . the noises, the unexplained movement of furniture and toys, the strange behaviour of the residents here, the CCTV camera inside the apartment to name but a few.

What the hell was I thinking of? Putting my daughter in danger, overlooking the freakiest of things just so we can live here at this address for a cheap rent.

Is it pride that's made me overlook the obvious?

I pick up the chair in the foyer and hurl it at the stained-glass panel on the right side of the door. It bounces back.

I sink to the floor, sobbing. I'm a prisoner. I can't escape this place . . . What the hell can I do to get my daughter back?

'Freya?' Audrey stands at the bottom of the stairs, speaking my name in her horrible, creepy low voice.

I stand up, ball my fists.

'You!' I bare my teeth and take a step forward, my distress suddenly gone. Instead I'm filled with a seething mass of fury that's telling me she knows exactly where my daughter is. 'Where is Skye?'

She holds her palms up to ward me off. 'You have to calm down, Freya.'

'Tell me where she is!' I screech and leap towards her. In the red mist I see a flash of skin, and two strong hands grab my forearms.

'Freya, Freya! It's me, Dr Marsden!' He sounds hoarse and panicked but is trying to keep his voice down.

'Get. Off. Me!' I struggle but he's stronger than I expected and he holds me fast.

'Do you want to see your daughter again?' he hisses, and that cuts through the red mist. I feel myself deflate in his arms.

Audrey steps closer, her perfume overpowering at such a short distance. This is it. This is where I become their next Sophie.

And yet . . . *Do you want to see your daughter again?* That means there's hope, doesn't it? If I play along and do as they ask, I can fool them into thinking I'm under their control.

I breathe again. It feels true to me. It feels like I can do it.

'That's better,' Audrey says in a sickeningly soothing way like I'm a child. It's all I can do not to slap her away when she strokes my arm and sets my clammy skin crawling.

Marsden lets go of me and flexes his fingers like they've seized up.

He looks at me, his face drawn and pale. In the dim light without the hall lamp, shadows play around his features, reducing his eyes to dark pools of nothingness.

'If you can stay calm, we can go upstairs,' Audrey whispers. 'We can see Skye.'

'She's not up there,' I hiss, trying, for the sake of my plan, to appear calm. 'Mark and Lily have gone, too. What have you done with them all?'

Audrey stares at me, then turns soundlessly and beckons me to follow her upstairs. I start to climb, looking back to see Dr Marsden standing there watching us.

At the first floor, all is quiet. Both apartment doors are closed and still, nobody is peering out. There are no signs of life. After all my screaming and banging!

What the hell is *this place?*

When we pass Lily's apartment on the second floor, I notice for the first time that there's a dent towards the bottom of the door, like someone had a go at kicking it open.

Is that how the Marsdens forcibly took Skye away from Lily earlier in the evening when I was out with Mark . . . by kicking the door in? I know Lily wouldn't willingly let Skye come to any harm. She might be in there herself, injured, needing medical help.

But we don't stop here. Audrey continues up to the top floor.

I shiver when we get to the top. My apartment door is still open, just as I left it, the landing still eerily quiet.

49

My heart cracks when it becomes obvious Skye isn't here, but a bolt of fury also shudders through me. My face feels like it's on fire as I turn to face Audrey.

'Where is she? Where's Skye?' My voice sounds measured even though I'm teetering on the edge of hysteria.

'It's important you stay calm, Freya,' Audrey says. She's fidgety and her eyes are constantly scanning all around her. 'This is exactly what we've been dreading . . . it's the reason we had the camera installed, to try and protect you. But you wouldn't listen.'

'What are you talking about? Protect me from *what*?' She's making no sense at all.

I run into my apartment, check all the rooms again. No sign of Skye or Mark. A noise outside on the landing has me rushing out again.

A small figure stands very still and apart from Audrey. I exhale with massive relief that she's here to help me.

'Lily, thank God you're OK! Where's Skye? Did they take her?'

Lily stares at me, and then she smiles. *She smiles!*

'Skye is fine, my dear . . . for now, at least.'

There's a quiet menace about Lily I've never seen before, and suddenly, I can't move. I'm frozen with fear and denial at the realisation that I've placed my trust, my precious daughter's safety, with the wrong person altogether.

'Where's my daughter?' I whisper. My whole body begins to shake. I clasp my hands in front of me to steady them. I don't want to show my fear, not now, not while I still have a chance to find Skye. 'I trusted you.'

My daughter has been with her for hours!

'Of course you did, everybody does.' She takes a step forward and I press my feet into the floor. I will not move from this place until I have my daughter. 'It's incredibly easy, you know, to gain that trust. Most people fall for the clichés of a trustworthy person: small, elderly, smiling, apparently caring. It works all the time for me, so you shouldn't feel foolish. You're not the only one.'

'Skye really liked you. Why would you want to hurt her?'

'Hurt her?' Lily frowns, apparently offended. 'I would never hurt the child. On purpose, that is. She's very valuable to me, you both are. I couldn't continue the experiment without your daughter, Freya.'

I feel sick to my stomach. 'Skye was your . . . *experiment?*'

She nods and slides a tablet out from under her arm. 'Your husband dying so inconveniently somewhat ruined our plans for Skye for a while. We thought she'd be too traumatised to be a solid subject, but looking on the bright side, you being alone turned into quite a gift. We've been watching you for some time, you see.'

All the creepy feelings I've had that someone is watching our every move, blaming Janine Harworth . . . and it's been them all along.

I shake my head, trying desperately but failing to process her words. 'But *why?*' I eventually manage.

'In the name of progress. Useful research is virtually impossible these days, we're restricted at every turn in a world obsessed by ethics and correctness. We need real research on real people. It's the only way to get results and make headway.'

She shows me a black-and-white still on her tablet.

'My grandfather carried out one of the most important pieces of research, and it's still highly relevant today. But he was vilified, labelled as unethical.' Her mouth twists into a tight knot. 'Here at Adder House, we are all committed to pushing boundaries in the area of psychology. We gravitated together in our early careers, have known each other for many, many years. The only thing we were missing were subjects . . . real people we could study in a controlled environment.'

I look at Audrey in disgust. '*All* the residents were in on it?'

'Oh no, those lily-livered fools tried to stop me.' Lily lets out a brittle laugh. '*They* didn't want to get involved in any useful, solid experimentation. Two residents even left the house. Cowards who wanted no part in my vitally important studies.'

'So, both me and my daughter, we've been your . . . your lab rats?'

'Well, that's an interesting way of putting it.' Lily throws back her head and chuckles. But I need more. There's so much that doesn't make sense.

'What were you hoping to get from this? There must be far more interesting people out there, so why study *us*?'

Lily takes another couple of steps forward. Her expression is so kind, so caring, completely concealing the dark heart that lies beneath it.

'My dear, you're very modest. It's touching, how unaware you are of your own uniqueness and value.' She splays her fingers and studies her short, neat nails, as though we're discussing the weather. 'Freya, have you ever studied your own family tree?'

'I was fostered. Family history has never interested me.'

'I can hardly believe that. You've never wondered or had any curiosity about where you came from?'

'It is what it is. I never knew any of my family.'

'Perhaps I can help you after all. Your mother was a teacher. Her name was Elaine Cantrell and she . . .'

How does she know all this?

Why would Lily go to the trouble of finding out my family history? I was telling the truth when I said I had no interest, and yet hearing her relay the facts so plainly makes me almost want more. But I can't let her lies distract me from getting my daughter back.

Lily's voice fades out as I try and distance myself. After the incredible deceit she's shown, I could never believe another word the woman utters.

'Anyway, I digress. The generations before that are of far more interest to me. I suppose you could say it's what binds you and me together.'

'I'm not bound to *you* in any way.' My lip curls as I look at her, detesting the vulnerable, kind image she displays to cover up her cruel nature.

Lily smiles. 'What a shame you never knew your great-grandmother, Freya. I see glimmers of her in you.'

'You *knew* her?' The words escape my mouth before I can stop them.

'Sadly I did not. But my grandfather, Professor John B. Watson, knew Beatrice and her son very well. Take a look at this.'

She turns to the tablet and taps something into the search bar. Soon, a grainy black-and-white video loads.

50

'Meet one of your ancestors, known in academic psychology circles as Little Albert.' Lily's tone is almost affectionate.

The short film is jumpy and a little blurry in places but I watch in fascination . . . and then in horror . . . as a man in a white coat – the professor I assume – assisted by a young woman, systematically taunts a small boy with a series of unexpected things.

The child is clearly distressed at the sight of a rat, a dog, and bizarrely, a man posing as Santa Claus. Anyone can see they must have ruined the poor child's life.

'The principle of classical conditioning was not a new one, even back in my grandfather's day. What he did was groundbreaking; to successfully imprint fear, a *phobia*, on to an ordinary little boy was staggering progress.'

'It's so cruel,' I gasp. 'Your grandfather was a monster.'

She frowns, obviously annoyed that I'm not displaying the enthusiasm she'd hoped. 'He was a genius, known as the Father of Behaviourism,' she hisses. 'And your own relation, Beatrice, she made it all possible.'

I shake my head. Look at Audrey, who seems powerless against this frail old lady who holds a power greater than the physical. Between us we could simply storm her, force her to tell us where Skye is . . . where *Mark* is.

'Little Albert's mother, Beatrice, was your great-grandmother, Freya.' Lily smiles at me with affection and I shiver. 'As Professor Watson was my own relation . . . Now do you see our beautiful connection? Do you see why it always had to be *you* and your daughter who helped me achieve my goal?'

Lily Brockley is quite obviously insane. I rack my brains trying to figure out what to do. I've no phone, I'm locked inside this madhouse. But my daughter must be here *somewhere*, else why bring me up here again?

Lily continues in the absence of my reaction. 'You, with your impeccable ancestral history . . . if we could breathe fear into *you*, condition *you* to be afraid, then we could do it to anyone. Don't you see what our studies could be worth? To teach new behaviours and discourage unwanted ones? To mould children into what we need them to be to fulfil their potential for society? To infect our enemies with fear . . . imagine that! The possibilities are endless.'

She takes yet another step forward and I step away, feel the banister against my back.

My fingers touch the metal filigree work that looks so attractive, but that Linda told me Sophie glanced her head on when she fell.

And here I now stand myself. Is this what happened to Sophie? Did she discover they were monitoring her every move, too?

She walks towards me clutching a syringe.

'It's time for you to sleep, Freya. We've come so far in our work here, I can't let it be ruined at this stage. If you cooperate, you can stay with your daughter . . . for a while, at least, until my studies are complete. I give you my word.'

Her word?

'You give me more *lies*, you mean.' I look desperately at Audrey as Lily walks forward and I press harder against the balcony. 'Please, make this stop now. She can't carry on ruining people's lives like this.'

I feel dizzy, vulnerable. I can rush Lily and try to knock the needle from her hand, but if Audrey assists her, she can probably sedate me even with a struggle.

'Think of your sacrifice as a wonderful gift to so many. We are not simply money oriented. We are psychologists, scientists, devoted to our field even when today's experts wish to discount our work, obsessed as they are with their political correctness, their human-rights legislations.'

I slide further along the balcony towards the wall at the end. She's completely deluded.

'What you're doing is unethical!' I shout now. 'You can't just do this to people . . . it's illegal!'

Lily shakes her head.

'Some of the greatest psychological studies have been unethical. I ask you, where would we be without them? Take Stanley Milgram's obedience experiment, or Philip Zimbardo's Stanford prison situational study. Both of these great men, now vilified and shunned by the very people they helped to progress. The ethical do-gooders still whine that Little Albert was not protected from harm. Barely a mention of the great strides in progress my grandfather made during his lifetime.'

'Skye!' I scream as loud as I can in the hope my daughter can hear me, wherever she is.

She lunges at me, the syringe held high.

'And now it's time for you to leave us, in the knowledge you have contributed to a very worthwhile experiment. As dear Sophie and little Melissa did before you.'

I duck down and jump behind her as her arm comes down, vicious and stabbing.

Before she can pull back her arm to attack me again, I push her as hard as I can, and with a terrific crack and groan of metal, the decorative balcony gives way and Lilian Brockley crashes down three floors with it.

The house seems stunned into deathly silence . . . And then, as Audrey and I look down on the apparently lifeless body of Lily Brockley, an apartment door opens and Matthew and Susan Woodings soundlessly step out on to the landing and stare silently up at us from the first floor, their faces without expression.

I rush to the stairs to make a run for it just as a figure appears on floor two, looking up at me as he rushes to the stairway.

Dr Marsden.

51

I run back inside my apartment and snatch up the heavy bronze hare Brenna bought us as a housewarming gift. *Where is Skye?*

I feel like I'm about to vomit any second, but I run back out on to the landing to find Dr Marsden waiting there. I never suspected Lily, but I've known all along in my heart there's something strange about him.

'Get away from me!' I swing the sculpture down and up in front of me. I am more than willing to smash it into his face if he comes near me. I'll do anything necessary to get my daughter back.

'Freya, please. Just settle a moment, the police and ambulance service are on their way.'

He's called the police? It doesn't make any sense.

Audrey appears from behind him, for the first time looking slightly dishevelled and wild eyed. When she speaks, her usually deep tone sounds weak.

'Lilian Brockley is our sister, Freya, she owns Adder House and we are all family here.' She glances down. 'Even Susan Woodings, my niece, has suffered with her nerves which has affected her pregnancies.'

'But you were part of this, too.' They can't all just shirk responsibility. They turned a blind eye to Lily's actions.

'It happened gradually, you see. Lily got the idea a few years ago, of carrying out real-life experiments on real people – experiments that would never be allowed legally for ethical reasons. But they weren't serious, didn't hurt anyone, and we were just observing.' He sees my shocked expression. 'I know what you're thinking, but she was far less ambitious about what she wanted to achieve then and her monitoring was fairly harmless.'

In his opinion! I'd like to speak to some of her victims.

'*That's* why you expressly brought me and Skye here? To be experimented on?' Emotion floods up through me like a tidal wave. 'You lied through your teeth, targeted me in the coffee shop. I confided in you and you knew we'd had a hard time of it since my husband's death. *I trusted you!*'

'I swear I didn't know what Lily had in mind. I didn't know about *this*.' He hangs his head. 'She promised . . . after Sophie died . . . it would never happen again. But I saw what she was doing to you and we tried, we really did try to help but—'

Audrey appears behind him. 'We realised she was getting seriously out of control. She was ill and we'd planned to get her medical help. But in the meantime, that's why we wanted to put the CCTV camera in your hall, to try and protect you from her, so we could see what she was up to.'

'We're so sorry, Freya. You were always kind to me,' Susan Woodings calls up. 'We never knew she was watching you to this extent.'

But they all knew something was amiss! They all knew Lily was disturbed but they put up with it to live in their comfortable bubble.

'What *was* Lily doing exactly . . . and why?'

'Infecting you with fear,' Audrey replies. 'She was recreating the Little Albert experiment all over again in a modern setting. It was particularly apt, she said, due to your family tree. In Lilian's disturbed mind, you and Skye were the perfect subjects.'

'How did she know all this stuff about me . . . stuff I didn't even know about myself?'

'We have a great-niece, a DNA expert who can track down the most distant ancestral connections. She alerted us to your genealogy as a matter of pure interest, she hadn't a clue how Lily would use the information.'

I feel so low and helpless. I reach out to him.

'If you're truly not part of what she did, I beg you to tell me . . . where is Skye?'

Without speaking, Dr Marsden walks past me and unlocks the door to the apartment next to mine. He opens it only slightly.

'This is where she observed you and spent her time.' He sweeps his arm to guide me inside. 'After you.'

I look at him warily. Can I trust him? But I have to know what's inside.

I walk through the entrance hallway of the apartment next door and let out a scream.

Skye is asleep on a single mattress near the window and Mark is lying on the floor with a head wound.

I rush over to my daughter, press my cheek next to her mouth. She's breathing. She looks pale, but she's breathing.

'She'll just be sedated,' Audrey says from the door.

I cradle Skye's head in my lap and let the tears of relief splash on to her face.

Then I lay her head back down gently on the mattress and rush over to Mark. He groans, barely conscious. There's blood down his face and spotted on the floor, but at least it looks like the wound is no longer bleeding.

'Looks like she was waiting behind the door when he broke into the room,' Dr Marsden explains. 'The ambulance is on its way.'

I look around me into a space that was once designed to be a lounge, where Sophie and Melissa lived. But Lily took it over to essentially turn it into a secret monitoring hub for Adder House.

On the wall adjoining mine, there are cameras showing every angle of my home.

Mark obviously missed some cameras in his search as there's a clear view of the lounge on one of the screens . . . and, oh my God . . . even the *bathroom*!

I turn and rush out, Dr Marsden running after me.

'Please, Freya, wait!'

I rush downstairs, past all the faces, some of whom I've barely spoken to, down to the ground floor. I run past Lilian Brockley's twisted, bloody body and barely give it a look. The front door is locked. I twist the lock, tug and pull at the handle, but nothing happens.

'I'm sorry, I can't let you go, Freya. I just can't until we sort this out . . .'

Suddenly there's a hefty banging on the other side of the door. I can see uniforms and torches through the stained-glass panels. I fall to my knees and begin to sob.

I have not written here for some time.

I have been unwell myself with nerves and have tried to focus on helping Douglas readjust after his ordeal at the hands of Professor Watson and Dr Rayner.

When my sister died, shortly after the experiment, my son and I moved away. Professor Watson's study made him very famous worldwide but fortunately, for us, there are a small group of eminent doctors who disagree with his Little Albert experiment and who have challenged his findings.

These people have raised funds and made it possible for me to give up work and care for Douglas.

He has been left in an awful state, afraid of everything . . . every object that is white.

It has been explained to me by our supporters that the professor had a moral obligation to 'de-condition' Douglas after the experiment.

He failed to do this and I believe he simply lost interest after writing up his findings, leaving my son emotionally harmed.

There are people who blame me for allowing Douglas to take part in the study in the first place and believe me, had I fully understood the implications, I would never have agreed to it.

But I did not understand.

I was pressured and convinced by Dr Rayner that it would be a harmless exercise with no ill-effects to Douglas. The professor was an eminent man who everyone admired. Who was I, a mere wet nurse, to defy him?

Now, we must try to build a new life. I find it hard to trust strangers but I must, in order to get the help Douglas needs.

I pray to God every single day that my son will one day fully recover and grow to be a kind and loving father himself. Everything Professor John B. Watson is not.

My son and I will be happy now. I can feel it.

EPILOGUE

Six months later

'I just knew deep inside there was something wrong when you wouldn't answer your phone,' Brenna had explained when I called her close to midnight on the day it all happened. 'When I thought about everything that had been happening there and Audrey rang to express concern over your confusion . . . I knew something wasn't right.'

Dr Marsden admitted to the police that while I ran downstairs to the garden to ask for help with the flies, he went in and opened the windows to get rid of them. They controlled almost everything I saw in there but in the end, he seemed almost relieved it was over.

'You can stay here as long as you like,' Audrey had said quietly as the police officers led her away. 'We want you to think about staying for good, rent-free, in an apartment of your choice.'

But it was a bit late for her to start to make amends.

Audrey was named in Lily's will as the new owner of Adder House. Dr Marsden is being charged by the police, but as he was unaware of the extent of Lily's activities, he's not expecting to serve a custodial sentence.

But I can't think about that right now. There's so much other stuff to get through. The door opens and Skye runs in. I stand up and wrap her in my arms.

Documents, including my great-grandmother's journal and footage the police found in the apartment next door to ours categorically proved that Sophie was groomed and hounded by Lily to the point that she became mentally ill. They discovered photographs taken of Skye outside her school and accounts of Lily sneaking into the apartment at night to rearrange things in Skye's room, hide things . . . all designed to make me think I was losing my mind.

It very nearly worked.

Sophie's sister, Linda, has been back in touch with me, and she is about to begin a challenge to the coroner's verdict of suicide and manslaughter, finally clearing Sophie's name.

Brenna walks over and puts her arm on my shoulder.

'I'm can't say enough how sorry I am that I doubted you, Freya. You were living a nightmare and I made it worse.' Brenna has been apologising for six months, but what she says next surprises me. 'I'm researching now, and when you're ready, I'll tell you the full story of how you were related to Beatrice and Dougie.'

I've already read and researched everything I can get my hands on regarding the unethical Little Albert experiment.

Watson and Rosalie Rayner were not objective in their evaluation of the experiment. They relied on their own subjective interpretations and opinions. They didn't de-condition Little Albert's fear. He may have lived the rest of his life in the grip of the illogical terror they had infected him with.

It makes my blood run cold and after reading Beatrice's final journal entry, if there is one thing I can do for my great-grandmother, it is to love and defend my daughter always, to the best of my ability.

I give Brenna a little smile and hug Skye tightly to me.

The door opens and Mark walks in. The head wound Lily inflicted has scarred his temple, but if anything, it makes him look even more rugged and slightly dangerous. Apart from that, he's back to his normal, healthy self.

Skye runs to him and he picks her up and whirls her around as she squeals with delight.

Mark has been an absolute rock to us. I've seen him every day and we're officially 'together' now.

He owns a small flat in Fulham that he's been renting out. Skye and I are planning to move in there when his current tenants leave. For now though, and until things settle down, we're staying with Brenna and Viv.

'Let's go to the park and see the ducks, Mummy,' Skye says. 'Me, you, and Mark.' It sounds like the best offer I've had all day.

ABOUT THE AUTHOR

K. L. Slater is the million-copy bestselling author of nine stand-alone psychological crime thrillers. Kim is a full-time writer. She lives with her husband in Nottingham.